THE OIL MAN

LEON PUISSEGUR

Savant Books and Publications
Honolulu, HI, USA
2011

Published in the USA by Savant Books and Publications
2630 Kapiolani Blvd #1601
Honolulu, HI 96826
http://www.savantbooksandpublications.com

Printed in the USA

Edited by Daniel S. Janik
Cover by Daniel S. Janik. "A drilling platform in the ocean" copyright Peter
Wollinga/Dreamstime.com (used with permission) and "Sten gun France
ww2-102.jpg" from National Archives Military Records in the public
domain.

13-digit ISBN: 978-0-9832861-5-8
10-digit ISBN: 0983286159

DEDICATION

I cannot help but dedicate this to all the people who in each of their small way have contributed to the idea of this book. I must also dedicate this book to my wife for putting up with me working on it at all the odd times of day and night.

The Oil Man

CHAPTER 1

On a normal Gulf evening, he would have entered the galley for a good meal after supervising the moving of pipe to the well, sometimes working shoulder-to-shoulder with the workmen on the drill floor. They were pulling pipe in and out of the hole to exchange drill bits because the formation they were drilling into some 250 feet below the surface of the Gulf of Mexico had changed. The hole would end up 36,876 feet deep in order to hit pay dirt, and it was rumored this pocket might contain as much as 50 billion barrels of oil. Of course, no one could really know for sure. The last well he'd helped sink went some 26,000 feet down and all they located was 600 million barrels of oil, having expected one to two billion, so it was always a proverbial shot in the dark. While the new 4-dimensional seismic equipment promised better images and more accurate projections, it still couldn't guarantee what was actually there.

John Marx was a self-made man. He'd worked himself through Texas A & M in petroleum engineering, and later through Stanford's Department of Energy Resources Engineering, but, in the end, there was nothing like the experience of working with a dedicated drilling crew and the thrill of the moment of discovery. He'd enjoyed working on contract to Rustic Oil ever since they'd returned to jack-ups instead of the more customary and expensive submersibles. Jack-ups like Rig Twelve, the particularly tall one he was standing on, were constantly animated by the ever-present hum from the hydraulics that kept the platform steady in all sorts of seas. This jack-up had three 400-foot long legs when fully extended, and was much more stable than submersed or floating platforms since, in an emergency, they could be plucked from the sea and moved elsewhere.

John paused on his way to an interior door to peer down over the rail into the beautiful, dark-blue water. Every so often he could see the flash of a hammerhead shark or the white ghost of a manatee, surrounded by all sorts of silvery, deepwater fish. The water seemed miles below yet John knew it was actually less than 80 feet to the surface of the sea.

A growl from his stomach reminding him of his earlier thoughts of a shower, food and some well-earned rest, he pulled back from the rail, tripping backwards over a small, black rectangular box lying on the slatted metal walkway on which he was standing. Looking like a malformed, two-by-two-by eight-inch black leather attaché case, John stared at it with curiosity, fully expecting it to reveal its purpose, which it clearly wasn't planning to do. Bending down, he plucked it from the rusty-red, wetted iron lattice and turned it around in his fingers. He looked both ways on the walkway to see who might have lost it. There was no one about.

On closer inspection, the padded leather box revealed the hint of a line dividing it lengthwise into two mirror halves. There were no visible hinges, stays, clasps or latch. Concluding that whatever inside was important enough to warrant a custom-made case like this, John slipped the rectangular box in a pocket and walked the remainder of the metal walkway to the nearest door. After securing the door, he proceeded to his quarters.

Placing the box on his bunk bed, he doffed his mud and oil-stained work clothes, tossed them into the white laundry bag at the entrance door to his room, took a quick shower, and slid into a clean denim shirt and jeans. Fingering the mysterious box one more time before tossing it onto his work desk, a second stomach growl, louder than the last one, commanded him to begin the quick trip into the mess hall to see what tempting delights their New Orleans Master Chef was offering.

On his way out, he hesitated, re-assaying the acuteness of his hunger against the pull of his curiosity, and decided on the later. Returning to his desk, he sat down to study the object further.

The unusual box obviously housed something of importance. The problem was, there was no obvious way to open it. Shaking it gently, he noticed a soft rattle, as if it contained a piece of wood, glass or metal inside.

Tracing a fingernail around the seam caused the top and bottom to separate slightly, just enough to glimpse an inner, protective lip denying him visual access to whatever was inside. Prying it further open with a letter-opener, the box hissed and the two halves actively separated, releasing the contents onto his wood-veneered metal desktop. A single, irregular shard of broken glass sang out in a pure, crystalline monotone as it struck the desktop and rocked back and forth.

Intrigued, John held it up in the sunlight streaming in through a porthole behind and over his shoulder. The fragment scattered the light like a prism into a rainbow of scintillating colors on the wall across from him. John sucked in his breath. The sound was immediately taken up by the glassine object and broken into thousands of delicate pure tones overlaying the aurora of colors. To say it was both visually and aurally stunning would be a gross understatement. The fragment was acting like a mixed light *and sound* prism, something he'd never experienced or read about. But most intriguing was the totality of the effect. Taken together, it felt as if the three-inch long, half-inch wide shard was trying to project something, to create something in the air halfway between the wall and where he was holding it.

Rotating it caused the shimmering mirage to change and its pure, ringing hum to disappear; returning it to its original position brought back the same aurora and sound as before. There was something… important…about this crystal fragment's unique abilities that spoke directly, though incomprehensibly, to him.

Once again his stomach rumbled. John replaced the crystal piece in its box. Momentarily satisfied, he would continue his investigation of the strange crystal after he satisfied his increasingly urgent gustatory needs.

As he got up to leave, he noticed his computer beeping softly inside a locker. Using the key about his neck, he unlocked it and retrieved a thin Apple MacBook Air, which he placed on the table next to the box, waiting while the computer finished booting up. One of the many perks—and there were many—the company provided was high-speed wireless for the workers' pleasure during their free time. Some companies didn't allow personal computers on their structures; he counted himself lucky to be working with a company as employee-friendly as Rustic.

As soon as the desktop screen coalesced, he clicked the flashing email icon to check what the beeping was about. Sliding back in his formed, plastic chair he watched the emails pop up, one after another, on the screen. The program changed beep tones to alert him that of the twenty-two new emails, one was flagged "URGENT." Scrolling down the list, he stopped at the flagged one with "FYEO - aoil" in the subject line. "FYEO," standing for, "For Your Eyes Only," was an inside joke that he and his longtime buddy, George Franks, who currently worked as a communications specialist back on land at Rustic Central, shared. John and George, after a prolonged drinking binge that began with an exchange of company gossip, imagined someday using what they learned to spin off a company of their own, and had, like junior James Bonds concocted a set of encryption codes known only to them. It was child's play, which neither was above enjoying. The "aoil" obviously meant "oil" which George had in haste misspelled. What was weird, however, was that the email itself was blank, without salutation or explanation of what was beginning to look to John like a practical joke of some kind.

Then he noticed the attachment. Clicking on it, his screen went momentarily dark, the file automatically unzipping, opening, and recognizing his computer, self-decrypting into...another blank document. John studied the blank document, moving the cursor as he did, until, running it over the center, it caused a pop-up box to appear that contained a composite image of a number of industry logos. A few he recognized as vociferous opponents of nuclear energy development. The others, while he didn't recognize them *per se*, from their logos, he could guess were involved in oil development, information systems, and global management or trade. The central icon around which the others clustered was a pictograph of a world with a sword thrust horizontally through it.

On a whim, John double clicked on the central logo and a small secondary window then popped up, asking him for an authorization code.

John was taken aback. This document was *doubly*-encrypted, and subtly at that. This second encryption key, of course, would be the one he and his buddy had long ago developed and agreed upon, which was the weirdest of all, since after coming up with it, they'd never used it. Despite the years, he could, however, easily recall it, having continued to imbibe their mutual favorite, "LA-31," Bayou Teche's "biere pale" whenever he could still find it. After typing in the name of their mutually-favorite beer and tapping "enter," the screen once again went black, then reappeared, this time in the form of an imaged memo.

The "To" line boasted George Franks' name. The "From" line displayed a name that was vaguely familiar to him: Leon Puissegur. The composite logo was still there, but the body now contained two highlighted text sentences with ten numbers sandwiched between. There was no signature and the two sentences on either side of the numbers read the same: ****DESTROY AFTER READING****.

If the discovery of the case and crystal hadn't sufficiently piqued his interest, then *this* certainly did. The numbers must be important, if only George's new girlfriend's measurements, or the Global Position System location of a new party "hot spot." Alternately, this could be another "conspiracy" joke, which George was inclined to play. Already doubting either of these first guesses, John felt himself wanting to believe the quizzical message was one that had been intercepted by George and forwarded specifically to him, given all the hoopla that he'd had to go through to open and read it. Furthermore, the general lack of inelegance would imply George hadn't had much time to do everything. That's when John noticed that the central icon in the composite logo had changed from a sword-pierced world to a representation of a perfect orthorhombic crystal. A crystal. Not unlike the one he'd just found on the platform deck encased in the specially-made, protective case. Perhaps the two…

No, he'd just gotten off an extended shift and was obviously more tired than he'd thought. The two events, other than both involving a crystal, one, iconic and intact, the other real but only a shard, had to be unrelated, serendipitous at best. Connecting them required reaching beyond serendipity into the intriguing realm of conspiracy theory. That was the rub: George knew John's mind was always looking for a new conspiracy theory when not occupied with work or family. That was the joke. In fact, his dabbling had recently become more of an obsession, one over which his wife, Ann, and close friends like George often chided him.

Taking the box back in hand, John carefully reopened it to inspect it more closely. It was indeed a piece of a larger crystal, and, when aligned vertically and rotated slightly, it certainly appeared like it could be a piece of a larger orthorhombic crystal, but…no, that was, again, too great a leap to too far-fetched a connection, given what little he actually knew. Still, the combination of factors caused him to register a tick in his brain to contact George as soon as he'd finished getting something to eat and caught up on his sleep.

The crystal, John decided, was actually the greater problem. What should he do with it? He'd found the box on the oil derrick, so logically, someone must have dropped it. Given its unique nature, that same someone would be looking for it. And that brought up a second problem: Who should he "return" it to? There was no "lost and found" on the platform, especially for objects of special value like this. The answer to his second question was obvious: He needed to bring it to the attention of the company man representing the oil exploration group who were currently contracting the platform. Most likely, it had something to do with the several visitors the group had been hosting recently. He immediately decided to leave the object locked in his room, and catch the company man on his way to grab something to eat.

After carefully replacing the crystal in its protective case, John, on an impulse, copied the mysterious and, by his most current reckoning, practical joke from the computer onto a thumb drive, which, for lack of a better place, he placed in the box with the crystal. Reclosing the box, he shut down his computer and placed the computer and box in his locker.

As he did, there was a sudden, very human knock on metal just outside his room door.

"John? You going to just sit there and stare at your computer, or are you going to grab some chow before it's all gone?"

"Grab some chow," John answered, locking the clothes locker with the key around his neck, and checking the lock to be sure. "On my way," John asserted to the open doorway, then got up and walked out the door with his friend.

"Hurry, man, or we're going to miss dinner. They're cooking up some nice thick Texas T-Bones tonight," admonished Josh Platur. Platur was a long-time friend of John's who lived a short way down the street from him in Violet, Louisiana, off Queen Elizabeth Court. John had talked his boss into offering Josh, who was fifteen years younger, and unschooled though experienced in the oil industry, a job as a roughneck on the same rig. They'd ridden together to the Rustic Oil Company compound in Venice to catch the company supply boat loaded to do a shift on Rig Twelve, aware that had the sea been rougher, they would have been riding a company supply helicopter.

Josh Platur looked like John's younger brother, though they weren't directly related, even acknowledging that everyone in rural Louisiana was related in one way or another within four generations. Josh sported nearly the same tall height and stocky build as John, but had auburn-blond, buzz-cut hair and intelligent hazel eyes set in a lean, worried-looking face dusted with soft facial fuz. The two walked together down the iron hallway to the dining room.

8

The dining room opened into a one-third-sized school cafeteria, similar to what one might see in a penal institution, but royally-appointed in terms of having the most modern gourmet cooking equipment available. Grabbing a tray and steelware from in front of John, Josh moved quickly down the line sniffing and examining the day's offerings, selecting generous helpings of what he considered "real food," in this case, a two-inch thick Texas sirloin steak, its borders extending well outside the over-sized plate, along with a side-dish of beans and another of grilled bread. Unfortunately it didn't include the customary two Texas Lone Star "long necks"—the most popular and, interestingly, one of the more difficult beers to obtain ashore outside of Texas.

"For Heaven's sake, leave some for the rest of us, Josh," John, waiting impatiently for Josh to move forward, admonished.

"Go to hell," Josh quipped back, grinning widely. "I can take my time to pick whatever I want. Now that I'm off duty, you aren't my boss." When John was the driller and they were on the derrick, John was everyone's boss unless the company man or the geologist was there. Then one of the two would take over giving directions, if he was dumb enough to get in the way.

"We've got plenty of time to eat and still watch the movie," Josh stated. "It starts in about thirty minutes. What's playing, do you know?"

"I'm right behind you, Josh, so you don't have to yell, and, no, I don't know what's playing tonight. Furthermore, I don't care."

"What kind you want?" a man dressed in angelic white with a tall chef's hat asked gruffly, interrupting John when he came up to the steaks.

"A big, juicy, T-Bone. Pan-fried, medium well."

"Here," the chef said, sliding an oversized slab of seared meat onto a plate that nearly took up all of John's tray.

"Jesus, Chef, what'd you do? Nuke it?"

"No, you sorry excuse for an oil man. The imaginary junior chef I'm breaking in fried it, and did a pretty good job if I say so myself," the man-in-white replied, pointing a long, two-pronged serving fork towards a stove with several pans containing sizzling steaks. "Eat and weep that you can't eat more. You'll find no better steaks than here on Rig Twelve," he stated, yelling, "Next!" in the same breath. It was pointless asking for anything else, there being no room left on his tray except for the requisite bottles of steak sauce and ketchup. John scanned the room, located Josh, and sauntered over, setting his steaming tray across from his lifelong friend.

"If you so much as touch mine, I swear I'll shoot you before we get home," Josh bantered, half-playfully, half-seriously, as he continued digging into his massive porterhouse.

"I could never do that to a young, starving man like you," John retorted with sincerity.

John went back to get a baked potato with all the mixings. Making his way back to their table, he noticed Josh, plate empty, eyeing his steak from across the table.

"Do it and I swear, I'll shoot before you can swallow," John ordered.

"Just joking, man," Josh replied. "I would never do that to an old man like you. Besides, I know you wouldn't shoot me here, you're too civilized." Josh pushed his empty plate and tray aside, debating in his mind whether to go back for seconds. In the meantime, John began cutting his steak into strips, shoveling them down like French fries.

"Got some new emails? I saw your computer out and you finger-pecking on the keys when I stopped by. You researching a new conspiracy theory?"

"Interesting you'd ask," stated John between mouthfuls. "I really don't know yet, but there *is* something strange going on. First, I find an expensive-looking box with a broken crystal in it, then, I get this blank email from George that's got a doubly-encrypted attachment that opens to a password we invented years ago. Serendipity, maybe, but I have a suspicion it's something dark and hush-hush that has to do with oil." John cut his baked potato into strips and smeared them in butter, waiting for Josh to comment.

"So you're trying to kill me after all?" Josh asked, acting like he was choking. "I almost fell for your crazy suggestion. Hell, I always do at first. So what exactly merits *you* a center stage ticket into another fictional conspiracy play?" Josh countered.

"Come on, Josh, I'm serious! I run across a mysterious black box, I receive an urgent email with an attachment containing a bunch of encrypted numbers that tells me to read and then destroy it, and you're not in the least intrigued? Just in case, I copied the attachment onto a thumb drive. I've stashed the crystal shard—that's what the black box contains—and the thumb drive in my locker for the time being. And, by the way, there was a series of company logos at the top of the attached document. The center one sported an idealized orthorhombic crystal just like the crystal from which the fragment I got would likely have come from. Orthorhombic. You get it? Not a usual shape for a crystal. One like psychics use. One like government and industry researchers use to store complex three-dimensional images approaching a yottabyte or more in size."

Josh's fork stopped in mid-arc, and he looked at John blank-faced.

"You know, Josh, a yottabyte—ten to the twenty-fourth power bytes—a quadrillion gigabytes!"

Josh's unspeaking mouth formed an oval "O." Getting his speech back, Josh said emotionlessly, "Yeah, of course. So this *is* another conspiracy theory! Look, man, we've been through this before. If you don't be careful, one of these days people are going to get wind of your crazy ideas and either fire you, or if one of your theories just happens to end up being true, kill you! I mean, maybe it's just a piece of someone's healing crystal or something. Maybe the email's another of George's practical jokes. I mean, it wouldn't be the first! Jeeze, sometimes I think you're so gullible, John. The trouble is, gullible or not, you always sound so…knowledgeable when you explain your theories. It's so damn easy to believe you. I mean, what if someone actually did believe you, and the conspiracy is somehow even partially true? Are you ready to live your life on the run from all the dark shadows in the world? Here, have some coffee. Maybe it'll bring you back to earth. 'Hello, John! Earth here'!" Josh chided offering his friend his coffee mug.

John stared at the mug and what little was left of his steak in silence.

"Look, John, if you really weren't supposed to receive that email, that alone would place you in serious trouble. I mean, you're not supposed to be downloading someone else's emails," Josh offered.

"I didn't download anyone's emails," John insisted. "It was sent to me by my friend, George Franks, and, yes, he and I've played tricks on each other before, but, Josh, I don't think that's what's happening this time. I think…I think this could be for real."

"That's just plain crazy! For God's sake, get some rest before you babble on. Think, man: How would George come across something so ultra-secret, and, even if he somehow did, why email it to *you!* For Chrisakes, why not send it to the FBI or the CIA or…some what-cha-ma-call-it military intelligence organization? Think, man! Why?"

John continued to sit silently as if contemplating an answer, then looked up. "Nonetheless, it *was* sent to my mailbox. The email appears to have originated from a guy named Leon Puissegur."

"Leon Puissegur? Isn't that the crazy oil man who's always writing about non-biological oil constantly being created in the center of the earth? Jeeze, that alone should throw up a red flag! Hey, speaking of Leon Puissegur, wasn't that him I saw walking our derrick earlier today? O-o-o-o-o! Now we can add a ghost to this whole fantasy! Or maybe he really *was* here, stopping by on his way to some 'secret' drilling platform where they're drilling for abiotic oil? What if the email and attachment were so secret, they were sent by Mr. Puissegur to himself for his meeting, and somehow your friend at Rustic Central got everything screwed up, forwarding it to you instead of him? Hell, what if the black box contains Puissegur's voodoo crystal for locating abiotic oil, and he accidently dropped it? That's just as likely a theory!"

"Yeah, Josh, and somehow, everything 'accidently' ends up in my lap. Me with just enough of a security clearance to work this rig. Besides, I don't know what the email attachment means. It was just a set of ten numbers. Okay, so now you're criticizing my 'conspiracy' idea while coming up with your own! Josh, let's let it go for now. All these coincidences are interesting, even intriguing, but I'm too tired to speculate further on what it all might or might not mean. And as for the Leon Puissegur thing, now that you mention his work, I recall running across his name from time to time on the Internet. Wait. Is this all a lot of Josh bullshit?"

"On the other hand," Josh said, baiting his friend further, "maybe it's a test. You know, a loyalty test or something in preparation for a big promotion. Don't laugh! It could just as easily be that, and if so, then what exactly do you plan to do with the email and crystal, John? I mean, you've got to at least report the box."

"I planned to stop by and inform the company man on the way here, but I got so wrapped up in the food and conversation, I forgot. He's probably gone now, so I'm thinking I'll mention it to him first thing in the morning before next shift."

"Okay, John, but don't say I didn't warn you."

"Warn me about what?" demanded John indignantly. "I don't get what exactly you think I have stashed away in my locker, unless... unless it was *you* who sent it! Jeeze, Josh, did you leave the box there and send that email to me? Is this payback for all the crazy jokes I've played on you in the past?"

"No, John, that I guarantee. I have better things to do then to set you up. Besides, I'm an ignoramus about all that highflalutin conspiracy stuff you're always spouting off about, *and* I don't know enough about computers to create an encrypted email attachment like that, especially one using you and George's 'secret' key. I do know a bit about that Leon Puissegur guy, but probably no more than anyone else on the rig. But I'm pretty sure I saw him on the rig, though."

"Then I guess I can count you out as the person who sent it to me," John said with finality, and looked nervously at his watch. It was already seven. John picked his tray up and Josh followed him to the clean-up area where they tossed their dishes and trays onto a conveyer belt.

"Come on, John. What with all the pre-movie commercials they show nowadays, we won't have missed any of the movie," Josh offered, tugging at John's shirtsleeve as they walked back down hallway.

"You go, Josh. I've seen the movies here so many times that I know what's going to happen before anyone says anything."

Josh slapped John fondly on the back of the head. "Okay, old man, you go and rest. I'll catch up with you later."

14

John didn't reply. At fifty-eight years of age, he was close to retirement. With thirty-eight of those years with Rustic Oil, he'd already put in enough time to draw his maximum, but Rustic, by this time, 'owned' his heart and soul. A 'foreign' outfit, New South Wales Petroleum, had hired the rig, and John felt responsible for protecting *his* American workers from foreigners and the way they had handled Blue Water Horizon when it blew several months ago. John had friends working on Blue Water Horizon rig, and he knew from the ever-present oil gossip that the 'company', meaning the company that had hired the rig, NSWP, had skimped here and there in order to better its profits. The result was that the rig hadn't proven as safe as it appeared on paper. His former driller-friend on Blue Water Horizon had paid for their misconduct with his life. Drilling was a risky business, even when the most stringent safety measures were upheld.

"Aw, come on, man! We've barely missed the opening," Josh said, stopping abruptly and breaking into John's reverie.

"No, you go. I'm going back to my room to rest," John repeated, giving Josh a quick wave as he turned towards his room.

John entered his room and climbed directly into his bunk, the day's exhaustion immediately overtaking him. It felt like he'd barely dozed off when klaxons throughout the rig began sounding.

Jumping to his feet, he merged into the stream of men walking worriedly but calmly down the corridor towards the main control office. As he entered the spacious area he noted several senior officials huddling around a pressure gauge panel with several red lights flashing. Workers were gathering in a semicircle surrounding the console area and murmuring. John's counter-part, Kelty Moss, was standing in the middle.

"The pipe just jumped sixteen inches into the air!" explained one of the men next to John, pointing at one flashing light in particular.

The needle on the gauge next to it was oscillating back and forth in the red "danger" zone.

John turned toward the man dressed in a dirty blue jump suit who had informed him, and was about to conjecture further about the meaning of the alarm. He was the mud man and his position in particular was suddenly critical. John, the most senior of the Rustic staff present, signaled the mud man to join him in the center of the group. "Have you thrown black magic into the hole?" John questioned.

"Already done, boss," the veteran oilman acknowledged coolly above the din. "I was warned by the super about a likely pressure buildup well before the pipe jumped, and on Kelty's order immediately threw some into the hole. It should be nearing the pressure source about...now." The mud man looked concernedly at his watch, then back at John and the control panel. The flashing red lights went off, the klaxon stopped, and the needle on the pressure gauge dropped into the yellow zone, indicating that the mud man's prompt action had bought them the necessary time to investigate the cause of the sudden pressure jump.

John wiped sweat from his forehead. "That was close." Turning to the NSWP company man who had just joined the group, he continued. "I strongly suggest you order an immediate survey."

"I've already ordered Dresser Legend, the most experienced contract 'event' engineer we know, out here as soon as possible. In the meantime, do you think it's safe enough to continue drilling?" Chris Longley, the company representative from NSWP asked, looking shaken but resolved.

"No," John replied curtly. "If you don't order the temporary suspension, I will, at least until the survey is completed."

Chris paled, then nodded his assent.

With Chris's consent, John turned his attention back to the mud man and continued. "Have the men clean everything up as best they can. The rest of you," John swept his arm across the milling crowd and shouted, "get to work! Kelty and I'll personally assist with any further problems until the survey crew gets here."

Kelty Moss pressed the "all clear" button on the console. Moss was well-trained, and this was his first 'super', meaning supervisor, assignment, having serving for years as the chief control operator, running the banks of computers that controlled the overall operation of the platform. He was also another of John's longtime neighborhood friends from Violet, Louisiana.

Finding his voice at last, Kelty yelled, "Everyone not on this shift is dismissed. Go back to whatever you were doing. The crisis is over," adding as he refaced John, "at least for now…"

John finished for his friend: "…and, Chris, make sure the survey people get out here ASAP. We don't want another Blue Water Horizon event. Kelty, have the men on duty secure the pipe where it is in the well."

"Consider it done," Kelty replied, as if suddenly reawakening from a nightmare.

"Gentlemen," John offered, deciding that now was not the appropriate time to bring up either shard or email with the worried company man, "I am going off to get some sleep. Call me if anything changes."

The Oil Man

CHAPTER 2

Joan Mistral, Dresser Legend's private secretary, was distracted by the dulcet tones of the dedicated New South Wales Petroleum answering device she carried 24/7. Standing behind Dresser, who was admiring the Houston skyline view from his Museum Tower high-rise, she quietly backed away to answer what was obviously an emergency call. Being constantly away on business, Dresser was calculating that the late night view before him was costing roughly a hundred dollars a minute.

At fifty-six years of age, Dresser had it all: this $10,000 a month hide-away apartment in Houston, a million-dollar-a-year expense account, a McLauren F1 street coupe in his private parking space, an Emtjet private charter Gulfstream V-SP jet at his call, and a beautiful private secretary to meet his other needs, all paid, of course, by huge retainers from NSWP and his other clients. In return, whenever trouble struck anywhere in the world, he was the one they called.

After a moment, Joan turned and placed the phone in his hand while caressing his cheek. Dresser ran one hand through his salt-and-pepper hair and answered. "Dresser here. This had better be

19

important." Having just arrived home after an onsite emergency survey of NSWP's Northsea One Platform near Stavanger, Norway, he was heavily jetlagged at four in the morning Houston Time.

"Sorry to call, sir, but we're experiencing a problem at Trojan Horse Well, Rustic Oil Rig Twelve, in the Gulf of Mexico. An hour ago, a pressure surge shoved a deep pipe sixteen inches back. We dropped some Black Magic down the hole and the pressure has decreased to cautionary levels, but the Rustic Oil super, a tool pusher named John Marx, has shut down the operation. I was told to contact you should anything like this happen."

"Is this Chris Layton with New South Wales?" asked Dresser. Joan slid a dinner chair behind him to sit. Dresser didn't wait for an answer. "Sorry if I sound brusque, but I just returned home from another NSWP emergency survey and I'm still adjusting. Work with the Rustic super. It's fortunate that he's also the tool pusher. Do whatever he suggests, and *don't* make the same mistakes as were made on the Blue Water Horizon. I'll call the flight crew and have them fly me to New Orleans, then grab a helicopter to Venice; the boat with all our tools and equipment will be enroute before I leave for New Orleans. I should be there in three hours. Keep in touch with me every fifteen minutes until the situation is under control."

Joan, anticipating Dresser's orders from what she was overhearing, was already on her cell phone talking with Emtjet. She was placing a call to Rustic Oil Central advising them to ready a helicopter to take them immediately to Rig Twelve, when Dresser put the cell phone on speaker.

"I don't believe you need to fly here, sir, and it's Longley, sir, not Layton, " Chris Longley explained. "It looks like a gas pocket, nothing more. Furthermore, your presence might draw the Department of Transportation's Pipeline and Hazardous Materials Safety

Administration's attention to this site, and with the current attitude of United States President and administration, the situation might be used as an excuse to shut down drilling in the Gulf. The administration's aware of the several...'problems' like Blue Water Horizon NSWP's experienced lately. It's obviously not my call, but I wanted you to be completely informed, in case your flying here happened to result in this so far non-event leaking to the press and going national."

"Hmm. Okay, Chris," Dresser said, signaling to Joan to cancel the arrangements she was making. "But let me know if anything new happens. Anything at all. I'll send Claude Askins' survey team. They're my best, and will present a much lower profile. How deep were we when it happened?"

Chris sounded relieved by Dresser's solution, and his use of the word, "we."

"We were down almost 35,200 feet, some 1,000 plus feet from where we ultimately want to be. I'll send you a report as soon as Askins gets here and I have more information. Right now, everything's stable."

"Very deep," Dresser murmured. "I'll call Claude as soon as I hang up. He and his team should be well into the survey by tomorrow. But before I hang up, do you remember the meeting we had with the 'other company' and their consultant?"

"You mean the one several weeks ago regarding a possible new source of oil?"

"Yes," Dresser answered, uncomfortable disclosing even the few details Chris was disclosing over the secure line. "I was on my way back from Stavanger when I was informed that one of the consultant's emails had been...intercepted. It contains confidential information relating to that meeting. NSWP Corporate thinks it was intentionally relayed by the employee at Rustic Central to someone on Rig Twelve but they're having a hard time pinning things down. Apparently the email was cleverly programmed to erase its pathway as it traveled."

Dresser cringed as he spoke. That information hadn't been meant for anyone outside the inner circle, including Chris. Dresser would need the man's help, however, to try to locate and contain the leak if he wasn't going to fly there and track it down himself. "If you come across anyone who reports having received an unusual, likely indecipherable email there on the rig, inform me immediately. Take care, and guard what I've just shared with you. And make sure you keep me up to date on that pressure problem," Dresser concluded.

"I will, sir," acknowledged Chris. "And, I'll keep my ears open about any strange emails." The line went dead before Chris had the opportunity to tell Dresser about another odd incident: the unexpected, unannounced and so far unexplained visit of two obviously important visitors earlier in the day. The first had arrived anonymously in a Rustic helicopter, to be hustled along the outside walkway and swept inside to the central conference room, departing on the same helicopter a short time later. The second visitor had arrived moments after the first in what looked like an NSWP corporate helicopter, departing before the first visitor left. Their meeting on Rustic Rig Twelve, currently NSWP Trojan Horse Well, if that was what it was, had lasted less than fifteen minutes. That seemed odder to Chris than any errant email.

Shrugging his shoulders, Chris returned his attentions to the control room. He could remember when control rooms had been a mostly empty room with a single, small panel. Now, oil platform control rooms were filled with banks of display panels that, together, oversaw almost everything that happened on the rig. The main processing computer was located below the control room in a constant seventy-two degree, twenty-five-square-foot room replete with tandem

Intel-based i7 processors, eight redundant real-time back-up computers, and a bank of dedicated, high speed fault-and-disaster-tolerant routers linked electronically and optically to both Rustic Oil Central and its current client, New South Wales Petroleum Corporate. One entire panel in the control room was dedicated to monitoring well depth, visually displaying the drill pipe superimposed over a caricature of the rig standing on the Gulf bottom, showing the pipe working its way down the projected borehole and into the seabed. Petroleum exploration had come a long way in the last ten years. Still, all the computers in the world couldn't yet replace an experienced rig super and tool man like John Marx.

Chris inspected the various gauges in the control room. Kelty, the current super, had left the room while Chris was consulting Dresser Legend. Chris didn't recognize the man taking Kelty's place. The man waved to Chris.

"Can I help you?" he asked, obviously not recognizing Chris either. "Name's Charles Staub. Kelty asked me to fill in for him while he takes a short break. Anything I can do for you?" Chris sighed, rubbed the tiredness from his dark brown eyes, and pulled a chair up next to the man.

"Glad to meet you, Charles. I'm Chris Longley, the NSWP rep," Chris said, offering the startled man his hand. "I don't usually end up interacting much with the evening and night shifts unless there's trouble. Would you please pull the pressure stats from the incident?" Chris could have called NSWP Corporate, but decided to use in-house data. He didn't want to run the risk of piquing any outside interests. Besides, it would give him the opportunity of impressing on this man that he, Chris Longley, was 'in charge' of the situation.

"Sorry, sir. Kelty mentioned that you were about, but he didn't describe what you looked like. So, welcome to the evening operation.

It'll take me a moment to pull that data up, but it's no problem." Charles worked the keyboard like a concert pianist, the LCD screen morphing as he typed to show the different pressures within the drill hole alongside a two-dimensional visual representation of the pipe. It showed an abrupt increase in both pipe and hole pressure the moment before the pipe jumped.

"Can you focus on the ten or so minutes before the jump?" Chris moved closer.

Charles again worked the computer keys like a virtuoso. The numbers on the screen changed to normal. "Does that do it, sir?" he asked.

"Now move the time slowly forward. I'm looking for any indication of a gas bubble," Chris explained.

"Sit back and enjoy, sir," Charles replied. Both watched the screen as he rolled his fingers slowly over the mouse ball until the pipe pressure suddenly increased. It happened so quickly that Chris, exhausted from the day's emergency, almost failed to notice an indistinct blur pass out of view well before the inner pipe had been abruptly displaced.

"Can you please repeat, slower this time, so I can see what that blur was?" Chris requested.

"Yes, sir. No one mentioned noticing any blur like that." Charles punched a few keys, and the pipe returned to its resting position. Run slower, the blur was more distinct, looking like a shadow moving snake-like but quickly through the adjoining rock, suddenly entering and traveling up the pipe.

"Can you go back again and freeze the screen where the blob first appears?" Chris entreated.

A moment later the screen showed a bubble-like bulge bursting into the hole. In the next frame, it vanished.

"Did you see that?" Chris asked, pointing at the screen.

"Yes, sir. I've never read nor heard mention of anything like that in all my years. It looked like a bubble of oil or gas bursting in from *outside* of the well. Do you want copies?"

"If you can, sure, but until the survey team arrives and they see this, I'd like to keep it between you and me. I don't know what we witnessed, and I want to be certain it's not an artifact. Can you save it as a video?"

"Sure, and I won't mention it to anyone until you tell me," Charles promised, copying the static photographs and then doing the necessary magic to allow them to be viewed sequentially as a movie. Finished, he handed it to Chris.

"You could go far in this business with the kind of discretion you've just displayed," Chris stated, adding, "I'll mention your name when I report this to my bosses at NSWP. The company rewards cooperation." Chris got up, patted Charles on the shoulder and, pocketing the thumb drive, walked out of the room. He wanted to return to the privacy of his room to more fully digest what he'd seen. It had looked like a spurt of oil bubbling up from below. An oil bubble, and if so, one of highly refined oil. To his knowledge, no one had ever reported such a thing. Maybe this was just the evidence his superiors were looking for.

In actuality, Chris ended up walking out onto the rig floor where, despite the hour, everyone was working feverishly. Under the banks of brilliant white xenon floodlights, roustabouts were cleaning equipment, roughnecks the pipe and pipe racks, the driller and his assistants the drill platform. Chris leaned over a side-rail to peer into the warm, brilliantly-lit gulf waters below. Fish were flashing around the wellhead attracted by the glare. Flying fish pierced the still water and sailed like a row of pelicans on outstretched fins, disappearing twenty feet away.

Switching from below to above, Chris looked into an inky black sky. The heavens looked as if a fistful of diamond dust had been haphazardly scattered across the sky. Then and only then did he begin thinking about what he would say about the 'oil bubble' he had just observed to NSWP Corporate.

Despite years of experience and rapid advances in petroleum technology, Chris knew that much of oil exploration still depended heavily on luck. Before, oil companies like NSWP would drill wherever they thought the oil might be, which sometimes meant ending up with a dry well unknowingly inches from where the oil was, and other times nowhere near any oil. Nowadays, oil companies had a better idea of where the oil was, based upon the interlaced, three-dimensional surveys by companies like Dresser Legend's and Claude Askins'. The drilling process had similarly improved. Seismic sensors within the drill pipe could often ferret out a collateral oil field, or areas that might fail in the future, allowing workmen to shore up a well long before an incident occurred. The biggest problem was locating and identifying an amorphous liquid mass miles below where all the experience and technology was concentrated.

Staring at the dark horizon, Chris saw a flash of red and green in the distance, and watched, intrigued, as the two colors descended and grew apart. Most likely, it was the morning workboat bringing food and supplies for the crew. The survey crew would arrive by helicopter, probably later in the day, eating up another of his promised furlough days. He was required by contract to spend as much time on duty as necessary to keep his bosses constantly advised during any incidents like this one. With the photos he was fingering in his pocket, he already had an idea of what had caused the pipe to jump, and, if it turned out as he suspected, his superiors would have reason to reward him.

Looking back across the rig floor, he noted underneath the derrick where the kelly, the pulley used to position new pipe, hung motionless. It was strange to see so much deck activity, without any drilling.

Chris stretched his arms above his head, yawned, and turned to re-enter the complex. Walking the deserted corridor to his room, he entered, then closed the door, pausing just long enough to look in the mirror at the streaks of gray forming along his temples and the crow's feet in the corners of his eyes. The stress of the job was getting to him. Wondering if maybe he should dye his hair back to its natural dark brown, he turned and sat on the edge of the bed. How much should he tell his superiors and the crew about what he suspected had caused the pressure buildup? What should he do about trying to find out who, if anyone, had received the email Dresser Legend had tasked him to locate? And what had the meeting between those two big-shots been about earlier in the day? Chris slipped off his shoes and climbed onto his bed, meaning to ponder while he waited out the few remaining hours to see what the new day would bring. Instead, the moment his head alighted on the pillow, he fell fast asleep.

The Oil Man

CHAPTER 3

Oh-five-hundreds hours might be early for many, but not John Marx. Even back home in Violet, he woke regularly at exactly that time, unless he'd been up partying into the wee hours with George, Josh or Kelty.

John rubbed his eyes and climbed out of bed. Leaning on the small wash-counter next to his bed, he turned on the water and splashed some on his face. A quick towel dry, and he looked into the mirror just above the sink to assess if any of the usual tell-tale signs of pulling the double shift persisted. Aside from his slightly bloodshot eyes, he decided he looked pretty good. On second look, his face appeared a little fatter then last year, which he immediately attributed to the increased sitting his bad back and knees dictated.

Staring at a single grey hair that had turned snowy white, John's thoughts drifted back to 1971, during the waning days of the Vietnam War. He had been training for a deep penetration mission to eliminate a particularly grievous North Vietnamese general. He and his spotter were positioned to jump out the open side-door of the chopper and rappel twenty-feet onto a plot of grass not more then ten feet square.

His spotter went first, and John had followed directly behind him. A quarter of the way down, the line was hit by a bullet or failed, he never knew which, causing him to fall the last fifteen feet directly upon his spotter. He would never forget the spotter's blank upward stare as three hundred pounds of man and equipment struck, cracking the spotter's neck in two. Feeling for a neck pulse seemed superfluous given the six inches of bone left protruding out from under the man's skull. John's own back felt as if he had been stabbed with a knife, but he wouldn't know all the details of his two herniated disks until later in 1990 when Veterans Affairs sent him to get one of the new Magnetic Resonance Images. Unlike even the newest petroleum industry ground imaging equipment, MRI's could discern between similar densities, in his case, separating out damaged cartilage, ligament, and other tissue His MRI showed one disk had shrunk fifty percent, it's neighbor, rubbing bone against bone from below. Several surgeries later, he'd been dubbed "fixed," but the injury still caused him pain, especially when it was humid, or when a storm approached. "Weatherman" his surviving 'Nam buddies at the VA hospital nicknamed him.

John slicked what there was left of his hair back with his hands, and checked his watch. It was 0530. He had about half an hour before he had to be either out on the derrick or in the central console area, depending on where he was needed most. He was a go-directly-to-work man, breakfasts reminding him too much of his 'Nam days. Eating anything in the mornings made him feel sick all day.

Retrieving laptop and box from his clothes locker, he placed the two side-by-side and thought while the laptop came to life. He wanted to relook at the message he'd received from his buddy, George, at Rustic Central. In less than three hours, George would be back on shift and he could call, either continuing the joke or, if it wasn't a joke, get as much information as he could about the email before informing the

NSWP representative, the "company man," Chris Longley, of the situation.

Removing the thumb-drive from the box and inserting it into the slot in his computer, the email attachment icon popped into view, patiently awaiting the decryption key his friend had obviously added. John no longer doubted that the email and attachment were originally from Leon Puissegur, the acknowledged "crazy" abiotic oil man his friend, Josh, had told him about. After the first decryption, John settled into a closer examination of the icon in the center of the otherwise blank letter: The symbol of the world with a sword piercing it. On close look, it wasn't just any sword, but a double-edged broadsword akin to those used by the Scots' highlanders but without a guard, more like the broadswords used by the Chinese in ancient times but straight rather than curved. Searching the Internet, he was able to identify the sword as a type of double-edged Japanese Tsurugi sword no longer in common use. A search for "world" and "Tsurugi sword" yielded an identical logo, that of the Dan Sogo Shosha Corporation. Apparently DSSC, as it was referred to in several obtuse Internet articles, was some kind of multinational super-corporation dealing in esoteric trade, information analysis and advanced computer data systems. Additional searches revealed associations not only with the expected array of computer corporations, but also multinational energy corporations including British Petroleum International (BPI), the parent company of BPI America, New South Wales Petroleum and, interestingly, a primary shareholder in Rustic Oil. Heady fodder for an avowed conspiracy theorist.

It was, however, two even more obscure Internet references to DSSC as a kind of international *daimyo,* an association of organizations that had appeared in tenth to nineteenth century Japan, the purpose of which had been to control the powerful samurai clans and the nobles' private land holdings—and thereby the government of Japan—that grabbed and held his interest.

John checked his watch. His shift would begin in less than fifteen minutes. Looking quickly at the ten numbers, he wondered what they might represent. If it had something to do with the unusual crystal shard and if the shard was optically activated, as it appeared to be, then it might be the dimensional bearings for directing a beam of light at a certain frequency into the crystal to shake free whatever might be concealed within. Then, the message might require further decryption, or it might represent a coded message, or George's cell phone number, or something purposefully devised by George to drive John mad.

Time was flying. John shut the computer down, closed the laptop, and returned it and the box containing the fragment of crystal and thumb drive into his locker. As he turned the key in the lock, he was once again surprised by Josh's smiling face peering in through the open doorway.

"John! After last night, I had to check to make sure you hadn't overslept. The helicopter with the survey crew will be arriving in twenty minutes." Josh held the door open until John joined him.

"I want you to work with the survey team from the moment they come on board till the moment they leave," John instructed with a clarity of mind that surprised Josh. "Help them set up the extra pulleys necessary to position and control their down-hole equipment, and make certain no one and nothing gets in their way. They can take over once they've off-loaded all their equipment; the bulk of their equipment came in by workboat late last night. Make sure everything is where they want it, and clear the ramps so they can set up all their tools. I want this survey done fast and right. I've got a feeling…"

"Meaning you want me to spy on them and report to you whatever they find," Josh restated candidly, as John turned towards the

32

control room.

"Um," John replied from a distance. Josh continued on his way outside to carry out John's instructions.

John walked directly into the center of the main console area. "I'm going out to meet the survey crew. I want to see who NSWP has contracted with to do the survey. I hope it's Dresser Legend, the guy they used last time. Despite the final outcome, he was good and fast."

Kelty Moss was double-shifting at the console computer, running the usual morning scans to make sure the servers and platform programs hadn't picked up any malware during the night. "Right-oh, John. If anyone asks, I'll let them know you're on deck."

According to the console clock, the helicopter wouldn't arrive for ten minutes, so he took his time walking to the helipad. Near the derrick, he could see Josh giving orders to several men to organize and stack the equipment that had arrived by launch last night. To his surprise, watching everything, including him, from a railing above was the NSWP company man, Chris Longley.

Above the helipad, the sky glowed a cloudless baby-blue. The horizon in every direction, however, seemed dark and moody. Heavy black clouds billowed threateningly towards the heavens. The air felt hot and humid, as if it might pour at any moment.

John continued to the heliport, each step feeling like nails were being driven into his knees and back. It was the damn weather. His back began to ache more with each jarring step. His final steps to the plexiglass-protected heliport walkway were living hell, and he stopped to catch his breath and look out across the Gulf towards the North. A red-gold speck was speeding toward him, the colors decrying it a Rustic helicopter. He looked at the windsock and noticed that the wind was coming across the landing zone from the East. so he anticipated that the helicopter would make its approach from the West for a more stable landing.

John leaned back against the railing, to be joined a moment later by Chris.

Chris asked the obvious: "Waiting for the survey crew?"

"Yeah. You, too?" John replied, asking the equally obvious. "Thought you might sleep in this morning after all of last night's activity."

"I'm a company man," replied Chris. "'No rest for the wicked'," he misquoted from the Bible's Book of Isaiah.

"Here like me to greet the survey team?" John continued, ordering his back and knees to stop their throbbing.

"Not actually," Chris replied. John noticed that the man was wringing his hands tensely as if the meager conversation were difficult. "I need their final analysis, and your multi-million dollar 'continue drilling' decision. Like I said, I'm the company man, remember?" Chris smiled weakly. "There's also another matter. One of some delicacy that I need to talk with you about." The reddish-gold speck in the distance had resolved into a Rustic helicopter, though the details stenciled on its sides were not yet visible.

"Last night I called Dresser Legend," Chris began. John acknowledged what he'd expected Chris would say with a nod. "Dresser sent the 'A' survey team–BPI's best–but declined coming, himself."

John's face dropped slightly.

"Don't worry. I've been reporting in to him regularly, though there's been nothing much to report since the incident. Dresser tasked me to…check if anyone on the rig had received an erroneous email. I promised I'd do so, and thought if anyone would know, you, the day super, would. Has anyone mentioned receiving a wrong or strange email to you?" Chris was taking extraordinary pains to make his

34

interest sound casual, but was an unaccomplished liar.

John startled. If Chris was talking about the email *he'd* received yesterday, then perhaps there was substance to his concerns after all. Still, rig-rental-company-be-damned, John felt disinclined to release *any* information until he'd had a chance to contact his friend, George. And what of the box with the crystal fragment Chris hadn't mentioned?

"Anything else missing?" John asked languidly, putting a hand to his forehead to wipe off several lines of sweat and, at the same time, lessen the glare from above.

"Nope. Nothing but the NSWP loss projections based on last night's fiasco," teased Chris.

"I'll let you know if anyone mentions an unusual email. Did you check with Kelty?"

"Yep. Just before I came out here to talk with you. Please let me know immediately if *anyone* reports such. I wouldn't want corporate to think I wasn't fully representing their wishes out here."

During their conversation, the red-gold helicopter had continued growing in size and taking on details. The humid air began to vibrate, then thump like a drum. The helicopter was one of the sleek new ones, French-made, like the ones the Louisiana Coast Guard favored for fast in-and-out work. Hovering above the pad, the pilot trimmed out the wind, kicking up a strong enough vortex to make John and Chris, despite the plexiglass protector, hold on to their hard hats. The helicopter settled and the engines began whining. The pilot shut them down abruptly—a little unusual, since, because of cost, most of the time the pilot would be expected to leave right away for another job on another rig. This one was obviously at the expensive beck and call of some important occupants.

The doors opened and three men jumped out. Number three, dressed in standard-issue BPI coveralls and wearing a Dresser Legend team baseball cap, walked directly up to John and greeted him warmly. "You must be John Marx. Mr. McClaussen talked highly of you on the flight out," said a tall, lanky man with dark brown eyes and perfect white teeth that made his long, stringy brown hair and Genghis Khan mustache look totally out of place. "I'm Claude Askins, engineer in charge of this survey. We were told to run a three-D survey and do a nuke check to make sure the pipe didn't side-swipe a gas pocket. Mr. McClaussen has asked Chris to escort my two men inside and help them temporarily stow our personal gear so we can get started as soon as possible." Aside from mentioning his name, Claude otherwise ignored Chris Longley. The two other men, also dressed in BPI working clothes and Dresser Legend caps, followed a chagrined Chris along the decking and into the interior of the platform.

John examined the engineer as if sizing him up, then shook the man's pro-offered hand, placing him at last. "Hey, I remember you. You did a survey on a former rig I was working on. You did a good job, and everything turned out fine. Your equipment is laid out on the deck. I suggest you get going on the survey. The shift driller and mud engineer are on deck, should you need them." John pointed out the two men to Claude. "We dumped black magic down the hole, so you'll have to do a bit of cleaning as you proceed."

"Damn," Claude cursed. "Black Magic is *the* worst drilling mud to have to clean off equipment. Still, I anticipated it and brought the necessary cleaning solution. This means, of course, it will likely take twice the usual amount of time to run the survey," Claude said, smiling at the thought of the substantial increase in final payment the Black Magic would afford him.

A big man—John estimated him to be six-foot-six-inches tall—climbed out of the back of the helicopter, straightened a custom-made, no-nonsense grey business suit, stretched, and began to walk over toward John and Claude. "That's the big boss, Mr. McClaussen. He wants to talk to you. I'll catch up later," Claude concluded, following in the direction his two colleagues had been escorted.

John stared at the giant man heading towards him. McClaussen stopped abruptly in front of John, extended a hand, and said in a deep, booming voice, "I'm Shaun McClaussen, owner of several of the oil companies that are sub-contracting your company's rig for this venture. I'm here to personally assess the extent of the problem reported by Chris Longley the other day. I usually bring an assistant, but there wasn't room for him and the survey crew. I wanted to come out with the survey crew to learn a little bit more about the people, yours, theirs, and mine, and determine their mettle. We've a lot invested in this venture, and I'm hoping to get the drilling back on track as rapid as humanly possible."

"Yes, sir, Mr. McClaussen," John replied, accepting the man's massive hand, while feeling personally taken aback. It was unusual for an oil executive to accompany a survey crew. It was even more unusual for the executive to also happen to be a senior BPI executive.

"Call me Shaun, John," the big man replied, shaking John's hand vigorously.

"Yes, sir…Shaun," John replied with obvious awkwardness. "May I show you around, sir?" he asked, sweeping an arm towards the walkway and interior door. "I'd be pleased to summarize everything that's happened so far with you."

Shaun McClaussen's steel-grey eyes bored into John. Then, as if dismissing something as unimportant, McClaussen continued with assurance, "I'm sure you will, John."

John took a deep breath. "You will probably want to locate yourself in either the control room or the executive conference room overlooking it. Go through the door, down three flights of stairs and take a right. The entrance to the Control room will be to your left and the executive conference room to your right. I'll be down to join you in a moment." John watched as the pilot secured the tie-downs necessary to hold the helicopter fast. The man then proceeded to approach John as if intending to follow McClaussen while maintaining a respectful distance between himself and the big executive. The pilot stopped abruptly as he was about to pass John.

"Hey! Aren't you the sniper that fell out of my chopper? Crazy John, the Weatherman?" John gave him a deer-caught-in-the-headlights look, not knowing what to say or do. Though he couldn't recall the man's name, he had recognized the man's familiar, thick Boston accent, so different from the usual mixed Texas-Southern-Cajun he heard everyday on the rigs.

"Come, John. You look like you just saw the devil," the pilot offered. "Forgotten your old buddy's name? It's Stan," the man said, offering a hand. "Stan Meyers."

John hung his head and shook the hand. "Stan. Jeeze, I'm sorry. With all that's transpired since the last time we met, and with the last couple of hectic days here on the oil platform, I did seem to have misplaced it. What are you doing flying Rustic helicopters? Last I heard, you were freelancing up in…Massachusetts, wasn't it."

"I was, but like most jobs today, it was all piecemeal contract work. 'Outsourcing' they call it, but what it amounted to was little money, no benefits, and no job security. I was lucky to get the job with Rustic. One Rustic pilot left for a better job and another retired. Not many pilots want to work down here running air-taxi service. I'm currently doing runs for the heads of three big oil companies down here: Rustic, NSWP and BPI. It was a coincidence that the survey crew needed to be hauled out here the same time as McClaussen. It's good to see you, but, hey, I should let you go. I know McClaussen, he's going to expect you and the company man to follow him like ducklings while answering a seemingly endless stream of questions."

John shook his head in disbelief. "We should get together later, today; it looks to me like you're going to be here for a while. By the way, here on the rig, I'm chief, cook and bottle-washer. Translated, that means day super, tool pusher and Rustic company man. Chris Longley is with NSWP, who are currently leasing the platform. He's, of course, the real 'company man.' Chris will probably be busy with McClaussen and the survey men, so when you go down below, ask for Kelty, and tell him I said for him to comandeer you a room." The two hugged genuinely but awkwardly.

John was about to release, when Stan whispered in his ear. "Something funny's going on. You hear about the Rustic Central break-in last night? A communications man was found dead. What's more, nothing was stolen as far as anyone can tell. Watch your back, John. McClaussen's not here just to supervise the survey and give them medals for a quick resolution."

"Thanks for the heads-up, Stan," John whispered back, releasing his friend and looking him in the eye. "Wouldn't happen to know the name of the person who was found dead, would you?"

"Franks," Stan replied. "George Franks. Didn't happen to know the guy, did you?"

John froze, stunned by the news of his friend's death, the man who'd sent him the email and attachment he'd planned to call later that morning. John had been counting on talking with George before deciding what, if anything, he should tell Chris. As Stan clanked his way across the metal catwalk, a tear wetted John's weathered cheek. Shaking off the shock as best he could, he followed Stan inside and made his way to where he thought Mr. McClaussen would be waiting.

McClaussen was in the center of the control room, towering

above all the workers, asking questions of anyone foolish enough to get within questioning range. As John sided up to the huge man, he overheard McClaussen asking a worker whether he or anyone he knew had accidently received an email with just the word, "oil" in the heading. John's reaction was to answer reflexively for the man, but he forced himself to pause, deciding instead to find out why corporate men like Longley and now McClaussen were so worried about an email. John was about to ask, when the imposing executive turned and looked directly at him. "Where's my new company man?" McClaussen boomed commandingly.

John, assuming Chris hadn't yet returned from escorting the survey team to their quarters and back to the platform, answered, "Chris Longley should be here momentarily, sir."

"You're not understanding me. That man's an incompetent fool. I sent him away and I'm looking for someone to replace him." McClaussen continued looking down from his high vantage. "I need to know the whereabouts of the top man representing Rustic."

John held his hands up and shrugged. "Then that would be me, John Marx, at your service, sir. I assumed you knew I was the Rustic company man in charge of the operation of this rig. So, now that you've found your 'new company man,' it's my turn to ask *you* a question, if you don't mind: Why all the interest in an email when we're sitting here on a potential Blue Water Horizon?"

Everyone in the control room stopped.

McClaussen motioned John to follow him out of the control room and into the executive conference room where he'd taken up quarters. Everyone in the control room could see McClaussen, through the large observation window, shaking a finger menacingly at John's chest while apparently yelling at him.

"I am here at the…request…of BPI. They've asked me to

personally investigate where and to whom an errant company email has gone. It was last sent from Rustic Central to someone here on this rig. The email was not meant for general distribution. It contains proprietary information—trade secrets—that, in the wrong hands, could adversely affect operations throughout the world." Despite the threatening demeanor and shaking finger, McClaussen talked as if he were reading a predetermined script. "I have been tasked with tracking down and...talking with...whoever received it. In fact, it's likely at this point that the receiver doesn't even know he or she has it or what it means. My job is to make certain it doesn't get distributed any further. If you hear anything, *anything at all*, about this email, be sure you notify me *immediately*. Me. Not the office, or that damned NSWP nitwit I just reassigned. Me. Do you understand? Me. Anytime..."

John looked away before answering, fearing the angry man before him might read in his face that he not only knew about, but had in his possession, exactly what it was McClaussen was after. A part of him felt obligated to tell McClaussen what he wanted to hear, but another stronger part was too shocked at the news of George's death. "I'll let you know the moment I hear *anything* from *anyone* about any such email...Shaun. In the meantime, I should get back to work with the survey team so we can find out why the drill string suddenly jumped back up the hole yesterday. How long will you be staying?"

"I plan to be here for the duration of the survey, to see and report back to corporate headquarters first hand what is found out. In the meantime, I need to keep looking for someone who has knowledge of that email." McClaussen paused for effect, then added, off-handedly, "An NSWP employee, a Mr. George Franks, was killed...murdered... last night. It's likely his death is related to the email. I'm pretty certain it was he who forwarded it here. It's an important email, John, important enough for the people above me to *order* me here personally, and for some to consider it more important than a man's life. I've had to...remove... several people, Longley being one, to progress the investigation. Did you know Mr. Franks?"

"Sir," John, relying on his authority as the new company man, said coldly, hoping to deflect McClaussen's question. "Could you please explain what you mean by 'remove several people'? And why?"

"I didn't remove them 'permanently,' like killing them, if that's what you're wondering, Mr. Marx. I temporarily re-assigned them to other duties so their actions wouldn't compromise my work. I'm not authorized to say anything beyond the fact that the information we're concerned about was in an attachment to the email, and should never have seen the light of day."

John visibly relaxed. "Then am I correct in assuming that BPI wants to make certain the information doesn't fall into, for example, the President's hands, giving his Interior Secretary an excuse to shut down Trojan Horse and other exploratory projects currently underway?"

"Well, John, what with the recent spat of 'environmental problems' BPI has been experiencing—this one included—it's no secret that the present administration isn't thrilled with us drilling here or around the USA," McClaussen said, seeking, in turn, to deflect John's questions. "No one at BPI wants yesterday's event to end up being the straw that breaks the camel's back." John walked over to a second, equally large observation window overlooking the platform. It looked from the gestures of the survey and drill crews that they were preparing to drop the probe down the hole.

Satisfied that he and McClaussen had reached an information stalemate, John decided to switch tactics and reassure the man. "If I run across anyone harboring *any* proprietary information like you suggested, I'll let you know immediately. Right now, however, I do need to get to that drill floor so I can make certain they have all they need to complete the survey quickly without further incident."

"Thank you, Mr. Marx," McClaussen concluded. "I will be in my private quarters should you have anything immediate to report. And, by the way, if that's Mr. Longley over there with the survey group, tell him I need to talk to him. Now." McClaussen turned on heel and exited the executive room, leaving John alone to reconsider what he'd been willing to reveal. Considering the overarching importance of preventing another Blue Water Horizon event, it struck John how disproportionately important the email and attachment seemed in McClaussen's mind. Tens of lives and the fortunes of hundreds of thousands depended on nothing further happening between now and when the results of the survey became available. What was really bothering him, though, was that while no one had died, as yet, from the drilling emergency he'd declared, one man already had over a mere email.

He'd successfully pried some information from McClaussen, deflected the man's questions, and bought some much-needed time to think about what he should do about the email. McClaussen, by removing Chris Longley, had in effect successfully isolated John. That meant the finger of suspicion was on him. For a moment, John's thoughts turned to his dead friend and buddy, George, who had apparently instigated the whole thing. His life-long friend, unmarried, reclusive George, was dead. There was nothing he could do about that. A feeling of bitter helplessness welled in his chest and throat. John countered the only way he knew: by focusing all his attention on the drilling emergency at hand.

John left the conference room, heading outside in the opposite direction to where Chris Longley, deck crew, survey team and equipment were congregating.

As he approached, he noticed the survey engineer, Claude Askins, cradling the business end of the survey equipment. The front-end sensory unit consisted of a small, black rectangular box, not unlike the one John had discovered on the catwalk. The unit was attached to a huge reel off to the side by a half-inch thick steel wire.

The wire, traditionally referred to as a wireline, making survey companies like Claude Askins' in the vernacular wireline companies, was actually made up of over a hundred wires encased in a hollow stainless steel cable. Inside the black-box unit were the most advanced sensors ever created. Readings would be fed topside and instantaneously interpreted on display screens indicating within a couple millimeters exactly where the sensor box was located in hole. Behind the wire operator, Claude Askins would sit surrounded by a plethora of jury-rigged electronic field equipment, each piece specially designed to further process and integrate the different signals into a single, three-dimensional plasma screen display. The sensors included passive receptive arrays sensitive to different electromagnetic spectra, and active transmitters that could shoot electromagnetic waves of varying wavelengths out into the surrounding formation and sense returning waves, ferreting from their strength and timing valuable information on the surrounding strata. The reel in this case had been custom made, housing 40,000 feet—almost eight miles—of wire enclosing over a hundred different sensor wires.

Making his way to where the survey team was, John positioned near Chris, who was standing next to the survey engineer.

"Let me know as soon as you're set up, Claude. I want to see what we encounter down there." Chris noticed John beside him as he finished talking.

"John! Come join us! I was just telling Claude I wanted to view the results in real-time with him."

"Sorry, Chris, but McClaussen wants to see you in his private quarters, pronto." John signaled towards the interior door he'd just come from with a thumb.

"Did he say what he wanted?" Chris asked, his face flooding with concern.

"No, but he grilled me about an email containing some information that BPI doesn't want anyone to see. Know anything about it?" John asked.

Chris looked forlorn. Neither colleague could or would countermand McClaussen's order, and with no way out, Chris stood, turned and, ignoring John's question, walked off towards what, from the look on his face, was a meeting with Death.

The Oil Man

CHAPTER 4

Chris paused at the special guest quarters' door, rearranged his clothes, swallowed and knocked. "Mr. McClaussen, Chris Longley here. You sent for me, sir?"

The door opened. McClaussen stood to the side and motioned Chris to enter. "Come in. We have something we need to discuss."

Chris entered a spacious and well-appointed suite, typically reserved for government officials who sometimes came out to personally experience what happens on an oilrig in the Gulf.

"Have a seat," McClaussen ordered, pointing to the sofa and taking a seat in front of a mahogany table upon which sat an open laptop, its lit screen hidden from Chris.

"How can I be of assistance, sir?" Chris asked, sitting as instructed.

"Well, Chris, first I want to apologize for the abrupt reassignment of duties. It's nothing personal, you understand, but I had to remove you from the equation long enough to determine your involvement, if any, in a high-level information leak concerning our determined oil reserves. Being our company man, you were the prime suspect in terms of being the recipient of that information. Knowing now that *not* to be the case, it is important that I—*we*—locate the recipient of the email and destroy it before it falls into the wrong hands.

"We now believe that the email contains a set of mathematical 'instructions' telling the recipient how to go about activating and decoding some critical information stored in a device. At this point, we've no idea what the device is, what it looks like or where it might be.

"BPI enlisted a corporation we've done business with before— Dan Sogo Shosha Corporation, DSSC for short—to assist in reconstructing as much of the email content and its course as possible. According to the latest DSSC report, the email appears to have originated from a visiting independent oil consultant named Leon Puissegur and was addressed to or intercepted by a low-level Rustic Oil Central controller, a Mr. George Franks. Franks was murdered last night. No one has any idea what Puissegur knows about the 'device,' how he found out about it, or why he chose to send the instructions to George Franks, if, in fact, he did. We're now certain that Franks received the email and forwarded it to someone here. We've successfully eliminated a number of BPI, NSWP and Rustic employees, yourself included, from the initial pool of potential recipients, primarily through surveillance, discrete trace-back analyses and personnel tests, as with you.

"Having eliminated those who would most likely have benefited from the information, we have remaining a small, but unremarkable list, including the survey team members who just arrived. Since they were ordered by you, I reassigned you to work with them, and had you watched to see if you would establish contact with anyone in particular.

"Our two problems are now four-fold: First, we need to ascertain the cause of the pipe incident last night and prevent it from escalating into a bigger problem while keeping it all under wraps. Second, we need to locate the recipient of that email before whoever killed Franks does. Third, we need to locate the email and destroy it. And finally, we need to figure out where the internal leak came from, and what ultimately this is all about. These are of immediate concern, because, whoever the recipient is, he or she hasn't come forward and reported it, which suggests to me that this person—or persons—is involved in subterfuge."

McClaussen stopped talking and sipped from one of two tall glasses of iced tea sitting on the table. Chris noted with unease that McClaussen hadn't offered the second to him.

"Well, sir, what can I do to help now that you've determined I'm 'clean'?" Chris asked testily. "And before you answer, I *do* have some information…"

"Stop right there, Chris. Whatever tidbits you may think you have to offer, I'm certain I already know them, and that they will pale before what I'm about to tell you next. It may or may not come as a surprise to you, but the total United States oil reserve is currently estimated to be three trillion barrels of oil and some one or two quadrillion cubic feet of natural gas. This isn't a secret. In fact, it's widely known that this amounts to around 600 years of energy resources hidden right here, in and around North America. BPI's problem, and thereby NSWP's and yours, is that the present administration is actively engaged in stopping us from developing these enormously lucrative oil and gas fields. I believe what is in that email is proprietary BPI information on some newer, better technologies for extracting the resources, information meant to convince the present administration to change its stand. More so, I suspect that the information would convince the present administration

49

to select BPI exclusively to develop these reserves."

McClaussen stopped and took another sip from his glass.

Chris sat, open-mouthed, taken aback by what McClaussen was suggesting. Was the man serious? Was BPI trying to court the U. S. government into allowing it a monopoly to develop the North American Strategic Oil Reserves? Could the email actually have encoded within it the necessary information to bring that dream to reality? If so, repossession of the email would be worth...what? Billions, even trillions of petrodollars. And how much did it cost these days to buy a contract on a human life? He'd heard the price had fallen in the current depressed world economy to less than a million dollars. No wonder George Franks was so expertly eliminated from the equation. But by whom? And if so, who would be next? Chris could think of any number of people: McClaussen, Askins, Marx...himself? Standing up, he walked in a daze over to the table and reached nervously for the second glass of tea. After a satisfying draught, he set the glass back on the table and began asking questions.

"Mr. McClaussen. With all due respect, what you're implying just doesn't make sense. BPI can wish all it wants to develop the North American Strategic Oil Reserve, but it could never happen. Nothing short of another world war could force America and Canada to begin using up their *strategic* oil reserves. A constant string of wars— Vietnam, Afghanistan, Iraq, Syria, Libya— hasn't pried it open, what less than a world war could? An *email?* There's many undeveloped oil fields left in the world, but there's no new oil. Once a field is opened and developed, it's slowly depleted—eventually gone forever. Poof!" Chris swept a hand through the air in emphasis, turning his back on McClaussen in frank disbelief.

Now it was McClaussen's turn.

"Chris, I've probably said too much already; certainly more then you were meant to know, but I've shared with you because I need your help to run down who here received that email! What if it's not about new fields, better access, or better extraction technologies? What if BPI could prove that, developed correctly, some oil fields in the world *won't ever be depleted?* What if BPI had proof that the North American Strategic Oil Reserve sat on top of a deeper, constantly renewing source of oil—a veritable abiotic oil 'factory' located in the outer mantle of the earth, producing oil faster than any known extraction process? What if the United States, in developing its strategic reserves, could suddenly and completely dominate the world's oil market? And even if that were not entirely true, USA and Canada wouldn't actually need to *produce* the oil, gas or gasoline for consumption, it would be enough that the world *believed* it could. Anytime it wanted, with the help of BPI."

Chris slumped back on the sofa, even more shocked and aghast. "You mean…"

"I mean we need to trace where that email went and make certain it's destroyed before it gets into *anyone* else's hands. You see, today's survey of yesterday's 'incident' may very well provide the additional support necessary to 'confirm' what many in the past considered a wild-ass theory at best. Abiotic oil isn't a new theory, Chris, it's just that it's been discredited over and over since it was proposed by Georg Agricola in the 1500's. Contemporary oil theory has it that oil is biological in nature, formed from kerogen, a mixture of heavy hydrocarbons from decaying biological matter compressed in sedimentary rock. The 'proof' of this 'no more oil formation' point-of-view has been based on the observation that all kerogens have a unique biological chemical 'signature,' and that it's been possible to locate new oil fields based on biotic oil theory. However, BPI, in association with several other large energy corporations has, for the last quarter of a century, been working closely with America's National Aeronautic and Space Administration and Russia's Glavkosmos to identify the origin of life—hydrocarbons—primordial oil—abiotic in nature—on other planets. Evidence of rich mixtures of abiotic hydrocarbons in the atmosphere of Saturn's moon, Titan, and in the atmospheres of Jupiter, Saturn, Uranus and Neptune, as well as recent questioning if whether the biological 'signatures' in oil might not come from thermophilic bacteria living *on* the oil being created abiotically in the earth's upper mantle, have all begun to re-raise the old 'chick and egg' question: Which came first, life or the hydrocarbons? Is the true source of oil biotic or abiotic? It's this very issue that's making it so hard for scientists to decide if there was ever life on Mars. That's not to say that the earth's oil is *all* abiotic, but it is to say that not *all* the earth's oil is biotic, and there's growing evidence within our corporate *daimyo* that says that in select areas of the North American Strategic Oil Reserve, billions of barrels of oil are being generated abiotically. Again, the science isn't as important as the perception: If people *believe* that America's oil reserves can't be depleted, then BPI can use that belief. That's what Leon Puissegur's visit here yesterday was all about. He met clandestinely with one of our BPI representatives to supposedly cinch the deal. The details of what they actually talked about and what, if anything, they accomplished in their short face-to-face talk, I'm not privy to. But I do know that they met, and what was on their agenda was some new findings on abiotic oil that he was supposedly carrying." McClaussen paused to give Longley time to process what he was disclosing.

"What's a *daimyo*?" Chris asked.

"A *daimyo* is a Japanese business concept whereby various companies, each holding one or more decisive pieces but none of them individually holding all of the pieces necessary to dominate a particular aspect of society, in this case, energy, join resources to accomplish a common end. BPI holds the key resources to discover, develop, extract and process oil and gas. Someone else, presumably Mr. Puissegur and his associates, hold the key information regarding abiotic oil necessary to unlock the reserve for exploitation. Someone else, perhaps a private space research consortium, has discovered the processes and conditions under which abiotic oil forms. Someone else has the political savvy and contacts with the present administration. All these companies are coordinated by a single 'under-the-radar' supernational corporation, I'm assuming Dan Sogo Shosha Corporation. These are, of course, just guesses, but given the last day and night's turn of events, I'm guessing not too far off the mark. What I know for certain is that BPI does not want any of this to leak out, especially to the press or public." McClaussen walked over to the large window that overlooked the platform below and stared, hands behind his back.

"I hope you understand the seriousness of this," he continued, not looking back at Chris, "and are careful not to share anything I've divulged with anyone else. I doubt anyone would believe you, and NSWP, BPI and our 'associates' would emphatically deny whatever you said, but in doing so, you'd be placing yourself in the center of a maelstrom in which your life would have no more value than that of George Franks'. But enough of that. We need to take action. Regarding the drilling problem, where exactly do we stand and how the hell did a Rustic Oil tool pusher come to shut down our operation?"

"John Marx is in charge of this rig which we are currently contracting from Rustic Oil. That makes him responsible for the safety of everyone on it. He's got thirty years experience, and that has made him cautious. A friend of his died as a result of the Blue Water Horizon explosion. He stopped a job a short time ago and saved the entire rig from destruction when a well pipe blew about six inches back up into the well. Had they continued drilling, the gas pocket they hit would have blown the well apart, destroying the rig and killing everyone on it. His prompt action not only saved the rig and crews, it later brought in a well with some two and a half million cubic feet of natural gas and some twenty million barrels of oil." Chris stopped talking, waiting for McClaussen to respond.

McClaussen turned from the window to briefly contemplate his new accomplice-by-default. The man was smart, but obviously not able to grasp the big picture. "We have no choice but to wait and see what the survey will show. I respect your opinion of Mr. Marx, and, if he really knows as much as what you say he does, perhaps BPI should make a move to acquire him. You sound like you and he are friends. Has NSWP made an offer for him to join?"

Chris wriggled uncomfortably, sensing a trap. Careful to address McClaussen's second, less loaded question first, he replied, "No, sir, it hasn't. NSWP was considering offering him a line position, but felt he was too close to retirement to make the offer profitable to both parties."

"'Would he be 'profitably amenable' to extending his retirement date for enough money, do you think?" McClaussen asked with contempt. "What the hell is all this double-talk about, Chris? Get NSWP to make him an offer he can't refuse and get him on our side. Maybe he would enjoy getting out of the mud to act as an advisor or administrator. Maybe he should have your job…"

"I'll check with the company…"

"Didn't you hear what I said? I *am* the company, Longley! NSWP is a shell subsidiary of BPI. We frequently use shell corporations like NSWP to do work like this that we don't want to draw undue attention to. That's why you're here. You've got your company's permission, man. Now do it! Talk with him. Find out what makes him tick and notify my office to make up a contract. This is too sensitive an effort to chance him possibly blowing it all. Get on it as soon as we finish talking. I want a signed contract in my hand by tomorrow evening."

"Now for our other problem: It's rumored that Franks also had a female acquaintance who was killed on Blue Water Horizon. I think it's conceivable that he wasn't acting as an industrial spy or selling company secrets for his own ambitions, but rather acting in defiance— a way for him to express his anger with BPI for causing the woman's death. The question is, who on this rig would Franks trust with the revenge information, and how can we most effectively and efficiently lay this problem to rest without arousing the public suspicion?" McClaussen re-sat in his chair and stared daggers at Chris.

So it all comes down to this, Chris thought quickly. *McClaussen brings me into his confidence just to maneuver me into either disproving his hunch or forcing me to provide the key piece of information he needs. Very clever. And if I provide that key piece of information? How would that change our 'new' relationship? I'd become an instant liability, one that, like Franks or his confidant here would also need to be "put to rest" as McClaussen had so eloquently expressed.* Chris made his decision. "Sir, from my experience here working with both NSWP and Rustic Oil, I think I can say that your being here will be regarded by the crews as a show of company support and faith in a potential emergency. Just how important this incident, the rig and your 'secret' mission to get that email back is, they won't have an inkling. I'll make sure of that, now that I'm in the know. If I may suggest, let's for the moment focus on giving Mr. Marx the leeway he needs to ensure a safe rig and operation (and, of course, to see if, as you say, the 'incident' will provide the 'proof' BPI needs for the abiotic oil theory). That would ease tensions and, I think, loosen tongues. In the meantime, I'll inquire what would motivate Marx to voluntarily come under NSWP's thumb. At the same time, I'll start discretely inquiring as to who on this rig considers himself a 'friend' of Franks—the kind of friend who Franks might believe would be smart, motivated and able to use the email information to exact the kind of personal justice you're suggesting."

McClaussen leaned back in his chair with deliberate nonchalance. *The man's hiding something,* he thought. *Maybe he's the one after all...* "Good enough. I'll continue working on the external, while you quietly work the internal. I will, like you and everyone else, be ostensibly watching the survey results and hoping they end up showing good production projections for this exploratory well."

McClaussen returned to the window, hands once again clasped behind his back. Facing East, he examined the clear blue skies above, the distant ring of dark clouds on the horizon, and the clear blue sea below. His thoughts, however, were already elsewhere.

CHAPTER 5

John slipped back to his room without saying or hearing a word. Given the shocking death of his friend, George Franks, John now felt certain the email he had was the one McClaussen was looking for. His conversation with the BPI executive left him feeling sad, angry and more intrigued than ever about what the numbers meant, and whether they were, as he now suspected, somehow linked to the crystal. If the two were related, then the numbers would likely have something to do with using the crystal. At least, that was his most recent thought. Whether he reported the two or not, he was in danger of being caught with them in his possession, and, if there *was* a connection between the email and the two, he was likely in mortal danger. As he rounded the last rail before entering his room, he ran into his friend, Josh Platur.

"Where you off to so fast?" Josh asked, blocking John's way and waiting for an answer.

John took a moment to catch his breath. "You remember the email I told you about? The one I couldn't figure out?"

"Your latest piece of evidence of another secret global conspiracy? Yes. And why are you looking so white? Is a ghost

57

walking the corridors?"

"In a way, yes," John replied. "Shaun McClaussen, the BPI executive—the hulk who got off the helicopter last— is here and he knows about the email Franks sent me—the one I told you about. The one I thought might be related to the crystal fragment I found. McClaussen just called me out. He knows George sent the email to someone here. He doesn't yet know who, or if it was opened. But I know, and now so do you. I also know that George is dead. Do us both a huge favor; don't let anyone know that I was the one who received it, and especially don't mention anything about the broken crystal, at least, for now." John unlocked the clothes locker and removed the computer and black box. "I need to be the one who tells McClaussen that I was the one who received the email, before someone else dies. Still, I don't trust him...so I want you to hold onto the thumb drive."

Flaberghasted by the nonstop revelations, Josh huddled closer. "He may search your room. I would, if I were him," he volunteered.

"That's why I'm giving you the flash drive. I can keep McClaussen busy between the survey, my continued interrogation, and his checking my room till tomorrow morning when our shifts here end. Once we're back at home, we can meet at my house and you can give it back to me. You have a problem with that?"

"No, John. In fact, it should work. It's common knowledge that I don't do computers. I don't even have one here, so neither McClaussen or anyone else would have any reason to suspect me. Suddenly I'm as curious about that email as you, now that I know the big guys are looking for it."

John slapped Josh on his shoulder in thanks. "If anyone asks where I am, tell them you saw me heading to my room," John opened the black box and handed Josh the memory stick. "Make sure it's well hidden. Once I tell McClaussen that I *was* the one who received the

58

email, after having noted my spam filter having erased it, their attention should remain on me. That should make it possible for you to move about without a problem. I just hope everything..." John turned on his computer, wiping from it all traces of the email. Everything looked good; if McClaussen asked again, he could say that he hadn't realized the email had been received and automatically deleted, and was the one McClaussen was searching for. If his laptop were examined, it would confirm everything he said.

While John was working, Josh chatted nervously. "I assume you've heard about our new visitors?"

"New visitors?" John asked, powering down the computer and placing it back in the locker.

"I figured McClaussen told you: He's called in some additional 'professionals' to help him with the search."

"Professionals? What kind of professionals?"

"Electronics professionals, I figure. After all, McClaussen's supposedly looking for an email. What other kind would he need?" Josh asked innocently.

John shrugged his shoulders, not wanting to make more of the rumor and his rising suspicions than either deserved. "I want to give you one more thing, Josh, that I want you to guard with your life. I'm not certain what it is, but I'm convinced it's part of the whole puzzle and ultimately why that email is so important."

John closed the rectangular black box without showing Josh what was inside. "I need you to protect this along with the thumb drive. It may turn out to be nothing. No one, even McClaussen, has mentioned it. I found it on the catwalk yesterday, before I discovered the email. I also need you to promise you won't look inside the box at least until I tell you it's safe. I'm concerned that having seen it might compromise you. Now, I need to get back on the rig. Did anyone see you come here?"

"No, the hallway was clear. I'll go back to my room and stash these someplace in my room for now."

"No," John decided. "I'd rather you kept them *on* you. At all times. Like you said, there's no reason for McClaussen or his new helpers to suspect you, and if your room just happened to be searched while you were out and nothing was found, that would lend further substantiation to your innocence. If you see or hear any suggestion that they're going to search our persons, which I sincerely doubt they'd do given it would send a blatant message to everyone that something was seriously wrong, find somewhere outside of your room to hide the box and drive temporarily. Then go back and retrieve them as soon as it's safe. Again, keep them on your person if at all possible. It's the safest place on the rig right now. Now let's get out of here."

With that, the two left the room, John taking a left down the back stairway two floors below to the derrick floor, Josh a right up one floor to Helipad Two.

The signature thumping of a twin-engine AgustaWestland AW139 Executive Jet Helicopter taking off muffled the normally sharp metal-on-metal clanking on the derrick as preparations for starting the survey came to completion. As the sleek red, white and blue helicopter, at over seventeen million dollars the most expensive in the BPI armamentarium, whisked off the helipad, another could be heard coming in. A BPI helicopter of the same make rushed in from the North, pounding the air and creating an uncomfortable, gut-wrenching feeling, that made Josh feel as if something distinctly bad were about to happen.

John was on deck near the cable reel, when he saw the two helicopters gracefully touch down, one after the other, just long enough to disgorge their human cargoes. Something told him that

McClaussen's superiors had figured out that he was the recipient of the infamous email. John took off his hard hat, wiped his brow, and began walking along the rail towards the executive office where McClaussen's "electronics professionals" would be gathering. It was time for him to let them know he had, indeed, received the email, since, if their new visitors were the electronics experts Josh had said, they would most likely have brought with them the IP address of his computer.

From behind the pipe racks John could see McClaussen standing just outside the landing area, waiting to greet the offloading men. Four husky, black-suited men got out carrying what looked like overnight bags, meaning they planned to stay awhile. The group headed directly for the interior door, walking officiously past McClaussen without stopping. The second helicopter dropped off two additional men, one younger and thinner than the rest, dressed in a polo shirt and tan slacks, the other trim but heavier-set, probably in his 50's, wearing an expensive grey business suit with a yellow silk tie. The younger handled the bags while the older was warmly greeted by McClaussen. John couldn't recall the older man's name, but he remembered having seen him somewhere before. He had to be important to warrant McClaussen being there to personally welcome him. The executive offered his hand, and McClaussen shook it gratefully. It seemed to John that in extending his hand, McClaussen had also genuflected slightly in deference.

John noticed the visitor say something to McClaussen, and could gauge its singular importance by the way McClaussen's eyebrows raised and his eyes widened before the handshake concluded.

Looking at the rail, John noticed his knuckles turning a pale white. Releasing the railing, he took a moment to unclench his fists, noticing the fine tremor that remained in his fingers even as he worked his hands. His stomach suddenly clenched, and he couldn't decide if it felt more like it contained butterflies or bees. In the end, it didn't matter. The only thing that mattered was what would happen to him and his friends during the next couple of hours. When he told McClaussen about the email, John had no way of knowing if he would be ignored, acknowledged, disciplined, fired or shot.

Looking up from his fists, he saw McClaussen hold open the door to the platform interior for the older man, then turn. The hairs on John's neck stiffened. McClaussen was staring at him. As their eyes met, John knew, despite the distance between them, that McClaussen *knew*. McClaussen broke eye contact, and followed his honored guest inside, leaving the younger man carrying the bags to awkwardly work his way through the door alone.

John closed his eyes and took a deep breath. When he finally resumed walking, the outdoor loudspeakers blared, "Mr. John Marx. Mr. John Marx. Please report to the operations room."

CHAPTER 6

"When Mr. Marx enters, I need you all to look harmless. Assure him with your smiles that he's not in trouble. When I noticed him standing near the pipe rack a few minutes ago, he looked...concerned. Of course, some concern would be expected. And how much of it is over the email, yesterday's drilling incident, my talk with him, or the progress of today's survey, we can't know. Not yet. Having witnessed you all flying in just now will add substantially to his concern. I don't want him going any further in that direction in here. I need him relaxed. Off-guard. Got it?"

All heads indicated their understanding, McClaussen's honored guest adding his assent. "According to Mr. Stein," McClaussen nodded at the man in the grey suit to his right, "Marx was the indented email destination, but as of yet, there's no indication that he's aware of that. For all we know, the email could be in a spam box on his computer. Even if it got past any filters, we don't know if he noticed, opened, read, or forwarded it. If he doesn't know anything about its contents, we wish to keep it that way." McClaussen addressed all six of the men gathered around the conference table in the executive conference

63

room. "And remember: As far as anyone on this platform is concerned, we are all here simply to look over Marx's shoulder, to observe and report, first-hand, the results of the survey."

John knocked three quick times, then opened the door and entered the room. He looked warily at the four black jump-suited men from the first helicopter, each moving backwards, silently and inobtrusively dissolving into the four corners of the room.

Maximum field and firepower positions, a voice in his head that had saved his life more than once before in Vietnam warned. Then he noticed the grey-suited executive from the second helicopter standing at McClaussen's side. The young assistant wasn't present.

These men all mean business, the voice in his head continued.

Wracking his brain, it abruptly came to him that McClaussen's honored guest was Howard Stein, former head of security for NSWP and later, BPI. John hadn't seen him for several years, and then, had assumed by the man's demeanor that he was one of those 'golden men' destined to work his way to the top. McClaussen's fawning meant Stein's current position in the corporate hierarchy equaled or exceeded McClaussen's, while Stein's quiet presence suggested to John that he represented a power higher than BPI—the proverbial power behind the power. John would have given anything to know who Stein was working for these days.

All eyes turned towards John as he stopped before the conference table as far from his adversaries as he could. It was clear everyone was waiting for an axe to fall. But from whom and where would it fall? Stein maintained his detached, immobile appearance.

McClaussen spoke first. "Please, have a seat, Mr. Marx. You seem a bit perplexed. Do not be concerned. You've done nothing wrong, and you are not under any obligation to be here beyond your much-appreciated cooperation. I'll ask Mr. Stein to explain what is going on, as he's more up to date on things. Mr. Stein, Mr. Marx," McClaussen said, stepping back, leaving Stein standing in the forward center of the group at the other end of the table.

John took a seat, glancing warily back at the door he'd entered. It was now guarded on either side by two of the four men-in-black. With a dispassionate flick of his wrist, Stein signaled the four guards to leave. They exited the room without a word, leaving John, McClaussen and Stein alone together.

So it's the old "Good Cop, Bad Cop" routine, John mused.

"I thought you might appreciate the gesture, Mr. Marx," Stein said with the smallest of snarls on his face. "As Shaun said, we greatly value your cooperation in this matter. By the way, John—you don't mind if I call you John, do you?—you look familiar. Have we met?"

Now they're softening me up, John thought. *These two are the real professionals.*

"Yes, sir, Mr. Stein...er, Howard...we met briefly when I first applied for a job with Rustic Oil. You were a new dock security guard. We said hello to each other almost every day the first couple of months we began working for Rustic."

Take that, you bastard, John thought, and smiled.

"Yes, now I remember: It was quite a long time ago. In Venice, Louisiana, if my memory serves me."

"It does indeed...Howard. That was many years ago."

Take that, you fake!

John knew the procedure. Stein would attempt to knock him off balance with friendly small talk, setting him up for the big one-two punch from his gorilla, McClaussen.

Stein straightened to his full height, which still left him dwarfed next to McClaussen. The two walked, one around each side of the table, to where John was sitting.

This is it, John concluded, bracing himself mentally and physically.

"John," McClaussen began. "Howard here's ascertained, with reasonable certainty, that you recently received an email from George Franks, and, furthermore, that it was the one I asked you about earlier with an encrypted attachment. What we don't know is whether you opened it, whether it is still located on your computer and whether it got forwarded to anyone else. As I mentioned before, this email is very, let me say it again, *very* important, and must not remain in any form in your or in anyone else's hands. It cost Franks his life; we don't want any further such incidents on our hands, or for any of this to leak out. Mr. Stein and his superiors believe the attachment contained information that could compromise not just NSWP, but BPI as well as Rustic and numerous other cooperating oil companies. And so I reiterate: You are not in any trouble, but in order to protect you, we must make certain, *now*, whether you accessed that email and where it is. Howard is…wishes to have…our specialists who just walked out of here look at your computer to make certain it is totally free of the offending email and attachment."

Translation: You're in deep shit and it's just going to get deeper, John thought.

He was distracted from following this line of thought by the sound of the door opening behind him. The same four men who moments ago had left the room re-entered, one holding under his arm John's laptop. John was about to object, when Stein snatched the laptop and placed it on the table.

Stein spoke with his back towards John. "Before you say anything you might regret, Mr. Marx, I want to acknowledge that you have every right to object to my men's preemptive acquisition of your computer. I need you to know that I ordered them to do so to

66

definitively answer the second and third of my concerns. In short, I did it to protect your life."

McClaussen started to say something, but John cut in, hoping to put off the need to answer the first and most dangerous of the three questions as long as possible. "I have always known that nothing on this privately-owned rig is private when it comes to company business." John settled back in his chair awaiting Stein's rebuttal.

Stein didn't disappoint. "Again, I want to assure you that my men were strictly ordered to touch nothing else in your locker other then your laptop." Stein opened the laptop and slid it in front of John.

"Would you be so kind as to awaken your computer and open your mail program?" Stein ordered more than asked.

While waiting for the computer to boot, John, curious if Stein and his men had already accessed his computer, decided to hold off answering Stein's first question as long as possible. "Other than him being a high school friend, what makes you think Franks sent *me* the *original*?" careful to stress the words "me" and "original" to add as much doubt as possible. "As far as me making copies, I use Internet Explorer, so there's always the possibility that someone used the infamous 'back door' to access my computer and pirate a copy. And how can you be certain I was the only recipient?"

Stein turned, cocked his head to the side, then smirked. "Clever boy. You seem to have an admirable knowledge of computers and computing," he replied, locating himself behind John where he could observe both the screen and John's fingers working. "I asked two of our governmental partners, the National Aeronautic and Space Administration and the National Security Agency, to help us trace the Internet pathways of all of Mr. Frank's emails. They enlisted the help of the National Institute of Standards and Security, NISS, who, with the assistance of the offices of the Computer Incident Advisory

Capability, CIAC, Defense Security Service, Office of Cybercrime... really, Mr. Marx, need I go on? Given the sensitivity of the situation, they were all too happy to assist. So, to answer your question, Mr. Marx, we traced one and only one such email and attachment from Franks' computer to yours."

NASA? NSA? NISS? CIAC? Office of Cybercrime? Why not the whole military-industrial complex, for God's sake? Why not God Himself? wondered John feverishly. *Who the hell really are Stein and McClaussen to command such power?*

"That's an impressive list of organizations you got to work together to 'protect my life'," John finally replied.

As soon as John's email program opened, Stein angled the computer screen to better watch over John's shoulder. As John scrolled through his emails, it became rapidly apparent to Stein that the one he and McClaussen were looking for wasn't there. Stein gestured to McClaussen who gestured to one of the four 'specialists.' The indicated man stepped up, and with John's permission, replaced him and began manipulating the program with lightening speed in ways that John couldn't follow. He watched as the man exited Mail and somehow accessed the primary operating system, then typed in some computerese that caused a window to pop up showing dates and times of all received communications. Among them was the email in question—at least John assumed such, given the string of red-highlighted code. The man looked up at Stein, and gave a nod.

"Well, Mr. Marx, my computer expert here has indicated that your computer was indeed the recipient of the email we've been searching for. With your permission..." Stein nodded back at the man, not waiting for John to respond.

The man gently elbowed John further aside and proceeded to exchange one alphanumeric phrase after another with the computer.

Several times the laptop screen flashed black, reverting moments later to blue screen, and finally another pop-up window with columns of all-white numbers and characters which the computer expert seemed pleased to see. The whole thing reminded John of a prisoner-of-war interrogation, where the prisoner was forced to spill out his guts, a little more each time, while the skilled interrogator not only openly gained access to everything, but erased all memory of the information and procedure as he proceeded. At the touch of a key, his computer went black and rebooted while Stein's computer specialist stood and stepped back, John's computer returning innocently to its original desktop appearance.

"Done," the man reported, obviously pleased.

"Thank you," Stein replied. Then he turned back to John. "My man assures me that, one, all evidence of the email has now been successfully removed from your computer; two, that he found no copies of either the email or its attachment anywhere else on your system; and, three, that there is no indication that you ever forwarded the email or the attachment."

McClaussen took the seat next to John. "I want to assure you, Mr. Marx, that nothing has been erased from this computer other then what Mr. Stein and his men were looking for, and that I—we all—deeply appreciate your cooperation. You may return with your computer to your room whenever you wish. I would also like to assure you that should anything said during this little meeting be heard outside of this room—and I have no reason to believe that would *ever* happen—the person attempting to spread such misinformation would not only be held liable for all resulting injuries, but would likely find the world a hostile and, how shall I say it, inhospitable place. On the other hand, I also want you to know that BPI is prepared to demonstrate its appreciation for your present and continued cooperation, through a series of 'incentives' and 'rewards' culminating, hopefully, in a generous lifelong consulting contract. But that's a separate issue for later."

As Stein and his men began what appeared to John preparations for leaving, McClaussen continued. "I'd like to add my own personal thanks, John, for your help in this matter. As I said, I look forward to continuing our conversation. We've much to talk about regarding your future with BPI and its affiliates. I'm always on the lookout for outstanding company men."

McClaussen dismissed John with a handshake, and after John left, returned his attention back to Stein, DSSC's director of security. "I lied," Stein admitted. "I'm certain he opened and most likely read both the email and the attachment. From what my man here could see, the attachment was doubly encrypted, and he appears to have broken through both encryptions. What we now know he would have seen was ten numbers. The numbers, of course, could represent anything: an international bank account number, or, my best guess, a further encoded message. I now have the numbers, but it may take us some time to tell what they represent. In the meantime, I need to get back to DSSC. However, this I do know with certainty: he made a copy of the email and attachment. It doesn't seem that he sent it anywhere, so whether he has since destroyed the copy, or whether it was copied to another device, we couldn't tell. The man's smart, Shaun, and he knows too much. For now, I want him watched. Discretely. Twenty-four/seven. His movements over the next twenty-four hours may provide us further clues as to what he knows, where the copy might be, and what, if anything, he's up to. I'll get back to you as soon as my colleagues at DSSC make sense of the numbers. It's important you not let him out of sight, and equally important you don't let him know he's being watched. Can you do that, Shaun?"

"Can and will; count it done, Howard. For that, I'll enlist Chris Longley's help. Then I can turn my attention to the second reason for my visit: determining whether the results of the survey that John Marx ordered can be used to support our abiotic oil scheme to takeover the North American Oil Reserves. It all depends on how much of what we find can be used to convince others that the interconnected strategic oil fields are being continuously replenished with abiotic oil from deep in the earth's mantle."

The Oil Man

CHAPTER 7

John had the nagging sense that he wasn't being told everything. Stein mentioned, or at least strongly implied, that he'd been able to locate and read the email, yet he didn't mention the "coincidence" of the original email being from Leon Puissegur, the chief advocate of abiotic oil, nor had he mentioned the meeting between Puissegur and the "other" man on Rustic Oil Rig Twelve earlier yesterday. He also hadn't mentioned anything about the mysterious box, which John was now *certain* was the key to what was going on. If Stein was holding back, then maybe he was hedging or outright lying when he'd said that the matter was concluded.

John, laptop resting in hand, hadn't gotten down the outside stairs when several of the rig workers gathered about him. "What's going on, boss? The high-up's pissed at your shutting down the well?"

John let out a nervous laugh. "No, It was just a matter of a misplaced email. It's all been resolved. We need to devote our collective efforts completely to the survey. It looks like the perfect time, too," John said, noting the survey crew had begun feeding the multi-functional probe into the well.

73

Josh appeared from within the crowd. "I hope you emphasized that none of us want another Blue Water Horizon!" The others muttered concerned assent.

John raised both hands, palms out-facing, gesturing for silence. "The meeting wasn't about what happened the other day. Like I said, it had to do with a company email that was mistakenly sent to me. For awhile, I thought they figured me for a corporate spy!" John chuckled as he waved the slim laptop in the air. In the petroleum world, corporate spies were dealt with quickly, seriously and without compassion. His further explanation would give the men something to talk about other than Blue Water Horizon.

"Come on, now! Let's all get back to work! If you don't have any, I'm sure I can find something detestable for you to do now that the show is over." It had worked; everyone began returning to the survey effort.

Josh looked around, making sure no one was within earshot. "So, what really happened, John?" he asked, following John down another flight of stairs and back inside the structure.

"Keep your distance, and attend carefully to your work," John growled. "I'm most likely being watched. There's a couple of things I need to do—quick—before McClaussen, Stein and Stein's men walk out of that conference room," he added, nodding towards the large window above them framing the six indistinct shapes looking down at him.

Josh followed John's eyes, looking discretely at the window then back. "Okay, back to work and mum's the word. But if anyone asks," Josh said, motioning with his head like John towards the window, "what should I tell them? I'm sure they know you and I are friends."

"I'm not so sure. And don't tell them anything more than I just told you and the other workers: You heard it was all a mistake.

Everything's fine now."

"Got it," Josh replied.

"One more thing before we split: When you get a chance, see if you can find out where this Leon Puissegur guy is now, and who he met with yesterday on this rig. Do it discretely, or don't do it at all."

"Can and will; count it done, John." Josh affirmed, slapping John on the back and saluting irreverently to look like any other worker following the super's orders.

John, for his part, acted indifferent to the laborer, walking on to the nearest door, re-entering the platform interior and moving deftly, computer underarm, to his room. Once inside and the door closed, he fired up the unit. What he needed right now was more information on the fragment, and the best way to do that quickly would be to access the Internet. If they were somehow monitoring his computer, they'd most likely be watching his emails. Even if they also knew about the fragment and were following his browser searches, what more would they learn than that he knew little to nothing? On the other hand, if they didn't know about the crystal fragment, which they hadn't once brought up in any of their "conversations," then his surfing would seem like a stressed out conspiracy-theory-man's ramblings. Either way, it was the only quick way to make further sense of what was going on.

Searching the Internet for "crystal, oil" brought up tens of websites on various petroleum companies with the word "crystal" in their name. It also brought up a Factsheet from NASA's Marshal Space and Flight Center on a space-based, zeolite crystal growth furnace. The Factsheet mentioned that zeolites, rigid crystals grown in space, could absorb many times their weight in liquid petroleum, rather like a sponge, while remaining hard as a rock. *Could the shard be from a space-grown zeolite crystal?* John wondered. *If it were, what would that have to do with Puissegur, "aoil" and a set of numbers? Could it be that "aoil," was Puissegur or Franks' name for oil held in crystals? It might even explain why McClaussen had been sent. They were drilling deep. Perhaps they were drilling and had hopes of striking a shelf of natural, oil-soaked zeolite? A great idea for a science fiction novel, but hardly realistic. Besides, McClaussen and Stein weren't exotic materials engineers, and there was no indication in this or similar articles that Claude Askins, almost as celebrated a survey engineer as Dresser Legend, had any connection to zeolites. It just didn't make sense.*

Diving further into the Factsheet, it became apparent that NASA, at least, was researching crystaline zeolites not as a way to produce petroleum products, but to store hydrogen and other forms of energy. Another quick Internet search, this time on "crystal energy storage," yielded a flurry of papers expanding crystals to not only storing energy, but information as well. *The logos in the email! They represented a consortium of energy, information and trading corporations! And the central logo: the world pierced by a sword? Perhaps the shard was part of a next-generation crystalline memory device?* Playing the devil's advocate, John did another search, this time on "crystal computer storage device."

This search yielded interesting, though seemingly unconnected results. A general article on "holographic data storage" was followed by several industry reports surrounding pioneering work in the field done by a Dr. Jacobs Thorstenson with Swedish Photoptics, a now defunct research and development firm. Thorstenson had been developing a holographic mass storage device that could store an unlimited amount of information in an orthorhombic crystal using a ruby laser to record and read the information. Unable to raise the next amount in a long series of venture capitalizations, Swedish Photopics declared bankruptcy and disappeared from public view. Thorstenson died not long afterwards under less than clear circumstances, supposedly taking his secrets to the grave. Several more articles, however, hinted that the defunct company had actually been acquired by and eventually absorbed into DSSC. There was also mention of a Dr. Alexei Sorolov, formerly of the Opticophysics Laboratory of the USSR Institute of Biophysics, in Academgrodok, the former Soviet scientific "brain city" near Karasnoyarsk in Siberia. Sorolov had apparently advanced Throstenson's work to allow storage and retrieval of information up to the yottabyte level using *normal* instead of laser light. Sorolov, an authority on holographic information storage, had sought and been granted political asylum in Japan. In the end, Sorolov ended up at DSSC, continuing Thorstenson's work. Sorolov was currently living in Texas, having retired from Infinity-Global Solutions, a Texas research and development subsidiary of DSSC, it's logo a world pierced by a broadsword. Further Internet searches yielded a picture of Dr. Alexei Sorolov at a recent international energy production conference standing alongside Leon Puissegur. The final piece of the puzzle fell into place: Sorolov's Linked-In phone number was the same ten numbers listed in the email!

John's search had become a race to see if he could contact Sorolov before anyone watching him made the same connections. His immediate problem was that there was no really secure way to contact Sorolov from the platform. John had to rationally assume that not only would he be watched and his emails bugged but that McClaussen or Stein would also have ordered all company phone calls to and from the rig monitored, at least for the immediate future. Cell phones had the illusion of security, but that was only an illusion: Any of the agencies Stein had mentioned could intercept cell phone calls from a given location and monitor them with ease. Since the Patriot Act, it was done every day under the general rubric of "terrorism surveillance." What John needed was a less traveled way to contact Sorolov—one that would be too insignificant for McClaussen, Stein or their superiors' to likely monitor. *Like Skype,* John thought aloud.

Another quick search and John located Sorolov's Skype moniker. The Skype directory reconfirmed that he was in Texas, so time zones wouldn't be a problem. A moment later John had located located him as "available" and not at the moment engaged in an online discussion. A moment more and he had him on audio-video.

"Doctor Sorolov? John Marx here. Could I have a moment of your time to pick your brain about an intriguing computer crystal information storage problem?" That should pique his interest without putting him off.

"Surely. And what is the nature of your problem?" answered Sorolov, his aged eyes displaying that blaze of curiosity that never leaves a real researcher.

"I understand that you're an expert on holographic computer memory devices—crystalline devices in particular, am I right?"

"Yes," Sorolov replied, his tone suddenly wary.

"I recently came across a half-inch by three-inch piece of what I believe was once a larger, orthorhombic crystal, maybe four to six inches in length. When a ray of sunlight touched the shard, it emitted a rich, pure-tone harmonic and simultaneously projected an aurora of colors into the air. Not on the wall, but in the air. It was as if the shard were trying to project an image of something that needed to somehow be brought into focus. When I rotated the fragment, the image remained unchanged but subtly shifted position." If the shard was indeed a piece of a normal-light holographic computer memory device, then Solokov, if anyone, would know. John chose to keep mention of Puissegur to himself for the moment.

Solokov didn't answer immediately. After a long pause, during which time the professor's age-lined face seemed to morph from suspicion to skepticism to interest and finally concern, Dr. Alexei Solokov cleared his throat and answered with a jumble of questions: "Who are you working for, Mr. Marx? DSSC? NSA? DARPA? Some other branch of the US government? And when and how did you... acquire...this intriguing piece of crystal?"

John, despite his rapidly growing excitement, replied matter-of-factly. "I work for Rustic Oil Company, subsidiary of British Petroleum International, which is related to Dan Sogo Shosha Corporation. However, I'm calling strictly as an interested individual. I found the shard inside a custom-made box laying on the catwalk of an oil platform yesterday, presumably where a couple of oil experts walked by on their way to meet each other for a meeting." After thinking, he added, "A meeting held in relative secrecy."

It seemed to take Solokov some time to process what Mr. John Marx, an unknown in Solokov's long list of scientific and industrial colleagues, was implying.

"Secrecy?" he finally asked.

"I assume such, as, at this moment, a British Petroleum International executive, and what I assume to be the head of security for BPI, along with at least one computer wizard and several musclemen, flew to the rig yesterday. Their stated mission is to observe a drilling survey I ordered, but their interests seem to lie elsewhere."

"A drilling survey? For what purpose did you call this survey?" Sokolov asked, his wrinkled eyes narrowing.

"I ordered a three-dimensional survey after stopping the drilling operation when the bore hole pressure suddenly jumped and visibly lifted the pipe. That's ostensibly what brought the BPI executive, Mr.

Shaun McClaussen, there, although I later discovered he had a second objective: to locate an errant company email. Howard Stein, the BPI security man and his associates showed up next after someone discovered that the encrypted email and attachment had been sent to me."

"I don't know any Shaun McClaussen, Mr. Marx, but I *do* know Howard Stein. He isn't head of security for BPI. He's head of security for Dan Sogo Shosha Corporation, and he's someone to be very, very wary of. If he's onto you…"

John decided this was time, if any, to play his trump and let the rest of the conversation proceed as it may. Interrupting Solokov, he stated with an audible waiver in his voice, "When I held the shard up in the room light it acted like both an optical and an auditory prism, casting a rainbow of colors throughout the room while emitting the rich, pure tone I mentioned. The email I received originated, I believe, from a Mr. Leon Puissegur, whom I suspect was one of the two oil men who met here yesterday. I believe the shard may belong to Puissegur."

Again Solokov retreated into introspective silence. "A piece of an orthorhombic crystal? Howard Stein? Leon Puissegur? You're certain about all this?"

"No, sir, I'm not certain. I'm running on a mixture of facts and surmises. That's why I called you. The encrypted message in the email matched your phone number."

John was surprised to see how calmly Solokov took the disclosure. He'd thought it worth at least a rise.

"Yes, well…" Solokov began, running a hand across an unshaven jaw and swallowing hard. "Leon and I go back…a long way. Thorstenson and I—I assume you know of Dr. Jacobs Thorstenson, a former colleague of mine?" Sokolov paused, expecting a reply.

"I only knew *of* him, having gotten to you through references to his and your collaborative work on the Internet. Thorstenson died…"

"He was murdered," Solokov said bluntly. "Found dead in his laboratory not long after DSSC hostilely acquired his private research and development corporation. He and I were rival research colleagues…friends, actually. We were working separately on developing holographic computer massive memory storage devices. Thorstenson developed a prototype that could, with the use of a laser, insert almost unlimited amounts of information into a perfect orthorhombic crystal. His device used transmission holography— shining the same wavelength laser light through the crystal—to embed and read the information. DSSC 'acquired' me during a visit to Japan, offering the two of us unlimited resource support. When Thorstenson completed his work, he suddenly died. I was kept on to advance the unit into a rainbow transmission device—one that uses normal white light instead of a laser to inscribe and read the information. As soon as that was accomplished, I was forced into…retirement. I say retirement, as I am well-kept, though constantly under guard, 'for my own protection.' I live these days in a comfortable prison, Mr. Marx, but a prison nonetheless. Skype and several other more advanced communication systems are my only remaining portal to the world."

"The man who forwarded the encoded email to me was my friend. He was also murdered," John added.

"There seems to be a rash of murders under the broad DSSC umbrella. I don't doubt that if word of the information about Leon's work, undoubtedly encoded on that piece of crystal you have in your possession, were to get out, there would be an epidemic of murders worldwide. You see, while Dan Sogo Shosha Corporation presents itself as a global trading corporation, it represents, coordinates *and now controls* a large number of 'cooperating' information and energy corporations all around the world, of which BPI, and your immediate employer are most likely included. DSSC is what Japanese global industrialists have historically called..."

"...a *daimyo,*" John interjected.

"You seem unusually well-informed for an 'interested individual.' So, what is it exactly that you would like from me?"

"Well, to start with, what value would a *piece* of a holographic computer massive memory storage device have? After all, it's just a piece, maybe only 20% of the original, and an irregular-shaped shard to boot. I assume that means it might hold within it a similar percentage of whatever information the whole crystal might have contained."

"Ah, there, Mr. Marx, I can definitely help you. You see, a unique feature of embedded holographic crystal memory is that the *complete database* is retrievable from any reasonably sized piece. That is to say, if the piece of crystal in your possession is what I think it is, it will contain a complete record of the *entire* database. That's one of the amazing properties of holographic crystal memory. And given what you've told me about its response to normal light, I suspect you have a piece of an advanced Denisyuk reflective holographic crystal. Such a device is activated when normal light is projected into the crystal. The 'image' of the information is reflected back towards the viewer, much as you described. I had the pleasure of working with Dr. Yuri Denisyuk at the Institute of Opticophysics before 'moving' to Japan and later being moved to the USA. He and Yusef Spasskov, his brilliant young assistant, created the Denisyuk reflective hologram. My small contribution at Infinity Global was to apply this form of inscription-transmission to computer crystals serving as massive memory devices. Interesting, no?"

"Interesting, yes!" John replied in amazement. "You mean a

shard, even a piece of crystal dust from a crushed shard, would contain the entire database inscribed on the original crystal?"

"Holographic crystal memory isn't quite *that* amazing, Mr. Marx," Solokov laughed. "There are minimum size limits, primarily having to do with the reading of the information from the crystal. For a Denisyuk normal-light holographic crystal like you've described, the fragment would probably have to be at least, oh, a half-inch-by-one-inch. If anywhere near 20% of the original, I believe your shard would prove more than adequate to retrieve the contents of the entire database. Anything less that than that—a shard of your shard, for example—might prove insufficient to be able to be read using today's technology. Tomorrow, who knows?"

"What about the contents, Dr. Solokov? You seemed to recognize the name Leon Puissegur. Could the information on the crystal refer to his work?"

"Yes. Well. Leon Puissegur and I also go back a long way. Leon is an oil man—an independent international oil consultant—championing the controversial concept that oil is not produced biologically, but abiologically. 'Abiotic oil'."

"You mean 'aoil'?" John asked, recalling the strange subject line of the email.

"Leon often called it that, to everyone's utter bafflement. I think he did it to get back at everyone for not…entertaining…his theory. In truth, abiotic oil is actually an old theory. I'm not an oil man, but from what I heard from Leon and the former USSR state-owned oil companies, Rosneft, and now Lukoil, with whom he frequently consulted, as well as my colleagues in the former USSR, the idea was developed by the Russian chemist, Dmitri Mendeleev, the world-renowned creator of the first version of the periodic element table. The theory that abiotic oil comes principally from non-biological sources has been hotly contested and was largely rejected until NASA began investigating life on other planets, and later the origins of life. Leon and other abiotic oil theorists held that the proto-chemicals necessary for life originally originated from abiotic oil. They had advanced the theory, using NASA data, to the point of calculating where exactly on this planet abiotic oil was being created. As Leon explained it, the key to proving or disproving the theory today no longer hinges on whether recovered oil has a biotic or abiotic signature, but whether it's possible to actually demonstrate *in situ* an oil field being replenished with abiotic oil. Leon told me the last time we met at a meeting that his calculations indicated a very high *probability* that the North American Strategic Oil Reserve was being naturally replenished with abiotic oil at a rate that would allow production-level extraction forever without depleting the reserve. Scientists and governments mostly rejected his ideas and data, so I suggested he might want to present his theory to DSSC, which apparently he did, and not so long ago from what you've said. Now it's my turn to speculate. I'm going to guess that what's on that shard of yours is probably his dynamic, four-dimensional map of the exact time-flow-locations of all the abiotic oil on the planet. It was a pet project of his. Only a massive holographic crystal memory device could store that much information. And if I am correct, then that piece of crystal you have is worth more than anyone could possibly imagine, if only for its incredibly persuasive marketing value when displayed. With that, one could..."

"...convince the US government to develop the North American Strategic Oil Reserve?" John interrupted.

"Certainly, that. And, if it were to prove true..."

"...like as a result of the survey I've ordered..." John added.

"...then, Mr. Marx, whoever possesses the information and gets it before the President of the United States, or any other world leaders for that matter, would hold in his hands the key to developing a monopoly on sustainable oil-energy on this planet."

"Now I understand," John concluded. "It's a win-win scenario for DSSC and BPI. It doesn't much matter whether the theory is true or not. Given the form and extent of the information recorded on the crystal it would be most persuasive. And, should anything suggestive of abiotic oil result from the survey we, and probably other oil men, are doing at DSSC/BPI wells throughout the world at this moment, like hitting a deep abiotic oil regeneration area..."

"...real *or* manipulated..." Solokov interjected.

"...then whoever holds the information holds *the* trump card," John completed.

"It's certainly something many would consider worth killing for," Sokolov ended.

"A few more questions if you don't mind, Dr. Sokolov. First, where do you suppose the shard came from in the first place? Wouldn't that mean that the parent holographic memory crystal had been shattered? Why would anyone at DSSC, assuming they created and held it, want to break it into pieces? Assuming the other pieces have a complete record also, why 'share' this one with me of all people?"

"All good questions, Mr. Marx, but far beyond my expertise and scope of knowledge to comment on. You have any other questions?"

"How would I go about determining if this shard contains Leon Puissegur's four-dimensional abiotic oil map of the world without risking my life and that of everyone I come into contact with?"

"Hmm. If you could somehow get the fragment to me here in Texas..." Solokov mused. "I maintain a private laboratory, and could read what's on it for you, but I'm under surveillance as I mentioned, undoubtedly by the very people who would pose a threat to you. Another option would be to locate Yusef Spasskov. I believe he's working at Petroleum and Geosystems Engineering at the University of Texas at Austin. However, the only way to *guarantee* your safety and that of everyone else would be to destroy the shard. Crush it. It would only require a hammer…"

"Other suggestions?" John asked, looking nervously at his watch.

"As I said, try to locate Spasskov. But watch out for Howard Stein. He's clever, ruthless, and tends to show up at the least opportune moments…" Sokolov abruptly stopped talking and blanched.

"Alexei, how good to see you, again. Imagine finding one of my oldest and my newest friends, here, talking together," Stein's sonorous voice echoed from over John's right shoulder. "I hope you don't mind my letting myself in, John; you seemed lost in conversation."

John looked over his shoulder at an evil-grinning Stein. "Well, actually…"

"Alexei," Stein cut in. "I think it's time for you sign off; I suspect you've provided Mr. Marx with more than enough to think about. We'll talk again soon, you and I…old friend." Turning back to John, Stein continued in the same, threateningly condescending voice: "And John, I think it's time for us to have a little chat of our own."

Dr. Alexei Solokov terminated the call without another word.

"I see you've been busy, John. It's been less than a half hour since we discussed how important it was that all further discussions about the recently recovered email and the circumstances surrounding it remain privileged information. *Not to be shared.* What of 'any person attempting to spread such misinformation would likely find the world a hostile and inhospitable place ' did you *not* understand?" Stein asked menacingly. "I expected more from a new company man." Stein's slowly thinning grin matched the viperous sound of his voice. "I sent Chris to find you, to share some good news, and what do I find?"

"I've been doing some 'company' exploring, Howard. You did ask me to call you Howard, didn't you?"

Stein's tight grin disappeared, and his eyes narrowed further. "I assume, then, that you were planning to share some good news of your own with me?"

"Yes, of course. But how much have you already heard?" John asked, regaining his poise at last.

"I suggest you assume I heard nothing of your conversation," Stein replied coldly. "Start from the beginning: Why call Solokov in the first place?"

John grasped at Stein's last sentence. Perhaps Stein had barged in at the very end and *hadn't* heard that much of his and Solokov's conversation after all. "You mentioned you were interested in where the email originated. Alexei Solokov is a world-renowned expert in computer information. I thought he might be able to…"

"You're not very good at this game, are you, John? In fact, your amateurish attempts at sharing as little as possible with me are what convinced me at our last meeting that you were *not* involved in high-level industrial espionage. The obvious conclusion is that you've some *personal* stake in all this. John, I must reiterate: Any attempt at involving others will end up putting them in mortal jeopardy. If you had just talked with me first before contacting Solokov. Remember Franks. Now I am obligated to dispatch a special security team to protect Solokov. I only hope it's not too late…"

Grasping at the straw Stein had tossed, John decided to build on the 'personal stake' angle in an attempt to ferret, if he could, how much Stein had actually overheard, and to further deflect attention away from Solokov. "I should have mentioned at our previous meeting that George Franks was a personal friend of mine. His death was a deep shock. I didn't know what to say at our previous meeting, and it's taken me awhile to…"

"I quite understand, and thank you for sharing your relationship with George Franks. We, of course, already knew of it, but I needed to hear it directly from you, without questions, coaching or cajoling, in order to better understand your…motivations, shall we say…in all this. Honesty is the vantage from which we will unravel this Gordian knot that appears to still be forming about us, and has yet to be fully revealed. There. You see, John? I'm not as difficult or bad as you might think. The welfare of you and all your friends, Solokov included, is of the highest priority for both of us. Now, if I may, I need to ask you where you think your friend, George Franks, got the email. And why he sent it specifically to you? As I said earlier, there's no indication at this point that he sent the email to anyone else. And please remember when answering that I've already assembled a surprising amount of information surrounding the incident, some of which, like you, I'm unwilling to share quite yet. I'm looking for you to make another gesture of good faith. Once we establish a venue of open sharing, then I can disclose more of what I know. Your information, for example, might provide independent corroboratation of some of what I have thus far uncovered, and provide further evidence of your 'innocence' at the same time. My information might provide you the same, as well as proving to you I'm not the enemy."

John thought for a moment. What Stein was saying had the ring of truth to it. Had he wrongly interpreted Stein's coldness and his need for 'independent corroboration,' as evidence of a conspiracy? On the other hand, wasn't it his own search for a wider conspiracy that had brought him to Solokov, and Solokov had clearly said not to trust Stein? Stein had also mentioned the "Gordian knot still forming around us" that was "yet to fully reveal itself" which implied that while Stein may indeed know more than what he was saying, he hadn't put everything together yet. Then again, there was the possibility that Stein was baiting him. Should he share all he knew with this security man, whom neither he nor Solokov really trusted, and continue playing the "innocent?" It wasn't yet clear to John what his own role in the whole affair was. John therefore chose a middle strategy.

"It seemed likely to me that the person who originally sent the email was trying to short-circuit some broader plan. Furthermore, George fully intended to send it here. Since I knew nothing about this, whomever it was meant for must have been here, on this rig and left. George, therefore, sent it to me, a trusted friend, planning to forward me further instructions as to whom to deliver it to. I'm assuming that he never got the chance to send them. I was on my way to report the email to Chris Longley when you and your men intercepted me. In answer to your questions, since George never had the chance to explain any of this to me, I'm just as unclear as you are as to the intent and implications surrounding the email itself, hence my Internet foray. I heard a rumor that a private meeting had been held between an oil consultant and a company man. No one had heard of anyone else visiting the rig that day, so I assumed the email was meant for one of them. I heard through the grapevine that the oil consultant might have been a fellow named Puissegur. My Internet search assured me that he was real, and involved in oil. I wasn't sure if it was a good idea to contact him directly—that would be more in your and McClaussen's arena—but I also wasn't sure if it all wasn't one big red herring, so when I ran across Puissegur's name on the same committee as that of the famous computer information wizard, Dr. Alexei Solokov, along with Solokov's Skype number, I took the outside chance of seeing if Solokov would happen to be available on Skype. He was. You know the rest." John held his breath, hoping the complex ruse would work.

Stein was silent for a moment, his face betraying neither his thoughts nor his emotions. Then he seemed to awaken. "So what exactly did Solokov have to say, other than to 'watch out' for me?"

John released his breath. The middle-of-the-road tactic had worked. Stein must have entered his room at the very last of his and Solokov's talk. Seizing the initiative, John replied, "Not much. Just that Puissegur was one of a proverbial legion of fringe oil lobbyists. Solokov said Puissegur had approached him about a crazy oil idea, and that the man seemed to be trying to get an oil company—any oil company—to take notice of him and the theory he was pedaling. Puissegur not being a company man, I reasoned that the email must have been meant for the other company person, of whom I have absolutely no knowledge, not even a name." There. That should repair any damage he'd done in calling Solokov.

Stein paused again, this time as if reflecting carefully on John's interwoven mixture of truth, obfuscation and deceit.

Stein nodded his acceptance. "Alright, I'll put Chris on finding the name of the company person. But for now, please, John, don't do anymore independent investigating. I've had a strong feeling all along that your actions, in particular, are being monitored. I don't know yet by whom, but given George Franks' sudden untimely death, I'm obligated to take every possible precaution. Is there anything else you can share with me that might help us along? Anything, John. Even a seemingly unimportant piece of information might prove of help."

It was John's turn to be wary. He couldn't explain it, but Stein's seemingly genuine request for cooperation made the hairs on his neck stand and prickle. There was something about the man that just didn't add up. "No, that's it. I hope my inquiry hasn't placed Dr. Solokov, Mr. Puissegur or the 'other person' in danger."

"I can't answer that, John, but I can assure you that by sharing your information with me, you've bought them each twenty-four hour protection. BPI has allocated extraordinary resources to me during this crisis to protect our companies and their people from harm."

It was the phrase "extraordinary resources," the word "crisis," and Stein's emphasis on protecting "our companies" from harm that, well after the man's exit, left John with an unshakable feeling of impending doom.

John locked up his computer and walked outside to a grating located just above the waterline, well below the bulk of the massive rig structure. Looking down into the clear blue water, he spotted a barracuda hanging around the leeward side of the wellheads, waiting to seize any unwary fish that happened by. The barracuda suddenly bolted from the shadows like a bullet from a gun and its victim disappeared in a flash of silver. John wondered how his friend, Josh, was faring, then, reflecting gloomily on how much alike the world was above and below the surface of the water, turned and walked back up the stairs to join the survey crew seventy feet above.

The Oil Man

CHAPTER 8

By the time John Marx reached the survey crew, Howard Stein, Shaun McClaussen and Chris Longley were already present on deck, trying their best to keep their collective eyes and ears on everyone and everything while remaining as inconspicuous as possible. Longley was huddled close to Stein, flipping through notebook pages. "We're past due for a routine inspection, sir. We could use the due inspection to justify checking any or all of the crew as they return to base for shore leave."

"Is Marx scheduled to be part of the shore leave group?" asked Stein.

Chris rifled through the notebook, then stopped, read, and responded. "Yes, assuming the survey is completed. His friend, Kelty Moss, is also scheduled for shore leave."

Stein nodded to McClaussen.

"Make it happen," McClaussen ordered, turning to watch the three crews—the rig crew, the company crew, and the survey team—laboring effortlessly together under John Marx's supervision. *The man was a born leader,* thought McClaussen. *Too bad...*

"Make certain the search includes all electronic devices," Stein added.

"Done," Chris replied crisply, turning his attention to Stein. "Your computer specialist is almost finished examining all the laptops on the rig, as well as checking on all transmissions that have come in and out of this rig the past couple of days. With your permission, I will assign him to the shore leave inspection team to check the electronic devices."

"Good thinking," Stein acknowledged curtly, as his computer specialist approached and stood stiffly at attention. "I take it you found something?"

"Marx is one chummy fellow. Pretty much all the workers on the rig consider him not only their leader, but friend also. In addition to Kelty Moss, he has another life-long friend on the rig by the name of Josh Platur. They travel together to their homes in Violet when on shore leave. Platur lives down the street from Marx. I took the liberty of asking Mr. Platur while we strip-searched him if he had a computer or if Marx had mentioned anything about computers or emails to him the last couple of days." Before the man could continue, McClaussen interrupted.

"Did Platur say anything—*anything* at all—that might indicate he knew about the email?"

"No, sir. But Platur did confirm to us that Marx has a laptop, which suggests to me that the information he provided should be credible. For example, he said Marx hadn't told him anything about an email, and I believe him. Platur doesn't own a computer. I cross-checked this with Kelty Moss, who also lives just down the road from Marx and Platur. When in Violet, all three frequent each others' homes for parties and such. They call themselves the three musketeers. Moss also doesn't own a computer. He said it would take too much time away from his 'active single life.' I found no indication that the email sent to Marx by Franks went to anyone other than Marx, nor did I come upon any indication that Marx had copied, forwarded or shared it with either of these two friends. Is there anything else you want me to do, Mr. McClaussen?"

"You did a fine job tending to all the loose ends. I've nothing further. How about your boss?" McClaussen looked inquisitively at Stein.

"Nothing more. Like Mr. McClaussen said, you've done a fine job here. Shaun will need your assistance at the base camp to search all shore leave personnel and their luggage to make sure no one's trying to sneak out a copy of the email. I think it's time for you and the men to head over to Rustic Oil base camp and await his further instructions."

Stein's computer man stiffened and nodded, then left to notify Stein's three musclemen to pack.

"Looks like your work here is pretty much wrapped up, Shaun," Stein ventured. "Will you be heading back?"

"No, Howard, I've been ordered to stay to report the survey results as well as squelch any rumors that might result. We're drilling exactly where Puissegur's model predicted an abiotic oil upwell should exist. If there's any possibility at all…"

The geologist in McClaussen fully understood. Experience told him that if they'd tapped into an abiotic oil source, it would be invaluable. On the other hand, gas pockets were infamous for causing drill pipe nudges, jostles and pokes, and in such cases, a spark could ignite the pocket into an explosive inferno as had happened on Blue Water Horizon. Either way, rig crews were notorious for spreading rumors whenever a 'find' happened or didn't, or an 'event' proved significant or not. Luck and safety were two things every oil man respected. Any rumor that an operation was "unlucky," unsafe, unsuccessful or in jeopardy was the kiss of death.

This "incident," however, was quite different. Not only did Puissegur's four-dimensional model pinpoint exactly *where* and *when* a deep abiotic oil source would occur—which was why BPI had ordered its subsidiary, NSWP, to drill here—but the model had also predicted the existence of upwelling pressure pockets at exactly this depth. If—and this was still a huge "if" in McClaussen's mind—Puissegur's abiotic model was actually correct, it would change the future of petroleum exploration. If BPI could produce hard proof that the North American Strategic Oil Field was sitting on top of thousands of such upwelling abiotic oil "fingers," constantly regenerating the oil field, that would surely convince an administration and Congress hungry for new funds, and an economically-depressed populace struggling under the burden of an increasingly out-of-control national debt to take action. If the President and Congress bought it, it would be the crowning achievement of his career, whether or not the abiotic oil theory was actually true. "If you stay, Shaun, then my work's finished, and that leaves me free to resolve several remaining problems. Once I do that, the project will be completely back in your hands."

"I can take care of things here," McClaussen replied, thinking of how well things had turned out so far, given the almost unbelievable reason why the email had gotten sent in the first place.

CHAPTER 9

Immediately below the platform, pipes from previous exploratory wells that were now in production hissed and rattled throughout their intertwining maze of angles, twists, turns, joins and bifurcations. It never ceased to amaze John how pipes carrying oil or natural gas from beneath the Gulf floor could assume such contorted shapes. Above him hung the majority of the crew quarters bolted to the production platform. Once the survey and drilling was finished, the deck would, he hoped, become an even more complex production imbroglio.

"John! I've been looking for you. The preliminary survey data are in. I bear good and bad news." Josh's ebullient voice was a welcome sound amidst the many.

"I was wondering how you were faring," John said, trying to imagine good news.

The two made their way together towards the mound of survey equipment that formed a roofless makeshift room within which two men controlled the reeling speed of the wire line into the drill hole, and several others hovered next to Claude Askins and the wall of readout instruments and gauges. The wire line was still being slowly lowered into the well with different types of tools being attached at marked intervals. The analytic equipment hummed and sang. Claude moved from panel to panel monitoring, analyzing and re-analyzing data as it flowed in from each sensor. Between the hole and the makeshift situation room were more stacks of electronic equipment to transfer and process the electronic signals from all the sensors into a single real-time visual display, complete with printed paper trail. It was Claude's job to make sense of it all.

Each time John ordered a survey, there seemed to be more equipment of increasing complexity. Even so, he could still spot-name some of the old reliables like the Martin Decker Unit sitting in front the cable drum. Its function was to measure exactly how many feet of cable were going down the hole by counting passing magnetic dots embedded in the cable.

John and Josh threaded their way through cables, equipment and men to a small building behind the deck-pipe rack, where a fresh drill pipe waited in readiness to extend the hole as soon as the survey deemed it safe.

"Those guys," Josh said, thrusting a thumb back over his shoulder towards where MaClaussen, Stein and his men were earlier, "literally tore my room apart. They even had me strip-searched to make sure I didn't have anything resembling a memory device taped or hidden anywhere. Thorough bastards, I'll give them that."

John stopped abruptly, almost knocking Josh down. "Did they find the drive or crystal?"

"Nope," Josh offered casually. "That's part of the good news. I hid it where no one would ever think of looking. You want to know where?"

"No!" John shouted, shushing at his friend the next instant with index finger over his lips. "Just be sure it stays hidden where they can't find it, and pay special attention when we reach the dock. One of the deck crew overheard Chris arranging for everyone going on shore leave to be searched by Stein's men at the dock immediately after they exit the liberty boat." John grabbed Josh's right arm and pulled him closer. "Any news about Puissegur?"

Josh's eyes dropped. "That's part of the bad news. Nothing— that's what I found out about him. Absolutely nothing. It's as if he disappeared off the face of the earth. Or maybe never existed. The guy's everywhere right up to when he appeared on the catwalk yesterday. Then, poof! He's nowhere! At least, I assume it was him. Hell, I couldn't even confirm that!"

John continued his grip on Josh's arm. "Nothing? You're certain of this? Not even a rumor?"

"Nothing at all, John…except for the fact that I couldn't raise anything at all, which, if he *was* actually here, *is* significant, I guess. Rigs are like sieves when it comes to secrets. It makes me question if it *was* him who visited here or…"

"If it wasn't him, then who could it have been? Who lost—or left —the box where I found it? I've been wondering whether the box happened to be there by accident, or was intended for me. After all, George sent *me* the email…"

"I'm afraid I've some other bad news before I give you the rest of the good: There's been another death. A guy named Alexei Solokov. Apparently you were talking with him earlier, at least that's what I heard Kelty Moss whispering to one of the junior controllers. He overheard Stein talking to someone about Solokov by cell phone. Kelty also mentioned it was a bit strange the way he'd heard it. The man didn't seem to make any effort to keep the conversation quiet. In fact, it seemed to Kelty as if Stein *wanted* him to overhear it. Rumor has it that Solokov was found dead in his Texas home late this morning. Nothing yet about how he died. The whole thing feels creepy and leaves too much to the imagination. It feels rather like a warning…"

"Dead?" echoed John blankly. "Then Stein was right about everyone I contact being at risk. I Skyped Solokov after finding on the Internet that he and Puissegur had met at a conference. He convinced me that the shard is a part of a crystalline normal-light holographic recording device, and I'm willing to guess that it was storing a four-dimensional map of the world showing where and when to locate the abiotic oil. It was apparently pieced together by Puissegur to demonstrate his theory. I'm also willing to guess that the information he gave me cost Solokov his life. The question is, who killed Franks and now Solokov? It could be any of a thousand competing companies. Hell, it could even be Stein!"

"Whoa, pardner. You keep trying to make this into a global conspiracy. Isn't calling an old scientist's death a murder just a bit premature…and unhealthy?"

"I don't know, Josh. I just know that there's more to this than what anyone is saying. I feel like an actor in someone else's play. Some people out there seem to know the lines but not me." John released his best friend's arm. "Promise me something, Josh. Promise me you won't go getting killed next?"

"I'll certainly do my best not to, but I recommend you watch *yourself*. Like I said, to me it feels more like a warning. It might not be a global conspiracy, but whatever's going on, George's murder and Solokov's death, if it is a murder, seem more to me like pre-emptive attempts at stopping the spread of information. McClaussen seems to be taking it all in stride, as if expecting them, and maybe more, to happen. The good news, John, is that Claude thinks he's discovered the cause of the pipe jump. He wants to fill you in personally on the details and his conclusion before telling anyone else."

At John's insistance, he and Josh parted from the shed through different doors at different times to minimize their being seen together.

On his way back to the survey area Josh visited the platform perimeter rail from which he could look down a hundred and twenty feet below at the glistening surface of the Gulf of Mexico. Because of the mess of pipes, men and equipment, the area occupied by the survey crew would be under constant camera surveillance to prevent a recurrence of a 1969 accident where an entire survey crew was knocked into the Gulf by a loose pipe. Two platform workers and one of the survey crew had been killed. Oil exploration at its best was always a risk in terms of both money and human lives.

John slid through the slit in the stacks of survey equipment that served as an open door to greet Claude. "How's everything going? Josh says you've found something."

Claude turned on his stool without moving the laptop balanced on his knees. He was using it to cross-check the huge mass of information displayed on the fifty-inch liquid crystal screen before them.

"There's definitely a gas pocket and it's located barely six feet from the open hole. I'm thinking you may want to cement this section of the hole before resuming drilling."

For John, Claude's reputation of understating a crisis had just been confirmed. For Claude, John's disappointment seemed out of place. He'd expected concern or worry. He had also assumed that John would quickly see the bad news for its good. After all, once preventive measures had been taken, drilling could safely continue.

"How big is the gas deposit?" John asked.

"Indications are that it may hold a few million cubic feet of gas.

You may want to inform Chris. Most exploration companies like NSWP like to hold small finds like this in reserve for future development." Claude said, stroking his Genghis Khan mustache.

"Are you certain it's a gas pocket and not a hot oil upwelling?"

"As certain as I can be," Claude assured him.

" Did you bring cement and cementing equipment?" John asked, finally accepting the survey engineer's statement for the good news it was.

"We brought everything, not knowing what we'd find, or what you and the oil man would decide to do." Claude turned his laptop screen toward John and lowered his voice. "John. Look at this," he whispered.

"What am I looking at here?" John asked, watching different color lines and shapes swirl across the screen as if they were all somehow connected in a dance of rhythmic color.

"Here," Claude said, pointing with a long-nailed finger. "See this dark blue area? That's the gas field that spit up your pipe. You see this blue reference color? This is how natural gas is supposed to look using the tool we have in the hole right now. The bright boys who designed this program assigned red to oil and the blue to natural gas; the other colors represent different types of rocks. The information you're seeing here is right now being sent back to the various companies who made the tools, and to the various regional and global centers that store petroleum information. The idea is to add to the world's knowledge base on different strata and rock types that contain or show up alongside oil and gas deposits. That way, someday, we'll be able to type in specific rock types and immediately locate the areas holding significant amounts of occult oil or gas, like using radar to locate where the biggest fish would most likely be lurking. What's interesting here is the reddish-blue color of your gas pocket, and the fact that the rock types surrounding it are not ones commonly associated with either natural gas or stratified oil deposits. This area looks and acts more like a natural gas field, but the color and rock strata don't correlate with that interpretation very well either. It's odd. Both professionally interesting and challenging. I hadn't thought of mentioning it to you or the company man until you asked whether I was *certain* it was a gas pocket and not a, what did you call it, a 'hot oil upwelling.' Now, I'm thinking that such an upwelling might look reddish-blue like this. There's always something new popping up in this trade."

John stared at Claude, trying to make sense of what he was saying. "In other words, you're *not* certain it's a gas pocket?"

"Yeah, well, if you hadn't asked, I would have said I was certain. Now that you've asked and offered an alternative, I can't be sure."

John took that as a "no." *So it could represent hot abiotic oil working its way up from the mantle.*

Claude turned back to his laptop, his fingers flying over the keys. A moment later the printer awoke—de DEEEE, de DEEEE, de DEEEE—and began printing stacks of numbers similar to what John was seeing on the wide screen display above. Claude gathered up the sheets and handed them to John. "Here. Give these to the oil man."

"Chris Longley," John corrected. "He's the NSWP representative, who, for a short time, Shaun McClaussen had me 'replace.' He's apparently back in McClaussen's good graces. In either case, McClaussen is expectantly waiting."

Claude whistled and raised his eyebrows. "Boy, do you know how to make things complicated."

John took the pile of papers and headed to the control office. On his way, he couldn't help but think of the risk in which he was placing his best friend. John reached the office as McClaussen was coming out, the two nearly colliding.

"Have you found something, Mr. Marx?" McClaussen asked, eying the stack of paper in John's hands.

"It's the survey report on the gas pocket we side-swiped," John said, shoving the paper towards McClaussen.

Deep lines cut across McClaussen's sober face as he accepted the stack, making him look old and worn out. "Let's go into my temporary office. I don't want the wind scattering this paper all over the rig."

John followed the shoulder-drooping giant, greeting Chris Longley as they entered the executive office.

"What have you got for us, Mr. Marx?" Chris asked affably.

"It's the survey engineer's report on the blowback." Spreading the paper out along the length of the conference table, John began reciting what Claude had told him, carefully omitting their whispered conversation while adding his own spin. "The engineer says there's a large natural gas pocket about six feet away from the drill hole. We need to cement that part of the hole to keep the gas from bursting through. He brought the necessary supplies and equipment, so I should have the cement job done well before the crew change coming up." John waited for objections or questions, and, hearing none, turned to go.

Looking anxiously up at McClaussen, Chris ventured, "What's the minimum cement necessary? We need to continue drilling as soon as possible."

John stopped and turned to face the two company men. "From what the engineer told me, we were damn lucky. Had the drillbit not been six feet below the formation when it blew through, we likely wouldn't be standing here discussing the situation. At best we would have been facing having to plug the entire hole, pull back and re-drill from a side-angle to bypass the problem area entirely. Either outcome would have been catastrophic. As it stands, it won't cost much in time or money to cement about ten feet above and below where we currently are, and then re-drill through the cement, allowing the cement to keep the gas out." John waited a second time to receive the authority to go ahead with the cementing. "If all goes well, the special cement should be dry enough to drill through in less than sixteen hours."

Both let out their held breath. While McClaussen gave the nod, Chris gave the order. "Go ahead. If you need anything—anything at all —just ask. Mr. McClaussen and I will catch a helicopter out later this evening. After I leave you'll be in total charge. You'll be both rig super and company man. I assume you can do that?"

John looked askance at Chris, then at McClaussen, trying to decide if this was meant to be the new job offer McClaussen and Stein had alluded to earlier. It would mean tens of thousands more income, something his wife would be pleased to hear. "No problem, Chris," John said, reflecting the wry smile on McClaussen's face. "I'll have Claude check and recheck his calculations and make a list of what he needs to plug the spot up. I'll keep you informed and notify you as soon as we're ready to resume drilling." John turned again to walk out.

"I'll take care of the paperwork," Chris added, confirming John's suspicions. "And John. Make sure there are no more problems. Oh, and before you leave, or I forget: Good job."

John's first reaction was contempt. But after thinking about it, he left the room with a new spring in his step. The day was proving full of surprises. Chris had never said, "Good job," to anyone, and then it struck him: *The man wasn't smiling, he was gloating. He and that bastard McClaussen were attempting to entangle him deeper and deeper in a rapidly growing web of murder and deceit.*

CHAPTER 10

Claude stood outside his makeshift survey center, waiting anxiously for John to return, ready to proceed before John even spoke. "It will take about thirty minutes to change over to the cement tool and position it. I suggested the men begin pulling up the cable and hosing it down as we pull it out of the hole. Figure another twenty minutes to clear the hole, and we can begin cementing," Claude said.

John smiled his approval. "Okay, Claude, NSWP has asked that we cement ten feet above and below the problem. Only after you call it safe, will we re-begin drilling. How much cement will you need?"

"The area in question's roughly two feet wide. Figure in irregularities and compaction and we'll need about…65 cubic feet. We've brought more, so we should be able to secure the hole."

John was about to reply when Claude motioned with his head for John to follow him to the back of the platform. After checking to make sure no one was around, Claude turned to John. "Here's something more you need to know, John. Scuttlebutt has it that you're involved in some kind of heavy-duty effort to damage the oil industry, specifically BPI. I assume you've heard about the sudden death yesterday of BPI

Chief Executive Officer, William Greyson? That makes three deaths in two days: George Franks of Rustic, William Greyson of BPI, and Alexei Solokov, formerly of DSSC. Do you see a pattern emerging? Word is that McClaussen and Stein were sent here yesterday to question you about some insider information you lifted. John, what the hell's going on? Rumor has it that if you are somehow wrapped up in all this and don't watch your back, you and anyone standing next to you may be next!"

"Really, Claude, you're outdoing yourself interpreting what's at the bottom of the well," John answered sarcastically.

"I'm serious, man! Greyson's death was just announced, and everyone's suddenly clammed up. The only thing McClaussen will say is that it has to do with large-scale industrial espionage and that the company suspects you're involved."

John was stunned. McClaussen and Longley had just offered him a dream job, at least so he thought, while McClaussen was, at the same time, spreading rumors of him being an industrial spy? John's mind shifted into overdrive. Claude was right: What the hell *was* going on? John hadn't contacted Greyson. He didn't even know Greyson aside from the fact that Greyson was at the helm of BPI. That would, of course, make him privy to, if not behind the scheme to open up the North American Oil Reserve to BPI. That alone might make it worth a rival company killing him. Conspiracy theories aside, it was sounding more and more like he, John, was being set up. But why? And by whom? Where in all this was Puissegur, and who was the company man Puissegur supposedly met with yesterday on this very rig? Would someone be next announcing Puissegur and the company man's deaths? And what about the doubts Claude had expressed earlier about the "natural gas" pocket being, in fact, some kind of intermediate between natural gas and a hot oil upwelling? Could it be hot upwelling abiotic oil? And what about the email and the crystal?

John, startled back to reality, realized he'd been staring at Claude's eyebrows, two thick brown bushes twitching on either side of the man's chiseled face. "Well, Claude, it…it's simply not true." Remembering McClaussen and Stein's warnings, he quickly added, "I did receive a sensitive company email, yes, but not through any machinations of my own, and Stein had a computer expert erase it from my computer." That was true. "I never got to read it." That wasn't true, but it was essential to say, given the situation. "I'm hardly 'wrapped up' in whatever's going on, and I'm certainly no industrial spy." That was untrue, given that Josh was secreting away a copy of the email *and* the crystal fragment. "By the way, how did you come to hear about all this, and just where does the President of BPI's death fit into this?"

Claude smiled, flashing his brilliant white teeth. "The first time, I heard it from some guys working the drill floor. The second time, I happened to be next to the pipe rack and overheard someone saying that you and he had almost been caught with some important information you'd acquired. It's all indirect and disconnected, I'll give you that, but you know how rumors spread on oil rigs."

Damn! thought John reflexively. *So who else overheard Josh and me talking together next to the pipes? Did this mean Josh might be the next to die? Damn it! Damn it! Damn it! I just need one thing— anything—to hold onto long enough to figure out what's going on and what to do next!*

"Listen, Claude. I don't need to tell you not to believe everything you hear on the platform. The work on a rig is generally pretty mundane, often dangerous and always stressful. Most of what gets said ends up either over-dramatic or blatantly wrong by the time it works its way to the end of a rumor-chain. If what you're hearing is true, then how come I'm not dead?"

"That's what I asked myself, and why I had to ask you."

Before John could reply, Claude continued, in his normal survey engineer voice: "I can have the plug in place in four to six hours. You'll have to wait the minimum sixteen hours before drilling through it though, and you'll need to drill with a six-inch bit, rather than the twelve-inch one you were using above the plug."

"Thanks, Claude," John replied, glad to return to actual vocational rather than alleged avocational activities. "That timeline shouldn't pose a problem. By the time the cement hardens, we'll have the necessary six-inch pipe ready. The main thing from my perspective is that we avert another Blue Water Horizon. On the other hand, I don't think six-inch pipe is going to go over well with Longley or McClaussen. They're planning to bore unusually deep. When you're finished, bring me the paper work, so I can sign off on it. In the meantime, I'll break the news to Longley and McClaussen. I don't relish telling them about the change in pipe…"

"I'll have the paper work and a DVD along with an updated printout on your desk by ten o'clock tonight. And about that unusual 'gas pocket,' John: I leave that to you to explain however you wish."

Claude and John shook hands amicably, and, as John turned towards the stairwell, he heard Claude murmur just loud enough for him to hear, "And good luck. You're really going to need it."

CHAPTER 11

A late afternoon Gulf sun blazed red as a fireball just above the horizon. John Marx steeled himself for his meeting with the mousy Chris Longley, and the physically and mentally imposing BPI executive, Shaun McClaussen. McClaussen and Longley were sitting at the conference table deep in discussion, but went instantly silent when John knocked and entered the room. Both stared, clearly unhappy with the interruption. Chris spoke first.

"What's going on, and how long before we resume drilling again?"

"Gentlemen, Claude Askins said he'll have a cement plug in place within about six hours. It will require another sixteen for the cement to harden, and we can then begin drilling through the plug. The only twist is that Askins says we will have to change to six-inch drill and pipe from here on."

McClaussen jumped from his chair and leaned forward, planting both hands firmly on the table. "Mr. Marx, I know that you know about our....'particular interests'....surrounding this well. If we find what we're looking for, we will need to extract as much as quickly as we can. The future of NSWP and BPI has become linked to the success of this operation. Dropping to a smaller bore isn't acceptable, and frankly, I'm curious as to what your involvement was in coming to this decision!"

"Mr. McClaussen. Given Mr. Askins' recommendation, we can't in good conscience do anything less. Both time *and safety* are of the essence. The resulting plug will be, in my opinion, adequate, but minimal. An expansion plug, a safer alternative that would allow us to continue using 12-inch pipe, would require double or even triple the time. Trying to drill around the anomaly would require days. The *only* viable alternative is to drill through the plug with an acceptably-sized bit. A six-inch hole and pipe leaves only three inches of concrete on either side to seal that section from intrusion. If we were to use anything larger, there would be a good possibility of a hot side-blowout, in summary, yet another Blue Water Horizon." *That should shut the man up*, thought John.

"We have no choice, Shaun," Chris muttered, cowering visibly before McClaussen's wrath.

McClaussen glared daggers and slammed a fist on the table. "Damn it, man! Who's side are you on?"

"When do you think we will resume drilling deeper?" Chris asked John shakily.

"My best guess is early Tuesday morning. I'll order the mud engineer to do a pressure test after the plug is in place, and again after we bore through it. I need to be assured that there'll be little or no shaking in either situation."

Chris stood, walked over to John, and placed an arm around John's shoulders. "Sounds like a good plan, John."

McClaussen watched the scene unfolding before him with interest. "There's been a change in plans, Chris," McClaussen abruptly cut in. "I'll need to leave early in the morning, so I won't be here to monitor things as I had hoped. Given the situation, I want you to remain here and keep me informed of progress." Turning to John, he finished with, "Is there anything more you need inform us of, John?"

Stunned, Chris's arm dropped limply from John's shoulder.

So the offer-he-couldn't-refuse was now rescinded. Well, if that was the cost of being the messenger of bad tidings, then so be it, thought John, who was hastily envisioning how to work the sudden change to his advantage. There was something wrong before, and something more wrong now. The situation had drastically shifted since the three had last talked, and, by John's reckoning, that had to be related to the death of Greyson. "I'll personally make certain that you are the first to know of any change in anything happening on the rig, Chris. Will you be ordering a certification inspection once the plug's in place and before we resume drilling?"

McClaussen and Longley looked concernedly at each other before Chris spoke. "I don't think that'll be necessary. I contacted the chief inspector with whom we usually work, and advised him that the situation was under control. That seemed to satisfy him, as long as I updated him regularly on our progress."

No inspections? Very clever. The two are obviously setting me up to be the fall-guy, should anything go wrong, making sure there are no external records to contradict whatever story was spun.

"Thank you, both. Now, I have to return to overseeing the operation," John said, wanting to conclude the increasingly awkward discussion as quickly as possible. Turning, he walked briskly away without waiting for permission to leave.

After the door closed, McClaussen stared menacingly at Longley. "Listen, Chris. No word of what we are about to discuss can leave this room. Understand?"

"Yes, sir."

"Things surrounding the email are suddenly heating up, and I'm certain Mr. Marx is withholding vital information, both about the email and the current drilling situation. I don't like duplicity within the ranks, so Stein and I have concocted a little surprise for Marx and his pals, assuming they make it through our onshore search unscathed. Greyson's death had changed everything. I need to return to headquarters as soon as possible. I sense Marx trusts you, which is why I countermanded my previous order to you to make Marx the NSWP company man. He's too smart and he knows too much. I need you here, in the capacity of the company man to watch him and his buddies. Stein and I had planned to isolate him and thereby pressure him into working with us, but it doesn't seem to be working. When I leave, I'm hoping Marx will approach you about what's going on. If he does, I want you to befriend him. In the process, I want you to find out what he knows, and at the same time prevent him from knowing anything more. Anything. Our companies' futures are at stake. At this point, any one human life is expendable. You understand?"

Chris, unclear if the threat was being directed at Marx or himself, shifted his weight uncomfortably. "I understand, sir. What should I do if he begins asking questions?"

"For God's sake, Chris, just tell him you don't know what's going on, but that if he wishes, you can contact me to find out. That should stop any questions from him. In fact, I need you to actually be in the dark about things for a while after I leave. That should make your answers even more convincing."

In the dark? Chris worried. *So NSWP wasn't going to be a key player or partner in whatever McClaussen, Stein and cronies were planning after all! And what about the death of BPI's Chief Executive Officer? This was beginning to sound like an emerging end-run, and*

114

those, like him, who were being end-run would end up not only a liability, but an expendable liability. "What will you be doing in the meantime?" Chris blurted out, wishing he'd not asked even as he did.

McClaussen's face darkened. "Mr. Longley, what I will be doing is, quite frankly, none of your business from this moment on. Everything you need know, you now know. Anything you will need to know in the future will be made apparent when the time comes."

"I understand, sir." Chris repeated, more clearly and more anxiously than before.

So it was an eleventh-hour end-run, and he and NSWP had been reduced to pawns in whatever was about to play out, Chris mused. *What can I best do to protect myself? Without more information, I'm little more than a blind participant, an easily manipulated, disposable puppet.*

McClaussen strode out of the room, silent, brooding, deep in thought while Chris, rocking nervously back and forth in his chair, tried without success to guess what McClaussen was up to. One thing he knew: McClaussen was a very dangerous man, and his partner, Howard Stein, even more so. It seemed to Chris that his only hope was in garnering John Marx's trust as ordered. The damnable email must be far more important than anyone was saying, and, if so, information surrounding it was the key to his remaining alive in the drama unfolding about him. He only hoped now that John would stay alive long enough to trust him, and that somehow in the process, he could come up with a way to save his own skin. It was time for Chris Longley, NSWP company man, to shake off fear, and do what he could to save himself and NSWP before it was too late. Now, how exactly could he most quickly gain John Marx's trust? That was the immediate problem.

The Oil Man

CHAPTER 12

John climbed slowly down the metal stairs, around the pipe storage area, and made his way back to the drill floor, thinking along the way. With Solokov gone, he desperately needed to contact Dr. Yusef Spasskov. John was convinced that in contacting Spasskov, he would place his and the man's life at risk. Still, what other options did he have? McClaussen was becoming more openly hostile, and Longley was solidly in McClaussen's camp. With Stein and his henchmen off the platform and therefore out of view, anything could happen. And John also had his friend, Josh Platur, to think of. Josh was secreting the crystal and a copy of the email on a thumb drive on his person. Any of these was reason enough for people to watch his friends, and if things got hotter, stop watching and take them out. Halfway to the drill platform, John's cell phone rang.

John paused, cupped the phone in his hands, and turned his back to the afternoon wind.

"Hello?"

"John, what's going on out there? Are you alright?" The concerned female voice on the other end was his wife, Ann.

"I'm fine, Ann. Just tidying things up for my leaving," he said buoyantly, hoping to deflect her worries and the interest of anyone who might be listening in on their conversation.

"John, two computer repair men came by asking to look at your computer. Is there something wrong with it? Did you schedule some repair work and forget to tell me?" He could hear his wife's voice quickly rising from concern to near-hysteria.

"Calm down, Ann. Did you let them in?"

"Of course not! I told them to come back when you were here. One of the men said there had been reports that our computer was infected with a virus that was contaminating other computer systems. When he threatened me like that, I definitely refused to let them in. I told him to get a search warrant!"

"You did right. If they come back with one, however, you're going to have to let them in. I think it would be a good idea to invite some friends over to stay with you until it's over or I'm back."

"I called the sheriff and he called Judge Evans."

John was surprised. "I'm glad that you did that, but, please, be careful interfering with these men. Thanks to your fast thinking, I don't expect they'll return until after I'm home early Wednesday."

"Are you suggesting that it's not about a computer virus, and that you're in some kind of trouble? Okay, John, exactly what are they after?"

"I don't know, Ann, and that's the truth of it. But whatever it is they want, it's not there, that I can guarantee. It has something to do with the oil company renting our rig and an operation they are engaged in. That's all I know, and all I want to know."

"Well, I sure wish *they* knew that, because these two guys looked like they would have enjoyed tearing the house apart with you in it if possible. They scared me, John. They talked and acted as if inhuman."

John glanced up at the window of the executive guest room where he could see Longley talking animatedly on the phone. His heart welled with a myriad of conflicting emotions, and he didn't have time to explain. "Listen. I'll take care of this when I get home. But while I'm waiting, I think I'll ask the company man why those thugs are harassing my wife while I'm at work."

"Thugs? From work? Now I know you're up to your neck in something. Still, I hope you can do something to keep them away. I told you, they scare me, John. I keep looking to see if they're parked somewhere on our street watching our house."

"If you see them again, Ann, call the sheriff's office immediately. You've already alerted him, so I'm sure he's already keeping an eye on the house. And after you call the sheriff, call up that old flame of yours who's on the police force. He's still around, isn't he?"

"John Marx! He's an old boyfriend! Nothing more!" Ann replied indignantly. "I don't want him involved, since I've already called the sheriff. They were rivals, you know."

"Why *not* involve them both? I think three on two is always better odds. Besides they'll both have your interests at heart."

"I guess if those two 'repairmen' give me anymore trouble, and you don't mind, I could call in the police, too," Ann said coyly, adding, when John didn't respond, "Okay, I will. I'm still a bit shaken up. I miss you, darling."

"I miss you, too, Ann. And the kids. Keep them home and busy in the back bedroom, and, as much as you can, away from windows. I'll see you late Wednesday evening. Be patient and wary. Keep your cell phone charged and handy. If they come back without a warrant, call out the troops and let the intruders know you're going to file charges against them for harassment."

"I'll do whatever's necessary, John. You know I will. I'll call you if anything further develops."

"Call me. Anytime." John folded his cell phone closed, and began walking back to the executive guest quarters, mad as hell. He was halfway there when an NSWP corporate helicopter swooped in. John watched McClaussen appear, walk casually up to it, throw in his bags, and climb in. As the door closed, McClaussen shot a sudden, furious look at John. John in turn shook his fist as the helicopter whisked off. His last image of the man was of two eyes smiling evilly down at him.

A few minutes later, John took a deep breath, rapped on the door lightly, then opened it and walked in. Chris Longley was at the far end of the conference table, still on the phone. Chris motioned for John to have a seat, and continued talking.

After a few moments, John interrupted. "I didn't come here to sit and listen to you chat, *Mr.* Longley," John stated sardonically, stressing the "mister."

"I'll call you right back," Chris said, and hung up the phone. "What seems to be the problem, John?" he asked cordially.

"I wanted to talk with McClaussen, but he just flew off like the coward he is, so you're going to have to do. I want to know why two men are harassing my wife?"

Chris seemed genuinely stunned. "Jeeze, John. I don't know what to say. I don't know anything about this, so I can't answer your question. Is Ann alright? I can call Mr. McClaussen right now if you want, and see what he knows."

"Listen, Chris: Ann's scared. I need him to call off his thugs before Ann does something foolish…like shoot them."

"I can call him right now. Then again…"

"Look, Chris, I don't have time for any games!"

"I'm not playing any games, John. Well, what I mean is that I

120

don't want to play any games. Something rotten is going on here, and I'm as much in the dark as you. Maybe more. If you really want to know what I think, I'm beginning to sense an end-run here, with McClaussen trying to shut NSWP and Rustic Oil—me and you—out. Out of what, exactly, I don't know, but John, I'm starting to get concerned for our lives." It was the way Chris stressed "our" that won John over.

" Well, then I guess it's alright if they show up again, for Ann to shoot first and ask questions later."

"I wouldn't recommend telling her to do that, but I would tell her to call the police if they so much as approach the house. Look, John, I really don't know what's going on any more than why McClaussen seems so hell-bent on pinning the email fiasco on you…and maybe me, too. So, do you want me to pass a message to McClaussen, or not?"

John took another deep breath and forced himself to calm down. "I guess not. But since you asked, what exactly *do* you know?"

Chris shook his head side to side. "Nothing more than I've just told you."

"Then thank you, Mr. Longley," John said ingratiatingly. "I guess I've nothing more to share than what I've already told you." John stormed out of the office, slamming the door behind him, whispering under his breath, "Fuck you, you little prick!"

The discussion hadn't gone at all the way Chris had hoped. Before John barged in ranting and raving about his wife being harassed—McClaussen had said he had a surprise for John, but surely a man like McClaussen wouldn't stoop to strong-arming a man's wife right out in the open, for God's sake. Chris had been prepared to share *everything* with John. It wasn't much, but it would have been enough to put Marx and his buddy, Josh, on alert. Instead, John's indignant

121

shouting had left Chris feeling more isolated and frustrated than ever. *Remember,* his inner voice reminded him, *people connected in any way with Marx have a bad habit of dying suddenly.* Of this, McClaussen and Stein had repeatedly reminded Chris, and Chris definitely didn't want to be next. "Fuck you, you big prick!" Chris whispered vehemently at the closed door.

John paced along the rail at the side of the building, scanning the rig and beyond where dark ruddy clouds blended into the dark blue of the sea. "Red sky in the morning, sailor take warning; red sky at night, sailor's delight," he mumbled sarcastically.

The most immediate problem, aside from his wife being harassed, was how to contact Sokolov's former Russian research colleague, Yusef Spasskov. Austin was not that far away, but it might as well be in Siberia, for all he could do about it. Josh was already overburdened, and likely being watched. Chris, he couldn't trust, despite his initial hopes on somehow swinging him over to his side. On the other hand, perhaps there was some way to trick the gullible miscreant into making contact with Spasskov for him. And if Longley were caught, well, he'd rather it be Chris than Josh or himself dying next.

He could ask Kelty, but Kelty, being naturally curious, a magnet for gossip, and a close friend and neighbor, was most likely being watched, too.

He could ask Claude Askins. Claude could probably even figure out a reasonable explanation for contacting Spasskov. A technical question, maybe. Spasskov was, after all, working for one of the most prestigious academic oil research and development teams in the world, and that would make a consultation believable at least. Something about their survey analysis, perhaps? With McClaussen and Stein off the platform, that should make it safe enough. All John needed to do was to somehow slip all this by Longley, so Longley the dog wouldn't end up reporting the contact to his master, that diabolical Shaun McClaussen. If McClaussen didn't hear it from Chris, then Stein wouldn't likely hear it, either. On the other hand, John reminded himself that every indication was that Stein hadn't overheard any of the details of his conversation with Solokov, and Solokov was nonetheless dead.

John also desperately needed confirmation that the email and shard were from Leon Puissegur, and the bigger issue was, indeed, all about abiotic oil. If he could just confirm that much, he'd have something he could use to make the lives of those persecuting him miserable, and those aiding him more secure.

John was still boiling over the threats to his wife and Longley's refusal to help him, and didn't notice Josh approach him from behind.

"Something eating at you? I haven't seen you this concerned since 'Nam." The mention of Vietnam jerked John back to reality. "Sorry, Josh, but I'm so angry at the moment, I could spit bullets. I'm certain that damned McClaussen sent some thugs to my house to check whether I had somehow squirreled a copy of the email and attachment on my home computer. In the process they ended up scaring Ann. You are right though: I feel like I did back in 'Nam when I killed the soldier rappelling beneath me. This is America, for God's sake! My wife is supposed to be safe in our home, and here I am, unable to help her when she needs me the most. Hell, it's my fault she's being harassed. Next time, these folks might as likely shoot as harass her."

Josh had to run to keep up with John as the man made his way to the drilling floor. "Yeah. I'm suddenly recalling what your VA friends said, and you have that same wild look in your eyes as they described. What are you planning to do?"

"First off, I've been thinking more about that damn email. It *has* to contain more than Solokov's phone number. Are you sure the thumb drive's safe?"

"They had their hands on it and didn't even know it. As a matter of fact, McClaussen and Stein both looked right at it. It's in a special place where even you won't find it. I can give it back to you anytime. When you realize where it is, you're going to laugh."

John stepped onto the drill floor and looked back at the office where he'd just been talking with Chris Longley. The man was standing at the window looking down at John. "I sure hope you're right, because I can see Chris watching me right now, and that means you, too. He'll probably let McClaussen know that you and I were talking. And speaking of talking, anything more about contacting Puissegur?"

"Nothing solid," Josh replied. "But these days that's good news. Ears to the doors, I have heard more scuttlebutt. I heard BPI recalled McClaussen."

"Recalled, eh? So that's what was actually behind his abrupt leaving."

"And I hear that Longley is in the doghouse."

"Really? He just tried schmoozing up to me using his Hogan's Heroes' 'I know *nothing*' speech. I actually believed him for a moment, but then it became clear he was trying to establish a one-way information highway: one-way to him! On the other hand, Chris has never been very adept at establishing relationships—his attempts at striking up a relationship with a woman never seem to last more than a few minutes—maybe he really is reaching out, Chris-style. Maybe…"

"Yeah, and maybe pigs can fly," Josh retorted brusquely.

"Maybe, in this case, they can. What if what I just experienced was a clumsy but genuine attempt to work together? We would have an inside channel to what's going on. I don't really believe that Chris is as uninformed and sidelined as he says. Not yet, anyway. If so, he'd likely be dead by now. Listen, Josh. Could you check him out? You'd have to invent a ruse. Maybe ask him for an unofficial explanation of what's happening 'on behalf of the workers' or something like that, and hint that you know things about me. Maybe that you *think* you saw me reading a weird email on my computer? That should be bait enough. Tell him you saw some numbers. That would prove that you saw something important. Then tell him you heard me mention it was some crackpot trying to place a virus on my computer. You saw me delete it. That would fit with everything that I've told them, and might open a door for Chris to talk with *you*, since he can't with me. It might also take some heat off me and my family, so I can maneuver better."

"Good plan. I've felt pretty useless, just hiding evidence for you. I've been longing to do something more substantial."

"If you can establish a 'mutually cooperative' relationship with Chris, perhaps you could wheedle him into contacting Puissegur? That could actually change the balance of power in our favor."

"I'm game," Josh replied. "I can't imagine them not suspecting me already, but who knows? They did a thorough search of me and my room. Thorough, but, of course, unsuccessful. If Chris is up there worrying about *us*, then maybe right now would be a good time for me to drop in and pay him a social visit."

"Let's separate first; give it a half hour or so. Let it seem like you've been brooding over what to do. Then contact him. Keep it low key. Don't divulge any more than we've just talked about, and *watch your back*. We don't know…"

"Yeah, yeah, I know. We don't know what plots he, McClaussen and Stein are hatching, either separately or together. I'm willing to bet McClaussen is busy trying to gather in the reins of BPI, while Stein chases down every last lead to the email in an attempt to secure

McClaussen's position in BPI and thereby his in DSSC. I'm also willing to bet those two vultures are using Chris as their platform eyes and ears while we're here, at the same time setting him up as a scapegoat, should anything flounder or fail."

"I think you may be right. If so, it's time for us to drive a wedge between the dangerous duo and their eyes and ears. I've never thought of Chris as the evil mastermind sort, but rather as a Peter-principle guy who's finally risen far above his abilities. If he needs a friend, now's the time for us to fill the bill," John summarized. "Okay, let's do it! I need to contact the Violet media as well as an investigative reporter I trust, a friend who writes for the New Orleans Times-Picayune, to be on hand just in case those goons show up at my house again."

"If this hits the media, you'd better be ready for a fight," admonished Josh, not at all surprised at the depth of John's resolve.

"It already is a fight to the death. Don't forget: Three men, Franks, Solokov, and Greyson, are already dead."

"You really think their deaths are connected?" Josh asked.

"Yes, I do. I know, everyone thinks I'm a conspiracy nut, but, Josh, I think this is the real thing, and I think it's big. Much bigger than we can see from our narrow vantage point. I think this is *really* big! And after what they tried to pull on my wife, I really don't care about the risk to me. They already know I know things. I'm already marked."

Josh let out a nervous laugh, "It always sounds so believable when you say it. Still, I can't believe the email's anything more than a corporate mistake they're trying to run down and cover up, and the crystal lost during a hush-hush corporate meeting here. I mean, what real evidence do you have that it's all connected, other than a bunch of wild speculations flying around in that fertile mind of yours? Maybe what's more dangerous is us running around like we know something, making everyone, McClaussen and Stein included, think we really do know something and that we're a couple of loose cannons. Man, that would be more than enough reason to harass us and get us fired."

"Or killed? No, Josh, *this one's for real*. I feel it. I can taste it, man. It's what I've been primed for all my life."

Josh didn't like where John's line of reasoning, if he could call it that, was going, so he decided to change the subject. Whether John was right or not wouldn't change anything for the moment. Even going to Chris with the story John suggested wouldn't place either of them in any more awkward a position than they already were. And, besides, John was his friend.

"Hey, remember you asked me about Puissegur, and I said I hadn't uncovered anything solid? Well, I haven't *located* him for certain, but Kelty reminded me that the man keeps a home in Violet, in the country, on other side of town from where we live. Kelty says he's normally reclusive. Hardly ever appears in town, and when he does, doesn't talk much. The word is that he's made more than a pest of himself at the various oil companies with his crazy oil theory, and they're all actively discouraging him from hanging around them. And now that I mention it, that's distinctly strange, given what you said Solokov said about having introduced Puissegur to DSSC, and his being here on the rig to meet with a company man. Doesn't jibe, does it? Kelty also hinted that the man's actions are being closely monitored. Puissegur's the guy who does the big fireworks show in Violet every New Years Eve. Does that help place him?"

"Yeah, I remember. He's so low profile that while the name sounded familiar, I wouldn't have ever placed him in our own hometown. Rumors aside, we should try and visit him on Wednesday after we go ashore. He could clear up a lot for us if he's hiding out at his house."

"He's there. At least, that's what I'm guessing from what Kelty says," Josh laughed, this time conspiratorially. "Okay. I'm ready, if you are."

John nodded, lazying up to the driller to give Josh the opportunity to break away unnoticed.

"Claude just finished the cementing. The equipment's being drawn up out of the hole now. He's told us to be prepared to drill through the cement plug around five o'clock in the morning tomorrow," one of Claude Askins' assistants updated John.

John focused his attention on the crew recovering the cable and equipment. One of the survey crew guided the cable out of the hole, while another washed it down, carefully removing chunks of mud and concrete debris.

"Let me know before we begin drilling," John ordered loudly, then walked to the back of the drill platform where Josh was painting a railing. John stopped next to a surprised Josh and looked around carefully before speaking.

"Josh, I need to be absolutely certain that no one will find that shard or memory stick."

Josh continued painting, purposefully not looking up or acknowledging John. His role in this intrigue had substantially increased, and he was, willingly or not, being drawn into John's conspiracy, and wanted to take every possible precaution. "What's the fuss?" he muttered quietly at his moving paintbrush. "I already told you no one would find them, no matter what they did. They wouldn't even show on an x-ray search, should Stein come up with that. Trust me: They're well hidden and yet always in plain sight."

"Sorry, Josh, but with everything suddenly converging, I need to feel certain. You're my best friend, and I feel guilty as hell involving you in this."

"Rest assured, John, that no one will find it. But thanks for the sentiment. You're my best friend, too. I stand by my friends."

Josh continued painting and talking, while John attempted a discrete visual search of his friend. "Thanks, Josh. But that's exactly what's making me reconsider asking you to talk with Chris. If I'm making a mountain out of a molehill, then I'm willing to take responsibility for my actions. But I fear my drawing *you* into this mess."

Josh looked up from his painting and grinned. "Hey, man. I'm in. Always have been. You can't shake me off that easily."

John looked back at him and returned the grin. "You missed a spot," he whispered.

Josh looked down but could easily see he hadn't, and they laughed uneasily together.

The Oil Man

CHAPTER 13

As the helicopter lifted off, McClaussen peered down at the troublesomely enigmatic John Marx shaking his fist and staring angrily back. *What was with this man, he thought, shaking his head in disbelief, and his "friends," Josh Platur, Kelty Moss, possibly even Claude Askins. And that hardly innocent, clueless wife of his—what did his men say her name was? Ann? Didn't they "get" where John was leading them? What didn't they "get" about George Franks and Alexei Solokov's deaths? It was like they were willingly standing in line, waiting to be killed.*

For a conspiracy nut, John Marx seemed surprisingly incapable of connecting the dots. And what about William Greyson's recent demise? Even a child could reason that when he, Shaun McClaussen, ascended to Chief Executive Officer of British Petroleum International, that crack-pot would be next in line to die. McClaussen need only engage his compatriot, Howard Stein, and the gadfly would be squashed along with anyone dumb enough to stand beside him. Where had common sense gone these days? Had John's generation entirely lost the ability to reason and scheme? The helicopter veered sharply to the North on it's predetermined flight path, the sudden shift in gravity interrupting McClaussen's reverie.

The man behind McClaussen offered him a headset. "Mr. McClaussen, you have an urgent call."

McClaussen positioned the unit on his head. "Yes? Who is this? What do you want?"

"Mr. McClaussen, this is one of Mr. S.'s men. My partner and I visited Mr. Marx's house as ordered. His wife wouldn't allow us in and threatened to call the police."

"Did she now," McClaussen chuckled, imagining a young woman in house apron, waving a frying pan in the air at the two heavily-muscled "computer repairmen." "I hope you've been watching her closely since."

"She locked herself in her house. A few minutes later, we were chased off by the local sheriff. The man knew we weren't computer repairmen."

"So Marx and his wife must have talked to one another..." McClaussen half-asked, half-stated.

"They did, sir, and there was nothing more we could do short of violence."

"Marx and his wife probably know everyone in a small town like Violet. Sit tight, and I'll see what I can do about getting a search warrant," McClaussen stated, his growing irritability clear in his voice.

"That's what Mr. S. said you'd say when he told me to contact you. We've taken a room at a local hotel on Paris Road in Chalmette. The number there is 277-3526. I'll register us under the name Roger Klein. We're to wait for your call."

McClaussen handed the headset back to the man behind him, and yelled above the noise of the helicopter, "When we land, I want you to get hold of a mister Sola Ming."

McClaussen's newly-assigned personal assistant nodded affirmatively while the helicopter pitched back to hover over Rustic Oil Central's helipad. The blades had barely stopped turning when a black stretch limousine pulled up. The driver dashed out to open the car door for McClaussen. As soon as McClaussen had settled in one of the limousine's generous leather seats, his aide handed him the car phone.

"Mr. Ming?" McClaussen inquired. "Shaun McClaussen here, soon to be CEO of British Petroleum International. I need a favor."

The limo squealed onto the highway leading to New Orleans.

Sola Ming was surprised and impressed. Listening intently, it took him a moment to process what Shaun McClaussen was both saying and implying. Ming, Chief Judge for the Fifth District Court of the United States, was loathe to accept or provide "favors," especially to powerful "special interests" men like McClaussen. Besides the obvious danger of being identified as an act of political self-interest, favors for such people usually required "special handling," and by definition, which usually involved personal expense or risk. On the other hand, having the CEO of BPI in his pocket was tempting, to say the least. Very tempting, Ming decided, as he continued to listen.

Ming scribbled a note to check out McClaussen's claims. A long-time personal friend of McClaussen, Ming was acutely aware of the millions of dollars BPI had contributed to his political war-chest over the years.

"What exactly are you in need of?"

"I need a federal search warrant against a Mr. John Marx who lives on Queen Elizabeth Court in Violet, Louisiana." Turning aside, McClaussen asked his aide for the address. The new aide was quick to hand him a slip of paper. "The address is 2524. I need to enter his house to search his computer for a company email and/or attachment containing trade secrets which we believe he forwarded to his home computer."

"May I ask why is this email so important?"

"Judge Ming. This email reportedly discloses details of a plan BPI is about to propose to the President and Congress of the United States. At the moment, this is a 'need to know request', and, I'm afraid, you do not need to know any more than what I've told you at this time. I can say, however, that if it were to get into the wrong hands, it could prove not only a corporate disaster, but a national embarrassment, if you understand what I am saying."

"Alright, Shaun, I'll do what I can. I know Judge Frederick Stone in the Fifth Circuit. I'll ask him to issue one for me. He's the least likely of my Judges to ask questions, being a hang-over from the previous administration. It may take awhile. I would like to say that the warrant will be delivered to you by Wednesday evening around 5 or 6 o'clock."

"That would work fine. I'll be in Violet then, and so will Mr. Marx. I want to personally thank you for your assistance in this very delicate matter."

Ming started to say, "You are most welcome, Mr. McClaussen," but before he could utter the sentence, the man had already hung up and handed the phone back to his aide. *Rude bastard*, the aide thought to himself, trying to think of how to best get in his employer's good graces.

Rude bastard, Ming grumbled to himself a hundred miles away, *but not a difficult request in exchange for a McClaussen political I.O.U.*

"Get me 'Roger Klein'," ordered McClaussen. The aide dialed the number and handed over the phone.

'Mr. Klein' picked it up on the second ring. "Hello?"

"Mr. Klein? I want you and your colleague to meet me at my New Orleans' office. I've ordered a search warrant for the Marx computer. As soon as I have the warrant in hand, we'll return together to Mr. Marx's house. I cannot stress how important it is to do this right. I've done my part. Now you and your man begin doing your part, understand?"

"Yes, sir, we can drive there by tomorrow afternoon, if that's okay. By the way, Mr. S. called just before you did and told me to assure you that at this time there is no evidence that the email was ever in anyone else's possession, and he'll make certain that no one carries a copy off the platform Wednesday. He said you'd know what he was talking about. The only 'loose end' then, is Marx's home computer."

"Good work 'Mr. Klein.' I'll be in Atlanta later tonight for some meetings, and in New Orleans by the time you arrive. I want to be there when you check Mr. Marx's computer. I want this finished by Wednesday."

"Yes, sir. And for what it's worth, I believe that Mr. Marx *is* cooperating, and that the email we erased on the rig was the one and only."

"Yes, well, we must be certain. I wouldn't have gotten to where I am today if I hadn't dotted all my I's and crossed all my T's." McClaussen hung up the car phone and slid back in his seat as the limo entered the Greater New Orleans Bridge to cross the Mississippi River. Out of the smoked glass window, he could see familiar tugboats hauling strings of barges up river towards Baton Rouge.

In fact, McClaussen loved New Orleans. The city mirrored him, presenting to the world a fashionable social face even while the business necessary to satisfy his unlimited ambition was being transacted in its dark bowels.

McClaussen vividly recalled that singular day in New Orleans when he became the owner of not one but three oil companies and several smaller drilling companies, which he had woven into a single multi-state corporation. His own personal empire. His legacy. Brushing off, as he always did, the fact that it had been his father who had actually planned and begun the whole process, McClaussen in his reverie could still hear the old man giving his final admonition: "Never allow information crucial to your designs to fall into the wrong hands. The next age is going to be one of information. In the next age, nothing will be as important for the wielding of money, power and control." His father had worked hard to build the informational foundation of the empire that was now his. McClaussen's lips thinned into a grimace. Thinking of the man always carried with it a wrenching pang in his gut from the premature loss of his father to exactly what the old man had predicted. In the end, the son had had to sacrifice the father, because the old man just couldn't keep his mouth shut.

"Mr. McClaussen, we're here, sir." The driver woke McClaussen from half-sleep and pulled the limousine up in front of the imposing One Shell Square building. At fifty-one stories, it was clearly the tallest and most imposing building in New Orleans. McClaussen brushed his thinning hair back, climbed out of the motorcar, and walked up the stone stairs, his aide following like an obedient duckling. Inside the ornate elevator, the assistant barely beat his employer at pushing the call button to his forty-sixth-floor office. Walking past rows of unacknowledged but awed employees, McClaussen called over his shoulder to the young man following him to book a first-class flight to Atlanta ASAP, as he fled into the quiet solitude of his private office. Easing into his executive chair, McClaussen sighed.

This was his "home," if it could be said that the increasingly international businessman actually had one. He turned in his seat to gaze through the floor-to-ceiling picture windows at the city, the Mississippi River and the low-lying parishes that, as new CEO of British Petroleum International, he would soon, in every sense of the word, own. His empire was about to expand into realms that in the past he had only dreamed of. It was too bad his father wasn't able to be here now to congratulate him.

The Oil Man

CHAPTER 14

Josh Platur was circumspect if nothing else, and called Chris Longley to make an appointment ostensibly to solicit the company man's help with a "small problem." He'd been careful not to mention John's name, or having association with John. Chris had been surprisingly amenable to the request, and invited him directly up to the conference room where Chris had been effectively sidelined by the irascible BPI executive and soon to be CEO, Mr. Shaun McClaussen. Josh stood before the door, smoothed his clothes and knocked politely. The brusque inflection in Chris's invitation to enter made Josh's stomach tense. This wasn't another conspiracy game. He was playing for his and others' lives.

Chris Longley sat erect in the chair at the far end of the table. "Come in, Josh. How's the survey going? What can I do for you?"

What can I *do for* you, *you mean,* Josh thought, as he approached the company man, kneading the edge of his removed hard hat nervously with sun-darkened hands. "We're waiting for the cement to dry. Everything's ready to re-begin drilling." Josh paused to let the "good news" sink in.

Chris visibly relaxed.

Now was the time: "I have a small problem that I'd greatly appreciate your help with."

"Just ask," Chris said magnanimously, enjoying the sense of power Josh's carefully constructed request was creating within him.

"A couple days ago, two individuals flew here. One, on his way back to his helicopter apparently dropped a pen, which fell through the metal mesh of the catwalk. One of the work men just found it. It looks undamaged. It has 'To Leon Puissegur—Violet, Louisiana—with deepest gratitude' engraved on it. It looks important."

"What kind of pen?" Chris asked, hiding his disappointment when the problem turned out to be so mundane.

"I don't know. I think it had the name of a mountain on it: 'Montblanc' or something like that, but it would probably be of even greater value because of the inscription..."

"That's a reasonably expensive pen. Probably a corporate gift. What did you say was engraved on it?" Chris interrupted brusquely.

"To Leon Puissegur—P U I S S E G U R—Violet, Louisiana—with..."

"Puissegur? I know that name, but can't quite place it. Violet? Isn't that where you live?" Josh's opponent's eyes narrowed.

"Yeah, that's why the boys asked *me* to try and locate him. You know, to let him know we'd found it."

Chris considered the explanation and couldn't find any reason to doubt it. "Do you have it with you?" Chris asked, to Josh's relief, apparently satisfied with the explanation.

"No. The fellow who found it has it stashed away, so it won't disappear. He said he'll turn it over to me when we've located and notified the owner. If you like, I can turn it over to you, but truthfully, the man who found it is holding it hoping there might be a reward in it for him. I thought, given all the security and such, it might be best for you to make the call and set things up. It would be a grand gesture by the company."

Chris humpfed in half-acknowledgement, half-disdain. Picking up the phone, he said into the receiver, "Marta, look up a Leon Puissegur in Violet, Louisiana, and call me back when you have him on the line. One of the workmen found a pen with Puissegur's name engraved on it."

"The workman who discovered it will stop by on Wednesday to personally return it to him," Josh hinted. "Let me know what he says, so I can reassure the workman."

"Not a problem," Chris assured. "Anything else?"

"No, just that," Josh reassured, making a show of awkwardly retreating as if in deference to Chris's position and power. Puissegur, of course, might deny it was his pen. Then again, it was more likely that if it was indeed he who "lost" the crystal shard, he'd catch on and play along. Either way, it really wouldn't matter what Chris and Puissegur said. As long as Chris made the contact, Josh and John would know for certain where Puissegur was and Puissegur would be alerted to their contacting him. Josh complimented himself as he backed out the door and returned to his work. It had gone much easier than he'd feared.

On the other side of the rig, John grasped the rail tightly when he spotted the outline of Josh exiting the conference room that Chris had reclaimed after McClaussen and Stein's departures. He had been going over in his mind the process involved in resuming drilling. It wouldn't be long before the cement plug hardened sufficiently. He had also been mulling over whether Josh had successfully cajoled Chris into contacting Sokolov and Puissegur for them. A ring from the company mobile phone on his belt bit sharply into both trains of thought.

"Marx, here."

"Mr. Marx. This is Mr. McClaussen's personal assistant. Mr. McClaussen asked me to inform you that he plans to personally hand the search warrant your wife requested to you at your house Wednesday. He hopes that you will make every effort to be there, so that the remainder of the email affair can be brought to conclusion."

As soon as the voice paused, John shot back. "Please tell your boss that I figured he'd find a way to obtain a search warrant. I would have been surprised, even disappointed, if he hadn't. And assure him that I've nothing at all that he wants in my room on the rig, on my person, or at home on my computer. At the same time, please notify him that I strongly object to his men attempting to intimidate my wife and trying to force their way into my home. He need only have asked, and I would have gladly given him permission to examine my home computer. I will be contacting the sheriff and police to be there to ensure there is no further harassment. And if I, my wife or any of my friends or associates are harassed again, in any way, he'll find the TV, radio and newspaper reporters I'm also inviting eager to take a statement from him." John hung up. *That would give McClaussen something to think about, especially given McClaussen's eminent bid for CEO of BPI. Corporate boards looked unfavorably on executives who attracted the negative attention of the press and public surrounding sensitive corporate issues. At this time, it was all about maintaining a balance of power, at least until he could obtain more information on what was actually going on.*

The moment he'd signed off, Claude Askins approached from behind.

"Claude! Tell me something good!"

"Just stopping by to say good-bye," Claude offered. "The scuttlebutt is that McClaussen is planning on bringing down some folks, and from the look on Chris's face these days, he must be one of them." Claude's mention of "folks" and "one" wasn't lost on John.

"Where the hell did you hear that?"

"From that helicopter pilot over there," Claude pointed at the silhouette of a man standing in front of a huge Sikorsky S-92 sporting BPI colors and logo sitting on the helipad. "About an hour ago, I received a call from BPI to pack and get ready to leave. The orders came from the top: Dresser Legend informed me that McClaussen is a shoe-in for the CEOship of BPI and called me home personally. Something big is going on, John, and the word is out that Chris, you and anyone you talk with are potential threats to the company. I wasn't supposed to say anything, but, hey: Bottom line is, we're oilmen. Remember what I told you about watching your back." Claude released John as soon as he'd finished talking.

"Thanks, Claude. I agree. There's something big going on and it's growing bigger by the minute."

"You really think it's all about an email?"

"I suspect that started it," John replied, hoping Claude would share more while waiting for the equipment and supplies to finish loading. "They say that the President sacrificed over three thousand jobs this year shutting down drilling and exploration wells throughout the Midwest due to safety and environmental concerns. They're desperately afraid of another Blue Water Horizon. I doubt the present administration could survive public outrage from another. In the meantime, if they changed course and encouraged development of the oil fields underneath our nation, they'd have to deal with the repercussions when the fields become depleted..."

"...unless there was evidence that a new BPI had developed the necessary technology to extract the oil without hurting the environment, and that the oil fields were being constantly renewed," Claude interrupted, completing what both were thinking, but reluctant

143

to state.

Claude placed a flat palm above his eyes like the bill of a baseball cap to better see how the loading of the equipment was going. One of his survey crew members, noticing, waved at him.

"Well, John, the equipment's loaded, so I guess it's time for me to be going. Call me when you're finished fishing and actually haul something in," Claude winked.

"I will," John said, not returning the gesture for fear of being spotted and endangering his new friend.

As Claude worked his way to the helipad, John noticed the pilot waiting impatiently. He couldn't be sure, but from the distance the man's profile looked amazingly like his old Vietnam helicopter-pilot friend, Stan Meyers, holding the co-pilot's door open for Claude. *At least,* John thought, *Claude is in good hands.*

John waved as the helicopter took off and headed for the coast of Louisiana. Returning his attention to the deck after the helicopter had disappeared, John could see a derrick man in the crow's nest getting sections of the six-inch pipe ready to toss in at the right moment. It would take several hours just to work their way down to the cement plug.

CHAPTER 15

The phone rang on McClaussen's Atlanta desk. If the view of New Orleans from his One Shell Square office was a kick, his view of Atlanta from his new British Petroleum International office on the fifty-fourth floor of the 700-foot tall Bank of America Plaza building on Peachtree Street was nothing less than breathtaking. The tallest building in Atlanta, the ninth tallest in the United States, and the forty-second tallest in the world, he was busy savoring how easy the CEO appointment had gone. McClaussen turned from the window and picked up the intoning phone.

"McClaussen here."

The reply, pleasant and feminine, was that of the only person who's mere voice made McClaussen shudder. If Stein was a hound of hell (and he was), then this woman was the devil incarnate.

"Have you finished taking care of the email debacle yet?" the Chief Executive Officer of Dan Sogo Shosha Corporation, DSSC, the parent company of British Petroleum International for whom McClaussen now worked, queried. The voice was musical and warm, but underneath the veneer, sounded hollow and cold.

145

"Miss Carol Bishop, how nice to hear from you. I…"

Carol Bishop cut him off abruptly in mid-sentence. "Do not, I repeat, do not *ever* call me 'miss', you fucking bastard, or I'll come over there and personally cut off your balls! And don't delude yourself into thinking I don't know about the long line of 'misses' who litter your path to the CEO's door. I never dreamed you'd rise to this level, or I'd have informed your wife about your fooling around. Hearing her beat the crap out of you and sue you for everything you've got wouldn't be punishment enough for…"

McClaussen decided it was his turn to cut in, if for no other reason than to silence the witch's diatribe. "Hold on, Carol. That's harsh coming from a sexual pundit like you. I don't deserve…"

"You don't fucking deserve to be crawling the earth, much less CEO of British Petroleum!"

McClaussen felt sweat forming on his temples and palms. It was true he'd never hesitated to do whatever he had to in order to attain his present position, including playing this vixen's sexual bimbo, for awhile making himself available day and night to her beck and call. Hell, it was more likely his wife would kill Carol Bishop before killing him. That would be fitting if nothing else.

McClaussen knew, however, that it wasn't Carol Bishop being suddenly deprived (or was that depraved) of his sexual attentions that was at the root of her anger. No, it was the manner in which it had happened. Eventually foreseeing the troublesome direction in which their rapidly-growing and wildly dysfunctional "relationship" was going, he'd simply not shown up one promised night or ever again. *What was that saying? Hell hath no fury like a woman scorned?*

"I acknowledge your…anger…Carol, and I don't deny that it's well-placed; however…"

"It's not anger, Shaun. I want your balls for dinner."

146

"Yes, well..." McClaussen found himself at a loss for words.

"And I will have them, if this email business isn't brought to a successful conclusion. *Now!* You've had enough time, and all I see are bodies and more bodies. *Dead* bodies! *Murdered*, for Christ's sake! You and that snake Howard Stein almost cost us everything. Our taking out Greyson was done professionally. Slick. Quiet. Did you notice? But because of this string of murders that you and Stein have affected, Greyson's death has shown up all over the papers."

McClaussen flushed red, focusing his attention on trying to move the topic onto—what had she called it—the "email debacle?" to keep her away from the infinitely worse "relationship" topic.

"Well? What have you to say for yourself?" she demanded.

McClaussen chose a neutral tack. He was never too proud to grovel if it ultimately got him where he wanted to be. "I'm working on it, Carol. It will be cleared up entirely by Wednesday evening. I..."

"Wednesday!" the voice on the other end of the phone line shouted. "What part of 'now' don't you understand? Come on, Shaun: Give me one good reason why I shouldn't deal with you like I dealt with that pansy-ass, Greyson! Or maybe you have a secret desire to see your wife trying to explain in all the proper social circles about some of those wonderfully compromising photos you were so eager to pose for, 'dear'."

Carol Bishop was a tough corporate woman who'd had to work her way up the ranks, not unlike her one-time middle-aged lover McClaussen, any way necessary. McClaussen had promised to leave his wife, hell, kill her he'd once promised at the height of mutual sexual ecstasy, so he and Carol would be free to forge more than an empire, more than a legacy: A dynasty. She'd never forgive the bastard for plying her affections, then, when it came time for him to actually leave that sodding socialite wife of his, coldly betraying *her* instead.

During the pause, McClaussen took a breath and admitted to himself that, as long as Carol Bishop held something over him, she would be his personal devil. Back before he'd introduced her to DSSC —oh, yes, it was in a moment of profound weakness hungering for a pretty new ass that he had introduced her to the corporate world. His reward had been for Carol to bind him in a sordid affair. He had, when they first met, unknowingly "rescued" her from a CIA black operation she was a part of that had gone awry. At least, that was her version of it. The two became instant, intense lovers. It was all quite unlike anything he had ever experienced, and frankly, hoped to never experience again. After he left her—given the intensity and… unusualness…of her appetite, he'd *had* to break it up. She had become, or he had made her, depending on one's point-of-view, a walking bomb waiting to explode.

"Cat got your tongue, 'dear'?" Bishop taunted. "If you and Stein can't handle something as mundane as copping an email, just tell me and I'll take care of it for you in my own way."

McClaussen squeezed the phone, aghast at what sounded to him like a barely veiled threat against his life. "Wait, Carol! Let me get a word in edgewise, will you? Okay, I'm going to get this done. Believe me."

"And just when will that be? After the fucking email goes public, like I'm thinking of doing with you?"

"I have everything under control. A federal judge is right now issuing a search warrant to check the home computer of the man who had it on his laptop. One of Stein's computer specialists who examined his laptop has assured me that no one else received the email, and it hadn't been forwarded. Just for good measure I had him erase the man's email folder. The email thing is done. *Finis.* Over. The home computer search I've ordered is just to be certain."

148

"Shawn, 'dear.' Why the hell are you going through all that, when you need only have asked? I would have ordered a couple of my own specialists to break in, wipe the computer's memory, and, 'just to be certain,' damage the disk? Computers suffer disk failures everyday. Why make it so complicated?"

"Two of Stein's men visited Marx's house earlier and, presenting themselves as computer repairmen, tried to get a look at the computer. The wife, however, got suspicious, and threatened to call the police." He stopped, waiting for Bishop to resume her raving.

"You shouldn't have allowed Stein's men to show themselves like that. For God's sake, Shaun, do I have to do *everything* for you?" McClaussen, noting a change in her voice from damning anger to partially veiled concern, decided to press the opportunity.

"Mr. Marx, the email recipient, was fully cooperative when we asked to see his computer on the rig, so Stein thought we could approach his wife similarly. When the wife resisted one of the men threatened her. I called them off. Hence, the search warrant, even though I'm confident we'll find nothing on the home computer. By the way, who sent the email in the first place. And why?" It was a long shot, but the change in her voice gave him the courage to ask. McClaussen was surprised when she didn't respond vindictively, and, instead, answered in the huskily alluring manner he'd over the years come to crave.

"The email originated here with a DSSC employee who was found dead the next day from a heroin overdose. Sad what people do to themselves…"

McClaussen startled. It was his turn to interrupt: "Jesus, Carol! What are *you* doing? You aren't working in black ops anymore!"

"Shut up, Shawn." The voice on the other side of the line had suddenly become cold and unfeeling.

"Hey! You can criticize me and Stein all you want, but as the CEO of a multinational corporation, it's not your place to…"

"It's not my place to what, Shaun?" she hissed venomously. "You're right. It's *not* my place. It was the place of that amateur friend of yours, Stein, to handle this kind of 'adjustment.' But he didn't, so I took action. That's what the CEO of *any* corporation is supposed to do." Carol's voice was diminishing. She was sounding temporarily mollified. "What are you planning to do about that nosey Dresser Legend survey engineer, Claude Askins? Did Stein not mention that Askins and Marx have suddenly become very 'buddy-buddy'? *My* informants tell me Askins has already second-guessed the abiotic oil affair. In my book, that makes him more dangerous than that stupid email you're supposed to have finished with. Keep trusting Stein, lover, and you're going to end up holding hands together in hell."

Despite the barbs, McClaussen felt a pull of desire awakening. "So you still care?" McClaussen ventured.

"Don't count on it, Shaun. Remember, I have you in some very compromising photos. You may be CEO of BPI, but DSSC, meaning me, controls BPI. Don't confuse confidence with caring."

McClaussen winced, the moment of desire having been replaced with a rush of adrenalized anger. "Right. *Too* right, of course. But Carol, the day is coming when, alone and isolated, you're going to make a mistake, a fatal mistake of your own. Perhaps you'll be tired or…distracted. And that will be the day, my dear, that I will get rid of you once and for all. I never imagined when we were together that you could grow into such a monster."

The voice on the other line fell silent, then hissed. "Go ahead, Shawn. Keep trying. That's the way I want to remember you: Trying and frustrated. Remember that I was trained to deceive and manipulate and control. Hell, I *owe* the CIA for happily getting rid of me and giving me the opportunity of learning real duplicity from you. Your first mistake, lover-boy, was not taking my advice when I told you how to take over BPI long ago. Your second was not taking my advice, period. There's no third mistake to learn from, Shaun. Quite simply, I can't afford you anymore, either."

"Big words for a broken woman, and, Carol, that's what you are: broken. I tried to fix you. I plucked you out of the clutches of hell, and gave you…everything. And what have you done with all I've given you? You've tried to suck me with you into your own past and present hells. I rescued you once. That's enough."

"My, oh my, Shawn! So, you've finally developed a real set! I do like that in a man. Just remember, they may feel free, but they're still in the palm of my hand. If you want to keep them, make certain you finish with that email by Wednesday, because, this I *will* tell you: That email, should it fall into the wrong hands, contains enough information to destroy you, me, the President of the United States, and perhaps even the nation!" The phone clicked and went silent.

McClaussen stared at the receiver in his hand, then slammed it into its cradle. *What the hell is wrong with that woman?* he thought, trying to shake the liquid disgust from his trembling hands. Out the window he could see an endless stream of cars plying their way in and out of Atlanta, and he wondered as he watched if he would actually be able to pull his part together—to create a smooth effortless traffic of oil out and money into BPI like the plan called for. Stein and his men worked directly under Bishop, and were there to do whatever dirty work was required. In return, Bishop or Stein, whether they liked it or not, were relying on him to grasp the helm of BPI, assume control, and ferret out who and what in the process would need "adjusting."

McClaussen, despite his shaken self-assurance, still believed he could do his part. Carol Bishop and Howard Stein would, of course, do theirs, too, but in the end, they'd have to be eliminated, as would Marx and anyone else who by intent or accident happened to stand in the way. All he, McClaussen, had to do for the moment was finger anyone in the way, and he or she would disappear—poof!—from the game board. When the time came, with very little manipulation it would be no easier or harder to convince Carol to get rid of Stein.

Carol, however, was a different matter. A clever, hurt, angry, infinitely-well-trained, loose cannon always pointing its muzzle in his direction, she could do little better in the long run than bring their past to an eventual showdown. When that time came, would the feelings of lust that her vindictiveness always seemed to awakened in him stand in the way of eliminating her before she eliminated him? Would he be able to move on, and remake his empire, his legacy, his dynasty with someone else? He could and would, he decided with finality. Carol Bishop was and always had been fatally flawed. The power was his and his alone to seize and control, and that *was* what life was really about, wasn't it? Oh, and he needed to call Stein about Askins.

CHAPTER 16

John stood erect, hands gripping the railing in front of him, watching the derrick crew move sections of drilling pipe across the rig like toys on a play set. They had finished drilling through the plug with no problem, and set extra rings in the cemented section to prevent the possibility of the pipe banging the sides of the plug. One could never be too safe. It was a beautiful Wednesday morning, the sun was shining brightly and there wasn't a cloud in sight. It was a great day, and a positive portent to his planned return to his home and family for a couple weeks of furlough.

John got up and went to his room to finish packing his bags. He had nearly finished when he heard a metallic tapping at his door. His muscles instantly tensed. Without waiting, Josh burst in, wearing a clean Hawaiian shirt and tan deck pants, hair slicked back like he was going to a party. "John! You ready, man?"

"Why are you all gussied up?" John asked, breathing a sigh of relief.

"An old flame called and said she had a surprise waiting for me when I return. Surprise—you know what I mean—it's her way of letting me know how happy I'm going to be tonight back home!"

John pushed Josh aside, peeked out the door and peered both directions down the hallway. Satisfied, he closed the door and grabbed Josh by the arm, pulling him close. Turning his radio on loud, he maneuvered close to Josh's ear. "I hope you have the flash drive and crystal well-hidden, because we *will* be searched, if not when we load up, then when we disembark dockside. I just want to be *sure* that they won't find anything. Our lives depend on you pulling this off, Josh."

Josh retreated, a big smile on his face. Nodding affirmatively, he maneuvered back close to John's ear. "I have it right now. Right here. In plain sight. Yet, I can guarantee you and no one can see or find it. And by the way, I talked with Chris and convinced him to call Puissegur—a brilliant piece of deception, if I do say so myself." Josh backed away from John and did a slow spin inviting John to guess where the devices were on him.

John searched him carefully with his eyes, but he couldn't see anything that might indicate that Josh was carrying the two items on his person. Turning off the radio and looking at Josh, who was wearing an even bigger smile than before, he stated, "You're one crazy magician. Okay, see you on deck."

Josh reopened the door and stood in the hallway, turning back to look at John. "Crazy like a fox, John. Crazy like a fox," he assured, then left.

John could hear the distinctive popping sounds of the blades from a large, tandem-engine helicopter approaching from a distance. *So, they're going to keep us close together and make certain no one jumps ship*, John thought to himself. That meant the search would be at the dock, so he could relax deck-side and during the flight. John grabbed his bags and made his way to the helipad to gather with the rest of the shift crew who were off-leaving today. As he handed his bags to the platform worker tossing everyone's gear in a back compartment, the man tugged his arm and pointed forward. "The boss gets the honor of sitting up front with the pilot."

John acknowledged the honor with a quick salute. Walking around the front of the monstrous Boeing-Vertol 234, he opened the glassine door, climbed in and strapped himself in place. Donning the usual flight headphones, a familiar voice appeared above the static. "How you holding up, pal?"

John looked to his left and found himself staring into two somber, bloodshot eyes. "I'm doing okay. To what do I owe this honor?" he asked his pilot friend, Stan Meyers.

Stan began his check down, flicking switches here and there. The engines jumped back to life and began whining. "The com's on private," Stan said into his headset microphone. "I don't have much time before I need to switch to public, so listen carefully. Claude Askins is dead. Something happened during the flight. What, no one knows for sure, but there was a sudden surge and the engine flamed. I fought the chopper down to about twenty feet above the water when the back section exploded. Everyone there died instantly in the fireball. Claude and I were thrown into the water. He died on impact. I somehow managed to survive, ending up with scratches and burns," Stan revealed an angry-looking, sutured slash about two inches long on the side of his neck. "The feds are tripping over each other collecting the wreckage, but it's a fool's errand. John, the chopper didn't malfunction. The board was all green and she felt fine under my hand. I know what an incoming round feels like when it hits an engine. The whole thing was well-planned and executed. When I heard you were scheduled to come back this Wednesday by chopper, I decided you needed someone at your side you could depend on. I didn't know if you'd heard yet about Claude. It happened over the Gulf quite away

155

from shore, and BPI's been playing every card possible to hush the whole thing up."

That makes four plus. How many more of my family, friends and acquaintances will die before this is over, John commiserated, his thoughts for the moment turning to his friend, Josh, sitting in the compartment behind him, carrying on his person the very thing which everyone likely died for. What of his wife, Ann, threatened, waiting expectantly for him to arrive home. And when he and Josh did arrive like the cavalry charging to the rescue, what could they realistically do to protect her and his family? It seemed to John like everywhere they went they brought Death with them. Even now, Death seemed to be snarling at his heels. John opened his mouth to say something, but closed it, words failing him completely.

"I see you *didn't* know," Stan said softly. "Well, I've got to switch to public communication, so think before you say anything further. And, John, I'm truly sorry to be the one to tell you about Claude." Stan twisted the throttle, pushed down on the pedals slightly harder on the left then the right in order to counterbalance the twisting force of the main rotors, then eased back on the stick. Like a sleeping dragonfly, the lugubrious mammoth slowly lifted up off the rig. Clearing the platform and derrick, Stan added more throttle, brought the nose down a bit, and began moving them forward at a faster speed. Once the helicopter was running straight at around 2500 feet, Stan slipped his headset off momentarily. "You want to fly her awhile?" he asked John, nodding at the co-pilot's control stick between John's legs.

John nodded in the affirmative, and reciprocated, sliding his headset off. "Sure. Just don't let the guys in the back know." John set his feet gingerly on the pedals and griped the stick. When Stan felt John take over, he stretched his arms out in the air and yawned widely, feigning tiredness.

Actually, it wasn't the first time John had flown a helicopter. In the Army, he'd originally trained, like Stan, to be a pilot, but the air hadn't appealed to him the way the solid ground always did, and, in the end, he'd opted to train for helicopter-based ground combat. Since Vietnam, John gladly took the second's controls whenever offered the chance, and flying to and from oil platforms in the rig supervisor's co-pilot seat often provided that chance.

The flight proved as uneventful as the announcement of Claude Askins' death had been troubling. Occasional shrimp boats whisking beneath them could be seen pulling their big trawls behind them, stirring the bottom mud, making it look from above like a boiling pot of dark brown coffee was pouring behind the net. As they got closer to the shore, platform after production platform popped into view with the usual two or three charter fishing boats plying the waters alongside them.

On the horizon, John noticed isolated glimpses of beach begin to join and paint a long white horizontal line, separating tens of flaming onshore oil towers from the grayish-green water. To his right, the landing pad emerged. Stan signaled with his hands and retook control of the helicopter, banking it around a small island to face southeast into the wind. He trimmed the craft, and the ground began creeping up. It was in that moment John made the hardest decision of his life.

Stan was an old and trusted friend. In Vietnam, he and all the other men had entrusted their lives to Stan, and the man had never let them down. John desperately needed someone to contact Spasskov at the University of Texas at Austin, and it was clear that John and Josh weren't going to be in a position to do that for awhile. Besides, he and Josh were being closely watched, he was sure. It was likely, however, that no one would think to watch a company pilot. On the other hand, something kept nagging. It seemed a little odd that Stan just happened to pop up on the derrick the moment when John most needed him. Wasn't the pilot supposed to go down with his chopper…or was that limited to captains with their ships? It was also odd that Stan alone had survived the helicopter crash. Still, Stan had always been known for his luck…

Against his feelings, John took the plunge. "I need a favor," he yelled above the noise.

"Anything for an old 'Nam buddy," Stan replied while continuing to expertly guide the helicopter onto the small pad beneath them. "What can I do for you?"

"I need you to contact a Dr. Yusef Spasskov. Yusef Spasskov," John repeated. "He's a research scientist with Petroleum and Geosystems Engineering at the University of Texas at Austin. Got that?"

Stan nodded, slipping a pen from his breast pocket, writing the name and place on his bare forearm. "Right?" he asked, showing John his forearm.

"Right," John affirmed. "I want you to bring him to Violet as quickly as you can. Can you finagle a company helicopter in all this mess without piquing their curiosity? Can you do that for me?"

"I'll do one better: I'll use my own heli'. She's small but can easily accommodate two. She's fueled and fast. If he's there, I could have him in Violet in maybe four hours. What do you want me to tell him?"

John hesitated. He was entrusting everyone's lives to Stan. His head said to trust the man, but for some reason his gut still resisted. "Just tell him a friend of Alexei Solokov needs his immediate help. Alexi Solokov. He'll understand, I think. If that's not enough, call me on my cell phone and I'll talk to him."

"Gotcha," Stan said, adding Solokov's name to his forearm and

158

resuming communications with Rustic Oil Central Heliport.

As the helicopter descended the last few feet, John noticed four burly men standing nearby, their black suits whipping in the rotor wash. They looked stone-faced, like Secret Service men waiting for the President of the United States. Even with the grass and dust kicking up around them, they stood firm, unchanging, resolute.

As soon as the two rotors stopped, everyone piled out of the craft and began matching up with their bags. The four men acted as guards and guides, walking everyone toward a small building that stood between the barbed-wire topped chain-link fence encircling them and their rides waiting on the other side of the building. The leader flashed a paper at the first person to approach the building, reading it loudly so everyone would hear that the men were performing a routine, unscheduled inspection ordered by BPI. The leader's voice and his body language related that their four greeters planned to do the inspection with or without the bag-owner's permission. The workers were guided into the building, one at a time, to spill the contents of their bags and pockets onto tables like those at security checkpoints at commercial airports.

Stan waved and took off, leaving John to shuffle slowly towards the building fourth from the last; Josh clearly wanted to be first, even though he would have to wait outside for John to ride home together. Josh passed through, John noted, without incident. When it was John's turn, he was subject to a more stringent inspection, two of the hulks holding him face against the wall while the other two painstakingly patted him down.

Finding nothing, the leader signaled for John to repack his belongings and leave.

Josh greeted John outside, sitting on the open tailgate of John's idling truck, swinging his legs back and forth as if totally bored.

159

"They really gave you the once over. Check it out, John: They're checking you again."

John let his eyes drift momentarily toward the building before climbing into his truck. Two of the black-suited men were watching him intently; the other two were exiting the building for a black Lincoln Town Car parked a short distance away.

"Figures," John said, shifting his eyes to the rear view mirror. "Big guys, big car. All the better to see what, if anything, they're up to." John signaled beneath the dash and mouthed, *They may have bugged the truck.*

"Good thing we've nothing to hide," Josh said, playing along, waving to the men while John pulled out of the circular driveway.

"For Christ's sake, Josh, don't egg them on. I want to get home to wife and family, not be pulled over and searched again."

"Don't be ridiculous, John. They've already searched us once. We're clean and they know it. There'd be no point in searching us again," Josh said loudly, sitting back and returning his attention to the road ahead.

Both let out a sudden belly-laugh as John made for Violet.

After a minute, John glanced into the rearview mirror, then cursed. "Damnation! They're right behind us! I'm betting their job is to make sure I *don't* get home to wife and family. Something's going to happen at the house, Josh. A showdown of some kind. I can feel it."

Josh turned around in his seat, watching the car behind them searching for the right moment to pass, and concurred. "It looks to me like these two are looking for trouble. Didn't you say that when we arrive at your place, the sheriff and police would be waiting?" The big black Lincoln behind them swerved and abruptly pulled back, John aggressively blocking their attempt to pass. "I don't know exactly what they're planning, but I'm thinking whatever it is, we need to keep the odds in our favor. We're on home territory now, so we should be able to lose them, don't you think?"

John smiled. "Agreed," he answered, blocking another passing attempt, this one on the right rather than the left. "These two are getting serious."

"You thinking of getting them to follow us to the ferry, then you and me sneaking off the ferry and watching while they sail helplessly away?" Josh said loudly and distinctly. He winked and mouthed, *Double switch: If the truck's bugged, we drive on while they wait onshore. We make sure they see two people who look like us get off...*

"Good plan, Josh. I don't like being followed and harassed." Then John continued loudly and distinctly, "We'll catch a taxi *and take care of our special business* on the way home." John added the "and take care of our special business" hoping to further motivate their tail into waiting to find out what their doubles were planning.

While John drove onto the ferry, Josh watched the Lincoln halt in the distance behind a shock of trees. Josh flashed the "okay" sign with his fingers.

The two henchmen got out of their car, one peering at them through binoculars, the other engaged in untwisting a black tube in one hand from what Josh assumed was a weapon in his other. John's added ruse had worked. Their followers appeared sufficiently motivated to question first and shoot later.

For twenty dollars each, two local walk-ons gladly donned John and Josh's jackets, hiked off the ferry and back to the waiting station to spend the money on a mess of boiled crayfish washed down with liberal amounts of local beer.

The two men-in-black patiently waited while the ferry finished loading and headed out onto the river. By the time they figured out they'd been had, John and Josh were half-way across the river.

"Definitely bugged," Josh confirmed, ripping a small metal package from under the dash.

John visibly relaxed, having lost the tail, at least temporarily defeating whatever plans the two ominous-looking men had made. It would be at least an hour before the next ferry, or two hours if they tried to drive to the nearest bridge. John sat back in the driver's seat and watched the opaque-brown waters of the Mississippi roil by. A log the size of a tree appeared, bouncing up and down in the river like the cork on a fishing line.

"Something eating at you?" Josh offered. "You look like you've lost your best friend, but, hey, I'm still here!"

"I thought I had everything under control until the pilot, Stan, an old friend from my Vietnam days, informed me that Claude Askins and the survey crew all died in an air accident. Shit, Josh, *everyone* I share *anything* with seems to turn up dead. I was thinking about how many others were going to die before this is over."

"Askins? Dead? How did it happen, man?"

"Stan said the helicopter flamed, and everyone in the survey party died in the fireball," John recounted, leaving off Stan's implication that the helicopter had been targeted all along. "He and Claude were thrown out. Stan made it, but Claude didn't. How many does that make including the survey crew? Nine dead so far? When will it end, Josh?"

More importantly, John thought, *how will it end?*

"I'm also concerned about what's waiting for us at my house," John continued. "That tail was put on us for a purpose, and I'm guessing it wasn't to greet us and guide us home. I'm guessing they had something else in mind, like maybe making sure we *don't* get home. If I suddenly didn't show up, Ann would be distraught, and the resulting chaos would shift the odds decidedly in their favor when they attempt to search the house. I'm concerned about you, my wife, my children, myself, hell, even Stan. How long before the next person gets knocked off? And what happens to all of us when this is over—when we're no longer needed? We know too much, Josh, to be left alive."

"What search of your house, man? You never mentioned anything about anyone waiting for us to arrive so they could search your house." Josh looked nervous. On the other hand, his best friend was focused, having avoided talking further about the threats John had voiced against their lives.

"Either McClaussen or Stein," John replied, "I'm not sure which, previously sent two men dressed as computer repairmen to check my home computer. Ann refused them entry. What tipped her off was not recalling me mentioning them coming. One threatened her. Ann threatened him back, saying she was going to call the police. They left. She called the sheriff *and* police, who alerted the local judge, who said he'd do whatever was necessary to make sure no one in Louisiana issued a search warrant, at least until I got home this evening."

"What else haven't you told me?" Josh asked, as they climbed back into John's pickup.

"A couple of things, for your protection. What I need to know right now is what happened as a result of Chris calling that Puissegur fellow."

Josh stretched taller, as if pleased with the pivotal role he was suddenly playing in John's heretofore private conspiracy play. "Chris called Puissegur to alert him that I had found a 'pen' of his on the rig that Puissegur'd allegedly dropped. I was hoping Puissegur would put it together on his own, and realize I was referring to the crystal. If he did, that would make things easy. He'd know we had it and wanted to talk with him. If he didn't, I figured we'd have piqued his interest enough to at least be expecting a face-to-face with us. Chris did it, as far as I can tell, totally unaware that he was setting up a meeting between you, me, and Puissegur. How well it worked, we'll find out when we visit Puissegur after dealing with your impending 'domestic issue'."

"I hope nothing's happened to Puissegur," John mumbled.

The two waited patiently for the ferry to drop it's ramp and the cars in front of him to off-load. Finally, the deck-hand signaled, and John slowly drove onto the heavy wooden off-ramp that creaked and groaned as if it might, at any moment, break under the weight of the vehicle. As soon as they reached the end of the ramp and made the top of the levee, Josh looked at John askance. "Check out across the road."

John reluctantly gazed at the old country store across the highway and saw two men dressed in black suits standing beside a black Lincoln. The two hulks were scanning the cars as they off-loaded from the ferry. One, noticing John's truck, pointed, and the two men disappeared into their car.

"One is shorter and the other huskier than the two we left behind," John announced. "This is a bigger, more organized operation than I anticipated. Someone's interested in doing more than just listening to our prattle. I'm going to guess these new guys will be more cautious, *and* more intent on doing whatever it is the others were planning on doing to us. If we could somehow get rid of these two, Ann, the sheriff, the police and the media will be at the house waiting for us. I tried my best to stack the cards in our favor." John grabbed another glance at the repositioning Lincoln as he turned onto the highway and headed north towards home.

"Maybe we could lose these guys in Braithway?" Josh offered.

"And just how would we do that?" John asked, noting Josh's confident smile and wondering what devious scheme was forming in his friend's fertile mind.

Josh looked back as a heavily-loaded semi-truck positioned itself between them and their tail. Using the truck as momentary cover, Josh brusquely ordered, "The road splits just up ahead. Take the left fork and head for the old Nickel factory."

"Yeah, so what then," John asked, as his truck screamed hard left, the slowing semi blocking their view of the following Lincoln Town Car, and also its inhabitants view of them.

"I have a friend who lives near the factory. He owes me a favor. Follow the river road, while I make some arrangements..." Josh flipped open his cell phone, speed-dialed a number and began joking and laughing with whomever he had reached. Abruptly closing the phone, he stated, "Problem solved. Wait and see what I have arranged for those guys back there."

John said nothing, focusing his concentration on driving as fast as his truck would go over the washboard-cut dirt road following the levee. Teeth clattering, it was everything he could do to not lose control and fishtail into the river. Behind his billowing dust cloud, he could just make out their pursuers, who, first taken by surprise, and likely having even more trouble negotiating the heavily pocked dirt road, were lagging further and further behind.

It took about thirty minutes to reach the factory. The Lincoln was now visible only by its own dust cloud. Josh, satisfied at last, directed John to stop and back off the dirt road behind a large clump of trees with a view of where the road made a sharp right curve. From their new vantage, it appeared as if the road disappeared into the river. Josh smiled and tapped John's shoulder, pointing with his other hand just beyond where the apex of the curve should be. A tractor was hauling a wagon into position in the road.

John reached out and gave Josh a high-five as they watched the distant pursuit car appear, shaking, skidding, barreling forward toward the surprise Josh had arranged. They watched as the dust cloud following the Lincoln changed from a light-brown cocky rooster tail into a dark black specter of death.

CHAPTER 17

Shaun McClaussen, having first 'liberated' himself from the thrall of Carol Bishop, and now ridded the world of her altogether, blew the sharp-smelling, rapidly thinning cloud of cordite from the nozzle of his silenced weapon, and slid his large frame into the executive chair in Dan Sogo Shosha Corporation's United States' Headquarters that had once been hers and was now his. From the eightieth floor of New York City's Empire State Building, the world looked satisfyingly his. A phone buzzed, causing the gun in his hand to morph into a phone handset, and the executive office into the interior of a Lincoln Royale limousine parked several blocks from John Marx's house. Forced out of his daydream, McClaussen reluctantly shook off the appealing thought of having finally gotten rid of his nemesis, and brought the phone to his ear. "Talk to me."

"Howard Stein here. The two men I assigned to Marx and Platur lost them at a ferry. My two backups picked them up on the other side of the river, but I've since lost contact with them. I..."

"You what? Jesus, Howard, I ask you to get rid of a couple of country hics and you go and *lose* them not once, but *twice*?"

167

McClaussen was in no mood to see the distance between where he was sitting and his pleasant daydream expand. "I asked you to eliminate them. I wanted them gone, removed, expunged from this last final act in the email farce!"

"Yeah, well, it's like this, Shaun: Most of my men are tied up with other 'pressing matters.' Still, I sent my four best to get rid of the two of them. Four-to-two! Marx and Platur were supposed to meet an abrupt demise on a dark, quiet, country road, their car careening off the road in their haste to get home," Stein replied, adding quickly, "Four of my best. Marx and Platur weren't supposed to reach the ferry, but, just in case, I positioned my other two men at the receiving end. The first two are still waiting for the next ferry. Thanks to the bug I had placed in Marx's truck, they overheard Marx and Platur discussing something they planned to do on their way there. My other two men picked up the chase, but haven't reported the kill as ordered. In fact, they haven't reported in at all. I ordered it all done low profile."

"With Greyson and Askins dead, Violet's sheriff and police on alert, two of your men missing, and the targets on the loose doing who knows what in anticipation of meeting here, I'd hardly call that 'low profile', Howard."

"Be that as it may, Shaun, I'm supervising a number of operations on this end that are taking up most of my manpower and attention. We agreed to operate so as not to attract any further attention. Remember, we've still got Puissegur to deal with. These two guys, Marx and Platur, just seem to keep getting all the lucky breaks."

"Spare me the lame explanation. I don't believe in 'luck' or 'breaks,' Howard. I believe in competence. That's what this whole effort is about: who is the most competent. Who will open, develop and control the petroleum reserves of the United States, and ultimately manipulate the world's oil supply. It's a game of competency, power, illusion and deceit. I'm doing my part. I'm waiting here, not far from Marx's home, federal search warrant in hand, to hear that Marx is taken out, or at least that the situation is in hand. Your job is to get the situation *back* in hand. No more fucking excuses, Howard! I need you to just do it!"

"There's no need for expletives. The situation *is* in hand; it always has been. In the end, where can these two go except to Marx's house? The man's wife has been threatened. He'll go there to protect her. That's the kind of man he is. That's *why* I had one of my boys frighten her. Your federal warrant trumps a sheriff and any policemen. You wanted to be *certain* that the email hadn't gone any further. Well, I've ordered the two men Marx and Platur lost at the ferry there. Wait an hour. Either two or four of my men will show up there with some good news, or, worst case, Marx and Platur will show up with four of my men in tow. Either way, you have the upper hand. Once we know Marx's home computer is clean, then Marx and Platur, if they're still alive, are living on borrowed time." Stein continued without pause: "I'd already made the necessary arrangements to remove them when the time came, just like I did with Chris Longley. You haven't heard about his 'unfortunate fall' from the rig, have you? But fall he did, poor man, and in the middle of the night when no one was there to help him. A drowning accident, Shaun, not another murder. Either Marx and Platur have already had a similar unfortunate accident, or they will soon. Trust me."

Stein continued without stopping: "By the way, Shaun, just before Chris…died…he mentioned that Marx's friend, Platur, had maneuvered him into calling Puissegur with a story about a missing pen that a worker had found on the platform. Watch yourself, Shaun. I'm not clear what Marx and Platur were up to, but I'm certain there's more to it than a lost pen. Puissegur may be scared, and a little crazy,

169

but he's not dumb. As soon as I locate my two 'missing' men and they confirm the kill, I plan to send them to Puissegur's place to keep an eye on him like they were before. Bishop says we've got all we need from him, so at the right time, I'll have my men quietly eliminate the old codger. He's such a recluse, I doubt anyone would even know he was gone, much less connect an accidental but fatal fall with us or what we're doing. Sit tight and wait just a bit, Shaun. I'll call you as soon as I know that Marx and Platur are no longer a problem and my four men are redeployed."

Shaun McClaussen threw the receiver at its dock. *Sit and wait? All I get these days are fucking excuses! Sorry, Howard, but I want this done right—and I can see to do that, I'm going to have to do it myself, and leave the mess for you to clean up later.* McClaussen tapped the glass partition separating him from his driver, and signaled for the driver to proceed to the Marx house. He'd go ahead and serve the warrant now with Marx's trembling wife watching, and a worried sheriff and some antsy policemen looking helplessly on. A very nervous wife, and the presence of at least two different law enforcement officials to witness whatever he found would be all that was necessary. Oh, yes, he'd also inadvertently wipe the entire computer memory clean like his expert had shown him, just to be sure. He may not trust Stein's motives, but he knew Stein was quite competent to finish off the two interfering oil workers one way or another.

McClaussen stretched his large frame on the slick leather seat as the limousine lurched forward. Scratching his chin, he thought momentarily of Carol Bishop and what she might try to do to him if he didn't put the email message affair entirely to rest today. The woman had shown herself to be cruel and heartless. She'd eventually have to eliminate him. In that, at least, he knew she could be trusted.

In the past, Shaun had entirely trusted Stein. The man had, early on, demonstrated an ability to act competently, effectively and decisively, but over time, his actions were revealing an occasionally haphazard brutish violent streak that was rapidly becoming a liability. Even so, Stein still had one redeeming attribute that outweighed his liabilities: He was the perfect scapegoat on whom he could blame all the violence after McClaussen ascended to the CEOship of DSSC, and, of course, if anything went wrong, he was also the perfect fall guy. *Yes, McClaussen assured himself, he would take care of the email problem, and, depending on how the chips fell, leave Stein to take the blame, but only after the man had finished all the dirty work.* McClaussen felt the car rolling to a stop next to the sidewalk in front of the Marx house.

Meanwhile, muscleman Crist Marcus and computer expert Hank Benniman, Stein's two professional gorillas who had botched the initial attempt at prying their way inside the Marx house, found no evidence of any memory devices on Marx or Platur during the shore 'inspection,' and who had been given a third chance to redeem themselves by eliminating Marx and Platur prior to the ferry fiasco, didn't prove as foolish as John and Josh hoped. The two hitmen had waited impatiently outside the ferry roadhouse for Marx and Platur to finish eating and call a cab. Instead, they ended up accosting two stuffed drunken backpackers wearing Marx and Platur's jackets exiting the ferry roadhouse. The ferry was halfway across the river when Crist, the 'brains' of the two, saw through the ruse, and called for backup from the two men Stein had originally ordered to watch Puissegur's house. It hurt Crist's pride to forward the contract, as well as the money, on Marx and Platur's lives. If everything worked, the backups would be waiting for Marx and Platur at the ferry dock on the other side of the river. While the backups took care of Marx and Platur, the two teams would exchange missions, leaving Crist and Hank to drive to Puessegur's house and continue surveillance.

Unfortunately, it didn't work out that way. Their backups had, indeed, given chase to the two oil men, but abruptly quit communicating. Sensing that somehow things had gone further amiss, Crist called Stein, who called McClaussen. Stein had just called back and ordered Crist and Hank to forget Puissegur and go to Marx's house to render McClaussen assistance. McClaussen: Neither Crist nor Hank liked the huge-framed, arrogant man who was the new CEO of PBI. In fact, McClaussen gave Crist the creeps.

The two had just turned down a tree-lined, suburban street in Violet, when Hanks spotted a dust-caked truck parked in front of the Marx's craftsman-style house with its large porch and dormer. A sheriff's car, two police cars, and a black limousine were parked along the sidewalk in front. Two brown-uniformed officers waited in the sheriff's car, and two blue-uniformed policemen waited in each of the two police cars—six law enforcement officers in all. The limousine's impersonal, smoked-glass windows revealed nothing of its driver or occupants.

Crist stopped two houses away and watched John Marx collect his bags from the bed of his old battered truck, and walk towards the empty porch. As Marx pulled out his house key, the front door burst open and two happily screaming children flew out and into his waiting arms.

"It doesn't make sense that a father loved by his children like that should be a problem," Hank said to Crist as they watched Marx return his children's eager hugs.

CHAPTER 18

Standing inside the doorway behind the two children, John's wife, Ann, smiled with relief, her arms crossed in continued defiance at the cars parked just outside her yard. John released the children, scooted them inside, and wrapped his arms around Ann. Ann returned the embrace, sobbing with joy. She'd kept the wolves from the door, now it was her husband's turn to take over. She never needed him more than now.

"Guess who decided to spend the night?" Ann said, sniffling discretely, as John gathered his bags and tossed them through the doorway. Two smaller children of exactly the same height, look and demeanor stepped hesitantly from the interior darkness. One grabbed onto John's leg while the other attempted to drag John into the house by the hand.

Inside, John's oldest daughter, Janice, greeted him with typical adolescent shyness. "Hi, dad. Hope you don't mind the boys. They've been asking about you since they came yesterday. They stayed up all night with us waiting for you."

John could hear fear contained beneath his daughter's reassuring words. He had deep feelings for his three children, and his two grandchildren, the twin boys Karl and Kirk. "No problem, Jan. I'm always glad to see the two knuckleheads," he said, rubbing each boy's head roughly.

"I no knucklehead, Paw-Paw," one of the boys declared indignantly.

"Okay, Kirk…" John started to say, but before he could finish the boy yelled back at him.

"I'm *Karl*, Paw-Paw. He's Kirk!" Each pointed mischievously at the other.

"I'm so sorry, Karl. You two look alike."

"He's lying, Paw-Paw. *I'm* Karl," said the other, thoroughly enjoying the game.

"Stop that, you know that game drives Paw-Paw crazy," Janice said, a hint of a childish smile appearing.

John patted all three, then grabbed Ann and gave her a second hug and kiss. "It's good to be home. I hope those two characters didn't upset things too much."

"It's not them, John. It's the viper in the black limousine with the federal search warrant I'm afraid of. Afraid, John! Afraid! Afraid for my life, yours and for our children. That man, whoever he is, is out for you. Why? What have you done?"

John ignored the question, asking instead, "Have you seen anything further of the man that threatened you?"

Anne pointed silently at a black Lincoln Town Car parked in the tree shade a couple of houses down.

"I see," John acknowledged. "To tell you the truth, I'm surprised they waited for me to return home. Those two tried to tail Josh and me when we left the dock, but we gave them the slip. Another pair took up the moment we got off the ferry, but Josh made a call to one of his friends down near the old Nickel Plant...."

"Should we expect them, too?"

"It's not likely," John answered with finality.

Ann didn't question him further. She didn't want to know what happened to them, she wanted to know what to do now. "What do they want?" she asked, lowering her voice.

"They're looking for an email sent to me by George. I don't think it was originally meant for me. I don't know all the details as to why or how it got to me, but it did, and these folks want every trace of it destroyed. They manhandled my laptop at work and erased the email, but I think they suspect I might have a copy on my home computer also." John averted his eyes and ran a shaking hand through his hair as he always did when lying, Ann noticed.

"So *is* there a copy on our home computer?"

"I didn't forward it, but I can't be certain that George didn't send a copy to my home computer as well," he said, this time looking at her directly.

The straight answer satisfied her, but only momentarily. "What was in that email that they're going to such lengths to rid the world of it?"

"I'm not sure, Ann, but it was encrypted. I...happened to decrypt it. The message was simply someone's telephone number, but I have the feeling the number represents something more. I just can't put my finger on it."

"This isn't another one of your crazy conspiracy theories that's gotten blown out of hand?" Ann asked dubiously.

"No," John replied, once again looking directly into her eyes. "I'm afraid it's real—deadly real—the tip of something much larger that these men and others are deeply involved in." John sat down heavily at the kitchen table, and watched the twins unpack his bags and gleefully toss his clothes all over the room.

"Boys! Stop that!" Janice, the family organizer, said, following the two misbehaving boys, picking up her father's clothes and trying to stuff them back into his bags.

"Don't worry about the clothes, Janice. I have to wash them all, anyway." Ann poured a glass of iced tea and placed it in front of her husband.

"Thanks, honey."

His voice sounded tired. *Dead tired*, Anne thought.

"You're welcome," she replied, her mind racing back to the five cars and their occupants waiting out front.

The doorbell rang, ripping at John and Ann's frayed nerves. John's stomach sank. "I'll get get it," he said, pushing Janice away from the door. "It is probably the goons."

Ann joined Janice across the living room as John headed toward the door. He stopped in the foyer and gazed through a crack in the long, vertical, stained-glass window at the side of the door. He could just make out a black stretch limousine rolling to a stop in back of a black Lincoln Town Car parked in back of the sheriff's car, the two police cars and his own truck parked in front of the sheriff's car. To John, it looked like a macabre line of elephants each one holding the next one's tail, all waiting impatiently in front of his house for the command to act. His neighbors across the tree-lined street were peeking through curtained windows and eyeing the scene. *Good,* thought John. *Time remains on our side, and the more witnesses, the better.*

"John, are you going to answer the door or what?" Ann asked, when the doorbell resounded.

"I figured I would make them wait a bit before I answer." The doorbell rang again, this time without respite. John moved behind the door and placed his hand on the doorknob.

Opening the door a crack, John could see the outline of the Sheriff, Ann's old high school flame. The man greeted him solicitously. "Sorry John. I hate to do this, but these three guys standing here with me have a federal search warrant, and I've no choice but to ask you to open the door. They want to look at your computer." Behind the sheriff, John could make out McClaussen's massive hulk surrounded by the two men who'd tried to tail him from the heliport. "The warrant's very specific: They're authorized to inspect your computer, and I'll be accompanying them to make certain they don't try to inspect anything else. It shouldn't take much time," the sheriff said.

John opened the door but held the screen door closed while he looked over the three men. Purposefully ignoring McClaussen, John asked, "Which of you two thugs posed as a computer repairman and threatened my wife?"

There was a long silence. John watched McClaussen shift his weight uncomfortably and nudge the man standing closest to him.

"I'm the one, sir," said Crist Marcus obediently. "I'm very sorry, sir. It was a difficult situation and I apologize if I spoke or acted inappropriately."

"Sheriff Grant, this man is to get off my property. If he tries to force his way back on it or in here, I'm holding you and those four police officers standing on either side of you to be my witnesses, if I end up not being able to curb my anger and do something rash. I hope you understand."

The sheriff turned to Crist. "This man's wife has already filed charges against you. I'd listen to him and leave now while the leaving's good." Two police grabbed Crist and escorted the grumbling man between them off the premises and into his car, the officers remaining at either side of the car's door.

John opened the screen door, allowing Grant, Benniman and McClaussen into his home. The three stopped abruptly when they noticed Ann standing to one side, video camera in front of her face following the men, it's red 'recording' light flashing.

Benniman raised his hands to cover his face, but before he could object, McClaussen slipped forward and handed John the warrant. "Where's the computer?" McClaussen asked, ignoring the camera, his voice flat and emotionless.

"The computer is in my room. Follow me. As you can see, my wife has the camera on and will be taping everything you say and do during the entire search. I assume you have no reason to object," John stated, more in the form of a challenge to McClaussen and Benniman, McClaussen's 'computer expert' he recalled from their earlier confrontation on the oil rig. Sheriff Grant blocked the way, waiting for McClaussen or Benniman to respond, while the two police officers, one on either side of the sheriff, scanned the house disinterestedly.

"I've no objection, Mr. Marx," McClaussen finally stated, gritting his teeth.

The sheriff moved to the side and John led McClaussen and Benniman down the short hall and into a small home-office with a single desktop computer. The sheriff and two policemen followed in single file, Ann behind them keeping the occupants within her viewfinder. Ann pushed and ordered an inquisitive Janice to take her two silent, younger sisters, Jennifer and Joan, and the two quarrelling twins out of the room, pausing in her shooting just long enough to direct them with a finger towards the back bedroom. They obeyed the finger, disappointed not to be allowed to be a part of the excitement.

As John moved to sit in the chair in front of the computer, McClaussen gripped John's shoulder with a hammy hand, directing him aside, then abruptly removed it as if John's shoulder were scalding hot. John was about to object to the assaultive gesture when it occurred to him that it had been faithfully captured by his wife. *Good,* he thought, praising his practical wife in his mind for thinking of shooting the video. More interesting, however, was the underlying message McClaussen's gesture revealed: McClaussen was feeling desperate. The bigger question, of course, was why. McClaussen needed only this last assurance to bring the email fiasco to closure. The obvious conclusion was that someone must be pressuring McClaussen, and pressuring him hard. The realization hit John like a brick in the face. *So there was a greater conspiracy after all!*

John reached forward and turned on the computer. Everyone watched at rapt attention while it booted. The moment the desktop appeared, Benniman slid into the chair, his fingers, for all their beefy appearance, attacking the keys like a concert pianist. After an unsuccessful search of John's email program, he swept the entire computer system for any signs of having received any incoming emails from any source during the last week. Once again not coming up with anything interesting, Hank Benniman relaxed and shook the tenseness from his shoulders and back. "There's nothing here, Mr. McClaussen. Nothing. The man's telling the truth."

At a signal from a still unsatisfied McClaussen, Hank resumed searching all programs and documents with a creation date within a week of the incident. "Nothing," Benniman reported again after a few minutes. "The computer hasn't been accessed, used or updated during the last couple weeks."

All eyes turned to McClaussen, who, with a look of mixed relief and hidden vengence, signaled Benniman with a tiny flick of his fingers. Before anyone could react, Benniman had entered a short string of alpha-numeric commands and tapped the "return" key. The computer popped and went blank.

John, shocked by the swiftness of it all, stared transfixed. The sheriff and police stiffened, shifting their hands to their weapons.

"I'm sorry, Mr. Marx, but I needed to be absolutely certain that the email, or any form of it, doesn't reside somewhere on your computer. All of the memory on this old, outdated computer accidently erased itself. I have already ordered BPI to replace it with the newest model complete with all-new software. I have also ordered that you be fully compensated for any...inconvenience...you and your family might experience as a result of the...accident." Handing John a business card, McClaussen continued. "Call my secretary, whenever. Having concluded our business, I need to return to my duties at BPI."

John watched McClaussen as he moved to exit the room, Benniman at his heels.

"And I appreciate your committing your henchman's illegal action and your lame excuse to tape," John, still stunned, goaded.

McClaussen shrugged without stopping.

"Oh, and, mind the reporters outside. They will undoubtedly want a detailed statement about what just happened here."

McClaussen stopped in his tracks, Benniman knocking awkwardly into him. It was John's turn to smile.

McClaussen glared daggers, then, resurveying the irritated sheriff, two policemen and still rolling video, shook his head, and huffed down the hallway.

"I only hope Josh was successful in getting the local TV, radio and newspaper reporters to come out to greet him on his way out."

The front door slammed shut, the collective yells of various news media representatives penetrating through the front door assuring John that Josh, as always, had delivered. It would be the biggest thing to hit Violet in a century, and everyone in New Orleans and Louisiana would soon learn of the CEO of BPI's dramatic "secret" visit to oilman John

Marx in his Violet home. The publicity should assure John, his family and Josh a measure of safety, at least for the time being.

John and his wife, the video still rolling, ambled up to the front door and opened it. Both black cars, surrounded by media, started up at the same time and drove off followed closely by the two police cars.

Sheriff Grant, approaching from behind, stood next to the couple. "Well, John, I don't know what that was all about, but I'd sure like to know the brand of computer you have that's so popular!"

"Thanks for coming out, Grant," John replied with a grin. "What happened was these folks lost something, and wanted to see for themselves that it wasn't on my computer. What makes me so mad is that I told them this before I left the rig. What you saw, Grant, was a poorly veiled threat towards me, Josh, and more important, Ann. This affair hasn't ended yet. They may try to meet out their threat with another less public visit, once the media is gone, so I'd be obliged if you would keep a close watch on the house for the next couple hours."

Sheriff Grant split a wide, toothy grin. "It would be my pleasure, John. I need to fill out a bunch of forms and report what happened here. I can do it all in my car. Normally it would take me a half hour or so, but I could easily stretch it out to an hour. Once I finish, perhaps you'd invite me in for some of those wonderful cookies you're famous for, Ann."

Ann slipped an arm though Grant's and, smiling sweetly, walked him back to his sheriff's car, the video-camera in her other hand dangling loosely at her side.

Behind John, the phone rang and Janice swooped out of nowhere to answer it.

"Yes, Mr. Josh. He's right here. Dad! It's Mr. Josh for you!" she called out.

John laughed at the disappointment in her voice. Obviously, she was expecting a more important call from one of her many teenage friends. The events of the day would provide her ample gossip for the rest of the week and then some.

John took the phone. "What's up, Josh?"

"McClaussen and his boys like the reception I arranged?" Josh asked, laughing heartily.

"McClaussen wasn't any too happy when he left." Josh acknowledged. "Thanks. Couldn't have done better myself."

"So, you want that flash drive and crystal now?"

"No, you're doing a great job. I want to go across town and check on Puissegur. Have you heard anything from my pilot-friend, Stan Meyers? I gave him your phone number. He agreed to fly over to Austin and check on Solokov's buddy, Dr. Yusef Spasskov, at the University of Texas, and, if he could locate him, fly him here."

"Nope, nothing while you and McClaussen were chatting. But I'll call you the moment I hear anything. By the way, now that all the excitement is over, I want to return to my house to shave, shower and get some clean clothes. How about I swing around in about an hour and we go hunt for Puissegur? Maybe I'll have heard from Stan by then."

"Okay," John agreed, his wife walking back into the house past him, exaggerating the sway of her hips and looking coyly over her shoulder at him.

John hung the phone up and followed her, while Ann shooed Janice away to the back room, asking her to entertain the other children for a while so mom and dad could get "reacquainted."

"What did Josh want?" Ann asked, placing the camera on the kitchen table and her hand on her hip.

"He wanted to clean up before we make a visit to someone across town. He and Sheriff Grant will be busy awhile…" John replied.

182

Ann looked squarely at her recently returned husband, a bedroom look in her eyes. "And I have something for you to do that needs doing, big man. You've been gone a long time, and I've had to do everything for you. It's time you thanked me," she said, taking John by the hand and tugging him playfully towards their bedroom. John, however, pulled back, and left for the living room.

"What are you doing?" Ann asked.

"I'm locking the doors. No need to have someone come in right in the middle of…" John cruised from front to back door, checking and locking each, humming a lilting melody. Making his way back to their bedroom, he found Ann already on the bed. Tearing off his clothes, he jumped on the bed next to her.

"Careful, wild man, you may hurt something."

"Right now, nothing could hurt me bad enough to stop."

John grasped Ann in his muscled arms, kissing her, taking in her familiar scent and taste, slowly, lovingly bringing her to the kind of wild ecstasy that only time apart can induce. John stroked her hair, her face, her shoulders, the curve of her breasts down to the gentle slope of her hips and thighs. Ann panted, shuddering with each caress, until she gathered her man in her arms and directed him into her. Their voices quickly became one, each groaning in ecstasy to the other's every move. They'd been apart two weeks—fourteen days—three hundred and thirty-six hours. It might as well have been years or centuries. It always led to intense lovemaking on his return. It was, in fact, how they made all their children.

Sometime later, Ann and John let out a long, exhausted communal sigh and fell to each other's side, slick with perspiration, finally satisfied. It was John who opened his eyes first while rolling on top of her again. Ann opened her eyes and stared intensely at the man on top of her. John smiled and announced, "I'm home."

After another session of lovemaking, John rolled onto his back, and Ann snuggled up to him, her head on his chest, making ringlets of his whitening chest hairs with a finger. "You know, John, forty years ago when we were first married this little patch was darker, but I love it just as much now as I did then. Even more. Just like I love you now."

John scanned her naked, glistening body. "And you haven't changed a bit since then. You're just as beautiful and wild a lover now as you were then. Remember when we first met? I drove up to your cousin's house out in Metairie on my motorcycle. You and your cousin, Betty, were standing near the street. You looked my way and smiled that smile of yours," he said, brushing her lips with his fingertips "And that was it. I pulled off the road, asked you your name, and since then our love has just continued to grow."

"I remember," Ann replied languidly. "I thought you were crazy. Betty said I shouldn't talk to you, but I did anyway, and I'm so glad I did. Look what we've built together."

John smiled over at her. "Yeah. Three kids, a small but cozy home in Violet, a boat to cruise the bayous together when I'm home…"

"John, let's go cruising this weekend. Or sooner. I love our home, but to be honest with you, I'd like to get away from here and all the craziness of the last week and today. What do you think? The kids and I can begin packing while you and Josh do whatever it is you need to do. The kids would love it."

"Sounds good to me," John agreed, thinking it better than sharing the house with Sheriff Grant, Ann's old and, clearly in the Sheriff's eyes, still smoldering flame. "I think Josh would enjoy coming, too. We could catch a mess of fish and enjoy grilling them outdoors at night. How would that be?"

Ann reveled in the boyish sparkle the suggestion had brought to her lover's eyes. Pulling the covers up she said coyly, "Sounds like a date. In the meantime, there's still more time before Josh and the Sheriff finish what they're doing…"

CHAPTER 19

Nothing was said between Crist Marcus and Hank Benniman as they made the turn from Poydras Street onto One Shell Square. Crist, still smarting from having been escorted off Marx's property by two policemen, squealed the car into the designated space in the underground parking garage, and the two took the parking elevator to the office where McClaussen, their boss, would be waiting. Their two other colleagues should have been standing in the elevator next to them, preparing to report to McClaussen on Puissegur. Instead, their contorted bodies were being exhumed by the state police from the mud-caked Lincoln Town Car recovered with great difficulty from the river. Crist swore under his breath at the thought. Hank stood stoic and silent. The four had worked together on numerous jobs. Marx was evening the odds rather quickly. Too quickly and decisively for Crist or Hank's comfort.

The elevator door opened and the two men were greeted by a secretary, who escorted them into an expansive waiting room. The secretary stopped in front of McClaussen's closed door, knocked, listened, then gestured for the two to enter, leaving quickly for the safety of her desk. As they entered, McClaussen swiveled around in his chair to face them.

"Sit," he ordered as if to two Dobermans, pointing to a leather sofa next to them. "I need to know what more you've found out."

Hank sat awkwardly, and spoke first. "Mr. McClaussen. As you know, I found no evidence of the email on Mr. Marx's home computer, and, with the system wiped clean, if there *was* anything, it's now entirely gone. I assure you…"

"You *assure* me. You assure *me!* You fucking well better be certain of what you *assure me*, Mr. Benniman, because as of this moment, my life, and therefore *yours,* depends on it! And as for you, Mr. Marcus, you stupid ass…"

"I'm sorry, Mr. McClaussen. I never meant to frighten the woman. Well, actually I did, but she set us up…"

"She *tricked* you, you moron! Don't you think I know? You're not smart enough to threaten her. I should shoot the both of you for failing." McClaussen stood behind his desk, braced his huge hands on either side of the desk, and stared down at the two men seated before him. Then he slammed a fist on the desktop. "When I give an order, I expect it to be followed, no matter what! Do you understand? Crist, get back to Violet and stake out Puissegur's house until I tell you otherwise. Hank, take another car and stake out Marx's house. Keep him in your sight at all times until you're prepared to assure me *with your frigging life* that he's not up to *anything* more. I don't trust that man. I've said it before and still believe it: He's hiding something—if not a secret copy of the email, then something equally damning. Slip up this time and I'll have you two 'replaced' with a couple of Stein's other men. You get my drift, gentlemen?" McClaussen re-sat, giving them a look calculated to terrify them into complete subservience.

"Yes, sir," both said in unison. Hank Benniman stood. Crist, still sitting, offered his nervous opinion. "Mr. Marx doesn't seem to me to be hiding anything at all, sir."

McClaussen turned his entire attention to Crist. "I didn't ask you what you *thought*. I asked you to do your respective jobs. If either of you spot anything amiss call me on my cell phone. Immediately! Use whatever force is necessary to make certain that neither Marx nor Platur contacts anyone further about the email or my 'visit' to his house. It's taken me hours to deal with the press. The whole email affair *must end here and now!* No screw-ups. If Puissegur or Marx walks on water, you do the same, you hear me? Now get out of here! It's my turn to, as you so adroitly put it, Mr. Benniman, *assure* a certain party that the situation is totally, completely, absolutely resolved."

"Yes, sir," the two replied in unison, hustling their way out of McClaussen's inner sanctum to the elevator. Inside the elevator, Hank broke the silence.

"Shit, Crist! McClaussen didn't sound just angry, he sounded like he's going screwy or something. Maybe the high altitude from his new position is going to his head. What the hell could be so damn important about a frigging email? And what exactly are we supposed to be watching to see if Puissegur and Marx do? I mean, how can we know whether they're communicating with anyone else, if all we do is sit out in front of their houses and watch them come and go? Do you really understand what we are supposed to be doing?"

Crist listened, looking at his partner dumbly as the elevator descended and the floors began chiming by. "Well, this I do know: We're not to question what this is all about, or what that email has to do with anything. We're to watch Puessegur and Marx, and call in anything unusual. That's my read. My guess is that the boss is more concerned about whomever *he* reports to than about us, otherwise, we'd be lying stiff beside our colleagues right now. We're paid to do as McClaussen tells us, and we're paid well for it. The way I figure, it's up to the boss—and his bosses and their bosses—to know what it's all about."

The elevator stopped abruptly and discharged its occupants. Neither spoke further, each eventually entering his car. What, after all, could either say?

Back in Violet, high above where John and Josh were finishing their customary post-shift ablutions in preparation for their journey to Leon Puissegur's house, a small, private helicopter with two persons aboard thwacked the air, the pilot looking for a place to land. His passenger, a balding East European dressed in blue jeans and a blue polo shirt, looked worried. The pilot, peering down questioningly out of the fishbowl front of the helicopter, looked even more worried. Stan Meyer shrugged and made another pass around the area. Minutes ago, he'd passed over John Marx and Josh Platur's homes, noting the dilapidated old truck parked in front of Marx's house. He'd tried calling Josh, but the man's phone seemed constantly busy. His passenger, Dr. Yusef Spasskov, an acknowledged genius in computing and petroleum geosystems engineering from the University of Texas at Austin, and he were engaged together in a loud discussion.

"I promised Platur I'd bring you safely to Violet, and, now that we're here, his phone's constantly busy, and I don't know where to land. I wonder what the hell's going on?" Stan yelled over the sound of the engine, making the explanation more as statement than a question.

"I don't personally know either Mr. Platur or Mr. Marx, but I do know Leon Puissegur. He lives not far from here. Over there in fact," Spasskov said, pointing off into the distance across town. "I need to talk with him now, if possible. Once I talk with him, we can go back to Mr. Marx and Mr. Platur's." Spasskov shouted back.

190

Realizing the hopelessness of trying to locate a place to land in a tree-lined suburban area, Meyers readily acknowledged his passenger's suggestion, and headed directly across Violet towards the country.

"There!" Spasskov yelled, signaling repeatedly down with a finger towards a sprawling, brick, ranch-style house below. The backyard consisted of an acre or so of grassy flatland, and appeared free of obstructions. Stan took a quick fly around, and not noticing anyone watching the place, proceeded to land in the field behind the house. The moment the small helicopter landed, Spasskov bolted out the plastic bubble towards the house. Stan took his time shutting down his helicopter, and watched as Spasskov pounded on the back door to Puissegur's house.

No one answered.

Satisfied the helicopter was secure yet ready to take off on a moment's notice, Stan Meyer reached behind his seat and slipped out his Vietnam-era Browning M1911 Colt Commander .45 caliber sidearm, and began screwing on a Nexus/Tactical III .45 suppressor that had been retrofitted to it. There was nothing quite like the stopping power of the old .45's even today.

After Spasskov pounded again, the back door opened to reveal a dapper, grey-haired man, about five-foot-six, with a bushy grey mustache and penetrating blue eyes hidden behind large-lens glasses. The two men recognized each other instantly and shook hands like old friends. Spasskov turned and waved to Stan to join them.

Stan climbed out of the glassine bubble and headed towards the two men, holding the silenced weapon behind his back.

Stan Meyer had done exactly what everyone had asked of him. Howard Stein had ordered him to do whatever Marx or his friends asked, and report their actions to McClaussen. When he'd told McClaussen about John's unusual request to locate Spasskov,

McClaussen had ordered Stan to do as he was asked, then eliminate the man. Then that bitch, Carol Bishop, who was busy taking control of DSSC, had called him. Unsatisfied with McClaussen's assurances that the email affair was quickly coming to an end, she had commanded him to do whatever *anyone* wanted so long as it resulted in the permanent removal of Marx, Platur and Puissegur. Everything was finally coming together at last. Now was his chance to fulfill all their demands at once. Well, almost. He'd still have to deal with McClaussen later. Strange the grip that Carol Bishop seemed to wield over men, but, then, he knew from recent experience that the woman was a tantalizingly inventive lover…

CHAPTER 20

Leon Puissegur woke, stretched and peeked out a front curtained window. The black Lincoln Town Car that had been waiting out there for several days was gone and hadn't come back. Good. Maybe the plan he'd set into motion was working, and the oil industry was preparing to acknowledge him and the abiotic oil theory he'd been touting for over a decade. It wouldn't be an easy transition from a non-renewable biotic to a sustainable abiotic oil world. All the basic assumptions and operational theories would have to be thrown out the window. Oil companies would have to be restructured. Universities would have to rewrite their curricula. It would be a different world, one in which global super-corporations like Dan Sogo Shosha Corporation would transition from a narrower petroleum to a broader energy and information base. Those that made the transition would determine the future. Those that didn't, well, they would be forgotten, despite past accomplishments.

A combination working oil man, theoretical geophysicist, and practicing computer specialist, Puissegur had, from the beginning of his career, taken an active interest in all aspects of oil theory, eventually tripping over an early nineteenth century abiogenic oil formation hypothesis. Initially proposed by three world-renown researchers, German naturalist and explorer Alexander von Humboldt, Russian chemist Dimitri Mendeleev, and French chemist Marcellin Berthelot, the crux of the theory was that oil was being constantly generated in the earth's fiery mantle, slowly making it's way to the surface, cooling, condensing and processing naturally into what was known today as oil. According to this new theory, oil, being a rich source of complex hydrocarbons, was the source of life on earth, food for the earliest archaebacteria, prototype bacteria without even a nucleus. The Abiotic Oil Theory initially languished for lack of supporting data, but was resurrected in the 1950's by Austrian-born, American astrophysicist Thomas Gold. But it was the United States National Aeronautics and Space Administration (NASA) that added the fuel to the abiotic oil fire with the discovery of large amounts of abiotic hydrocarbons on other planets. Gold reasoned that if oil precursors could be found throughout the universe on planets without known lifeforms, then that was further evidence for abiotic oil being a likely source of not only life on earth but oil as we know it today. Scientists in the former Union of Soviet Socialist Republics strongly supported this view. The rest of the world did not. In the end, it had been up to Puissegur and a handful of dogged scientists to carry on and advance Gold's claims.

And advance the theory they did. Several months previously, Puissegur had visited with British Petroleum International's Chief Executive Officer, William Greyson, and found a strong corporate ally, not so much because Greyson believed in his abiotic oil theory, but because, after several high level meetings, Greyson and the BPI board members became convinced it was the key they'd been looking for to unlock the North American Strategic Oil Reserves to development. As such, it really didn't matter whether the abiotic oil theory was "true" or not, just that the President of the United States, his advisors, and the American people *believed* it to be true (and who wouldn't want to believe in an unlimited source of petroleum energy these days). Desperate hope and unlimited greed, Greyson was convinced, would open the Reserve to exploration and development by BPI.

According to the theory, with well over two trillion barrels of oil lying in wait beneath the currently recognized oil fields located in Utah, Colorado, and Wyoming, BPI, as the principle advocate of this new and enticing theory, would be positioned to be a dominant world player, first in the petroleum sector, then in the energy and information business, an expanded role Greyson envisioned for BPI. The vision had quickly proven so large as to require other global "partners," and eventually a super-corporate structure was necessary to coordinate their activities. The Dan Sogo Shosha Corporation, DSSC, on the surface a global trading leader, was, now, underneath that facade, a consortium of the most aggressive energy and information corporations in the world.

Greyson had invited Puissegur to be present before a secret, joint meeting of DSSC and BPI's boards, the result of which was that Puissegur had been contracted to create a global abiotic oil "model" that would visually incorporate all the data BPI had on biotic oil alongside the abiotic oil regeneration areas Puissegur was predicting, to form one integrated, three-dimensional holographic projection. DSSC had marshaled its vast computing resources to further capture Puissegur's model into a single, solid, orthorhombic crystal that served as the memory core for a next-generation, normal-light, holographic reader and projector.

The unit proved a quick and astounding success. DSSC's ability to project Puessegur's three-dimensional rotating images into the air,

195

like a ghostly movie running from the past, to the present, and into the future, had proven the visual clincher that Greyson needed. Though few biotic oil engineers had moved to adopt Puissegur's theory, everyone who saw the projection had to admit it was eminently *believable*, and that was all that BPI actually required to set into motion it's plans for development of the United States Strategic Oil Reserve and, eventually, assume world dominance in the field of energy and information.

Puissegur had been scheduled to meet surreptitiously one final time with Greyson on an oilrig, Rustic Oil Rig Twelve, one of several sites where BPI was in the process of sinking several extraordinarily deep exploratory wells in hopes of drilling into an upwelling mantle fracture containing abiotic oil. Greyson had, in fact, bankrolled one of BPI's lesser known subsidiaries, New South Wales Petroleum, one of three oil exploration and exploitation companies owned by Shaun McClaussen, to do the exploration. If abiotic oil was discovered, then Greyson would have the field "proof" he desired. If not, it didn't matter: with a combination of holographic showmanship and sleight-of-hand, he'd "prove" the theory enough to talk the present administration and it's money-hungry politicians into opening the Reserve to BPI. It was a big-money, high-stakes venture, but one Greyson was more than willing to bet his and his company's future on.

What Greyson hadn't counted on was the unlimited greed that his scheme awoke within DSSC's most aggressive executive officer, Carol Bishop. It was Bishop and Bishop alone who foresaw that with such resources, real or imagined, DSSC could be reformed into an energy-information monopoly, tipping and eventually controlling the balance of world power. Thrust into the arena of world power and domination, DSSC would need a new, more aggressive leader—one like her, better versed in power tactics—at the helm. The trouble was that everyone in

DSSC and BPI, including Greyson, didn't yet know that they needed her.

Sensing that Greyson, once he "sold" the idea, would likely proceed to ensnare or eliminate any troublesome futurists like her from his new order, she covertly had a single copy of the crystal made, then smashed the original in a dramatically violent display at a board meeting that left two stakeholders dead and the rest in fear of their lives. The next day, amidst a quickly accumulating number of additional bodies, beginning with the nobody George Franks, she had Greyson eliminated, and elevated the killer, Stein, to DSSC's Chief of Security. Their co-conspirator, Shaun McClaussen, her ex-lover and current nemesis, whom she elevated to the position of CEO of BPI, alone stood in her way now. That and the stupid email which, through cleverness, she had her enemy, McClaussen, running down. As soon as McClaussen reported his success, Stein was to kill him. At the same time, her new lover, Stan Meyers, the best private helicopter pilot in the consortium, and now her covert hitman, would get rid of that meddling fool, Puissegur, who started it all and could, theoretically, bring it all down. Then Marx and Platur. Then Stein. Then all she'd have to do was tidy the house up a bit and finish entrenching herself through fear and intimidation into the center of power at DSSC. That would be her revenge against all the men who'd used *her* on their way up the corporate ladder at the CIA. It would also be her ultimate achievement, and she'd do it without that misogynist, McClaussen, fuck the man! Hell, fuck them all!

The Oil Man

CHAPTER 21

John and Josh loaded up John's battered-looking truck and set off for Puissegur's house a little less than an hour after the altercation with McClaussen. Both felt rejuvenated, though for distinctly different reasons: John for the long-awaited return to his family and the hotly anticipated tussel in the hay with his beloved wife; Josh for the long, hot shower and uninterrupted half hour of peace and quiet. Ann waved them off while the children continued to pack for the unexpected holiday on the Marx boat, a holiday that would begin as soon as the two buddies returned from their "errand."

Josh updated John continuously on the way to Puissegur's house: Yes, the local news reports on McClaussen's "visit" had been picked up by the national media and were generating intense national interest. John's investigative reporter friend from the New Orleans Times-Picayune had called, and Josh had agreed they'd meet at Puissegur's house. Yes, Claude Askins and Chris Longley's deaths had hit the news, sending rumors flying about Rustic Oil, NSWP and BPI's involvement in the "mysterious string of deaths." No, he hadn't heard anything yet from Stan Meyers, but he'd been quite busy on the phone, and expected Stan's call anytime now. It was Josh's opinion that, given the publicity surrounding all these events, they were "relatively" safe.

John nodded, acknowledging each update. He didn't nod, however, at Josh's conclusion regarding their safety. John didn't *feel* safe, and, inveterate conspiracy theorist that he was, suspected the worst was yet to come. His suspicions were confirmed when he noticed a familiar-looking black Lincoln Town Car with a single person in it traveling one street over from where he and Josh were, their courses parallel.

"Bandit at nine o'clock," John stated without emotion.

"Yeah, I noticed the car a couple blocks back. But why would someone be going our way *ahead* of us? You don't suppose our houses are bugged…"

"It's possible, but I was careful at home not naming Puissegur," John stated.

"And I didn't say anything about him aloud to myself while at home," Josh added, checking the bundles piled in the back bed of the pickup truck. "You don't think he's on their way to…"

"I do," John cut in. "I think he's making a beeline to Puissegur's place just like us, which re-affirms my hunch about Puissegur. I'm guessing Puissegur was there on the rig just before me, and the piece of crystal is his. The crystal's *got* to have something to do with the email. The two—the crystal fragment and the email—must be related somehow."

John slowed down as he approached Puissegur's house. The black car was parked across the street, but the man inside was making no visible effort to get out.

John veered off onto a side road to avoid being spotted, and parked across the street from Puissegur's huge back yard area, in which he spotted a small, two-man helicopter parked.

"Looks like Stan anticipated us. Let's hope Spasskov's there, too. Did you bring the email and crystal fragment?"

"Of course. Like I said before, it's never left my body..."

"Yeah, great. Just keep it and the memory stick hidden, wherever the hell they are, until I tell you, okay?"

"Okay," Josh replied with a grin.

John and Josh climbed out of the car, and walked around to the back of the truck. Unwrapping one of the bundles, John brushed off a 12-gauge Mossberg 500 sport shotgun he favored for hunting, and handed a smaller package to Josh. Inside the second package was a Marlin Model 336C deer rifle with spotting scope. One of the most popular hunting rifles in North America, this hard-hitting, lever-action, .35 caliber version was known for both pinpoint accuracy and quick reload. As they crossed the street, John situated Josh next to the helicopter, instructing him to keep his eyes on the curtained windows and back door. Then John walked the short distance, and, raising a hand to knock, abruptly halted. The door was ajar. After checking to make certain both barrels were loaded and the safety off, John tipped open the door with the toe of his shoe and slipped in.

It took a few moments to regain his sight in the dark kitchen. There was no one in there, but he heard voices coming from the adjoining living room. Three men and a woman. The woman sounded scared. One of the men's voices he recognized: Stan Meyers. The other two he didn't recognize, though one had a distinctly European accent, while the other was that of an older, local man. The local man, he figured, would be Puissegur; the foreigner, quite likely Spasskov. Puissegur and the foreigner were on the left side of the living room, talking about computers, crystals, holograms and abiotic oil. The third man, Stan, on the far right side of the room, fell silent to listen. John placed the woman next to Stan.

"So DSSC was able to create a yottabyte crystalline memory device?" asked the distinctly Eastern European voice.

"And to embed within it all of the information I've gathered on abiotic oil and it's likely locations. All into a time-space database, that, based on past changes, can now predict when and where the abiotic oil upwellings are all around the world," completed Puissegur. "Then something happened. DSSC's power structure abruptly changed. I was at a secret, high-level meeting of the boards of directors of several of the largest daimyo members. A woman, with the help of several assistants, seized the crystal memory device and shattered it. In the confusion, I was able to secret away the largest piece. Several guards wisked me back here, and constantly provided two bodyguards by DSSC's new Chief of Security—a man called Howard Stein. I remained here, under what has amounted to house arrest, until the day of the meeting between myself and Greyson.

"While waiting to hear from Greyson, I contacted Alexei Sokolov, the man who created the crystal memory unit, and, after swearing him to secrecy, disclosed that I had a fragment of the memory crystal. He told me that a crystal shard of this size would likely contain the entire database—a quirk of holographic crystal memory devices—and told me how to manufacture a special box for the fragment, which I did, here in my machine shop. It was my intention to return the fragment to Greyson at our meeting.

"From the moment the helicopter set down on Rustic Oil Rig Twelve, I suspected something was wrong, so while stopping on the catwalk and commenting on the view, I let the box slip from my fingers. If my fear was ungrounded, I figured I could return in a few moments and recover it. When I met Greyson, I was glad I parted with the box. Greyson was pale and fearful. He said the woman seizing power was ruthless, and felt he was marked for death. I whispered to

202

Greyson about the fragment, and expressed my concern about who would discover the box. We figured a derrick workman would most likely discover it and turn it over to the rig supervisor, who would, in turn, give it to the company man. Greyson felt the company man would likely be watched because of our meeting, so suggested I send an email to the company communications handler, who would alert the supervisor running the oil platform.

"We exited separately. Greyson took the first corporate helicopter, and I took the second. The pilot seemed quite curious about my visit, and kept pumping me for information, which I wasn't inclined to share. That's him over there," Puissegur concluded, pointing at a smiling, thin-lipped Stan Meyer, who continued carefully hiding the silenced weapon behind him. While Puissegur was talking, Meyer had slowly positioned himself so that he could simply raise his hand and eliminate both men. He appeared disinterested in the woman, presumably Mrs. Puissegur, standing next to him, and unaware of John in the kitchen.

"Thanks to my email, the communications man is dead. So is the company man. So is Greyson. So is Solokov. What have I done? Who's next?" asked a bewildered Puissegur.

"*You*," replied Stan, revealing his weapon and pointing it at the two men across the room. "Orders."

The woman next to Stan screamed, and Stan reflexively swung the weapon to point it at her. "You, too, if you don't shut up!"

At that moment the front door burst open and an adrenalinized Crist Marcus surged into the room in response to Ms. Puissegur's continuing, blood-curdling scream. Stan swept his weapon to his right in a 180-degree arc pointing it now at the surprised intruder and squeezed off a shot. The silenced Colt Commander flashed brightly, leaving suspended in the air a sickly white halo of burnt powder. The massive bullet thudded loudly into the door jamb creating a shower of splinters, barely missing Crist's neck.

As Stan prepared to squeeze off a second shot, Crist pulled out and leveled his .38 special. The two reports were like a single crack of lightening and thunder in the confined space. Stan flinched, his aim going slightly off center, but his bullet grazed Crist's left upper arm. The impact of the .45 bullet threw Crist solidly against the shattered door jamb.

Puissegur and Spasskov had dropped to the ground. The woman, pie-eyed at the horror unfolding before her, stood frozen with both hands to her ears and continued screaming.

Stan was about to swing his weapon to the left to stop the woman's yelling, when John stepped forward with lowered shotgun.

"No more!" he commanded. "Both of you drop all your weapons! Now, or I'll shoot!"

Crist's gun clunked on the floor. Stan leveled the elongated automatic pistol at the woman's midsection and shifted behind her, using her as a shield. "Try, and the woman dies," Stan growled, eyeing the door where John was standing, the way out to the helicopter and escape.

"Shoot, and *you'll* die before you can squeeze off another shot," John bluffed.

Crist, standing unsteadily, hands in the air, backed against the nearest wall.

"Out of the way, John, or, I swear, the lady dies!" Stan repeated, pushing the woman towards John and the archway between living room and kitchen. "Come join us in the living room. Now. Next to those two quivering oldies. Quick, before I change my mind and start shooting again."

John looked at an ashen-white Crist, who was cradling one

profusely bleeding arm with his other, then at the two men cowering on the floor, then back at Stan. He couldn't believe it. Stan Meyer, his lifelong friend, for God's sake! What the hell was...

"Move away from the doorway, John," Stan threatened, shoving the tip of the silencer up into the suddenly silent woman's abdomen, pointing the tip towards her heart.

John eased over towards the two men lying on the floor, his shotgun leveled at Stan.

Stan moved into the archway and began backing out of the living room into the kitchen, pulling the frightened woman with him.

"My wife..." Puissegur managed to say.

"My guest for a little helicopter ride," Stan said, releasing the woman just long enough to make certain the kitchen door was open behind him.

Puissegur and Spasskov stood shakily up.

"And now it's time for me to say goodbye," Stan said coldly, swivelling the nozzle from the woman towards Puissegur and Spasskov, and began to squeeze the trigger.

Stan's chest suddenly erupted in an explosion of blood, bone and flesh, and he staggered forward, wild-eyed, bouncing off the once-again screaming woman. Before he hit the floor, the six heard the loud bang from outside the back door.

John barely had time to swing his shotgun from Stan to Crist, who was bending over and reaching for his gun. "Don't even think of it," John growled.

CHAPTER 22

"Get his weapon," John Marx ordered, and Leon Puissegur instantly obeyed, pointing Crist Marcus's handgun back at its owner. "Watch him carefully. If he moves, shoot him in the other arm. If he moves again, shoot him in a leg. After that, shoot wherever you wish, but make sure he's dead."

Leon Puissegur and Yousef Spasskov looked at each other in disbelief.

"Shoot him if he moves, or he'll wrestle the gun from you, at which time, I guarantee, he won't hesitate to shoot first and apologize later," John warned. Crist's face morphed into a feral snarl.

Ms. Puissegur was standing stiffly in the kitchen exactly where she'd been standing when Josh Platur had shot her hostage-taker, Stan Meyers. Shaking off her shock, she added, "Do it, Leon," with grim, determined finality. Walking stoically over to join her husband, she grabbed the weapon from Leon's hand and moved the point of the gun from Crist's unwounded arm to his head. Time stopped. No one breathed. Ms. Puissegur's hand began shaking. With a prolonged sigh, she placed the gun back into her husband's hand, slipped behind him, and began quietly sobbing. "He would have shot me...or you...or Yousef. Don't give him another chance. If he moves, kill him for me."

That was all Leon needed to hear. His eyes cleared, reflecting an inner change from astonishment to resolve. Crist painfully raised both hands higher.

Keeping Crist always in view, John backed towards the kitchen and signaled out the door for Josh to join him. There was no further need to guard the helicopter.

Josh joined the five, keeping the barrel of his deer gun pointed at Stan's bleeding, motionless body, until, kicking the body with his foot and getting no response, he felt certain the man was dead. "A real work, this one!" Josh muttered. "Hope you aren't planning on joining him."

Crist nodded slowly in the negative, careful to make no sound or sudden movement.

"Good," Josh confirmed. Looking back at Stan Meyer's body, Josh offered, "I would never have guessed..."

"I did," John replied. "When Stan explained to me how Claude had died, I began doubting. Thank you for saving the day."

"'Aw, shucks'," Josh replied, feigning embarrassment.

"For the moment, let's tie this one up. Leon will keep him under guard while Dr. Spasskov and I look over the email message and crystal shard."

Crist tensed. "Yes," John continued, directing his comments at one of the worst of McClaussen's men, "Your boss was right all along. I have both the email and the object of the email secreted away. And, what's more, I plan to use them and this situation against him."

"But where...?" Crist began. Puissegur outstretched his arm and began to squeeze the trigger.

"I wouldn't say another word if I were you. Besides, it's none of your business," John interrupted. "I just wanted you to know that your efforts had failed. McClaussen won't be pleased when he discovers you let the email slip right through your fingers."

A look of fear passed across Crist's face, while John and Josh proceeded to tie him, groaning, on his side, on the floor. With his wife encouraging him, the front sight of Leon's gun never wavered from Crist's forehead.

"Mr. Puissegur," John began after testing Crist's bindings, "I need to know for certain what was in the email. I recognized the numbers were Solokov's phone number and Skyped him, hoping to avoid anyone knowing. After he was murdered, I wondered if he and I had been set up."

Leon Puissegur collapsed into a recliner, resting the body of the gun on the hand rest, and sighed. "You weren't set up by me. The phone number was a special one Solokov gave me. If anyone called that number, Solokov would assume that I had been successful in saving a readable piece of the crystal core memory. Your Skype call must have partially alerted him. Unfortunately, he was eliminated before I could re-acquire the fragment and meet with him. The information on the shard is worth…well, any number of people's lives if you believe the information on it is true, and I do. From the moment the memory crystal was shattered, I knew if word got out I had a readable fragment, wheels within wheels would begin turning, all directed at either recovering or destroying the fragment, depending on how whoever wanted it most imagined using it."

"So," John asked, turning to Spasskov. "Can you make the crystal dance?"

"If it's as large a fragment as Leon says, then the answer is, 'yes, I can.' I could do it right here, in this very room if I had the fragment," Spasskov assured. Josh looked hopeful; John, wary.

"First we must call the police," Mrs. Puissegur inserted boldly, staring at the body that was continuing to bleed on her kitchen floor.

"Yes," John agreed, looking from the lifeless body to the tied-up henchman. "But first, I need you three, Josh, Yousef and Leon, to help me confirm that what I have is indeed the real email and fragment. Josh, where are they?"

"Check this out: I told you everyone was always looking right at them," Josh bragged, reaching down and undoing his belt. Freeing it from his waist, he held the painted-brass American eagle belt buckle in front of them, grinning from ear to ear.

"I still don't see anything, Josh," John ventured.

Josh twisted the buckle, and the back popped open revealing two small objects wrapped in light cloth. Josh put the belt on the table, and held the flash drive up in one hand and the shard in the other. "I told you no one would see it or find it. The buckle has a lead lining, making it difficult to see inside even when x-rayed."

John shook his head in amazement. "Where did you get that from?"

"From The Spy Shop in Violet. You don't have the corner on the conspiracy market, you know. Some of us are just more discrete."

All four laughed heartily. Crist craned his neck to see the thumb drive and shard, glaring painfully and angrily at him. Josh handed the drive and shard to John with care, then flipped open his cell phone and called Sheriff Grant.

Grant answered barely through the first ring, as if waiting for the call, and, listening, informed them he'd make the necessary call to the police and emergency medical service. After reassuring Josh that he had visited John's house, and that Ann and the children were fine, he instructed everyone to stay where they were until help arrived.

John, in the meantime, handed Leon the thumb drive and

Spasskov the unwrapped shard. Leon clutched the thumb drive firmly in his free hand. Spasskov gripped the crystal fragment between thumb and index finger, held it in front of and slightly above his eyes, and examined it against the brightness outside the open kitchen door.

"This will work," Spasskov declared. "There are no internal fractures, and there's enough crystal here to preserve the entire database."

Spasskov turned, directing a ray of sunlight streaming from behind over his shoulder, then twisted the fragment in the light until it suddenly flashed. Everyone's attention turned to the man-sized sphere that materialized out of thin air. Mrs. Puissegur gasped. The earth, its insides visible to the core, rotated slowly before them with what looked like thousands of rivers of red underwater streams flowing up from the mantle, collecting in abiotic lakes and pools beneath and within the crust, some touching the millions of smaller green biotic pools located throughout the crust.

"The world's entire supply of oil," Leon said flatly, as impressed with the hologram now as he had been when he first unveiled it. Placing the gun on the arm chair cushion, he walked over to the table, and inserted the drive into his laptop. After typing in a short decryption key, the ten numbers in the message morphed into ten blocks of code. "And here's the code string needed to manipulate the image through time."

Spasskov stared briefly at the blocks. "Indeed. Everything is here. It only requires a small amount of equipment, which I've brought with me in the attaché case over there, to make the crystal fully functional." Spasskov walked, crystal in hand, to the attaché case on the living room table and opened it. "We're almost finished."

"It's not over yet," John pronounced as he watched in awe. "McClaussen's man here will eventually be missed, if he isn't already.

211

We still have to deal with McClaussen and Stein, and apparently the ruthless new CEO of DSSC, too, hopefully before they deal with us. Yousef. You continue. Make sure everything works, and protect the case and its contents with your life. Josh. You and Mrs. Puissegur keep an eye on our captive. Leon and I have something we need to take care of right now. We'll take Stan's helicopter. As soon as you finish your report to Sheriff Grant, induce him to take you and Spasskov to my house, and the two of you watch Ann and the children. I'm concerned for them. She's tough and street-wise, but they're still the most vulnerable point of our plan."

"Right," Josh answered, retrieving Crist's handgun from the armchair cushion, aiming it at Crist and handing his rifle to Leon.

Crist had stopped bleeding and was straining at his bonds.

Mrs. Puissegur opted to make coffee and tea while they waited for the sheriff, police and ambulance to arrive.

John and Leon stepped over Stan's body, John cradling his shotgun, Leon shouldering Josh's deer rifle. Leon was still stowing his rifle and buckling up when John awakened the helicopter and they disappeared into the blue sky.

CHAPTER 23

Hearing a piercing scream from inside the previously silent Puissegur house, Crist called McClaussen while checking the gun he normally carried in a small-of-the-back gun holster to make certain it was loaded and ready. McClaussen quickly agreed Crist should take all action to protect Puissegur, at least for the time being. The result of Crist's heroics had left him wounded, hog-tied and gagged on his side on the living room floor with his own gun pointed at his head by an irritatable-appearing Josh. When Crist didn't report back, McClaussen, anticipating trouble, called Stein, who ordered Hank Benniman to the house to find out what had happened. Benniman arrived outside the Puissegur house just in time to see a small helicopter take off from the back yard. The front door of the house was open, and the interior silent, dark and foreboding.

Figuring the worst, he rushed the house, stumbling over the writhing body just inside the door. Rolling to his left, he pointed his thiry-eight special unknowingly at Spasskov, the nearest silhouette.

Mrs. Puissegur, unaware, walked into the living room, screamed, and dropped the coffee and tea tray.

213

The living room erupted in gunfire.

Spasskov jerked forward onto the table, his forehead falling with a liquid thud against the makeshift keyboard inside the attaché case. Josh winced as a bullet dug into the flesh at the top of his shoulder, leaving a hot, searing furrow. The man at the door dropped to the floor behind his bound and struggling colleague, Josh's first bullet slapping soundly into the center of Crist's flailing chest. Crist moaned and fell silent.

Josh's second shot slapped Benniman's gun out of his hand, throwing the weapon against the doorjamb and rebounding it onto the floor at Josh's feet.

His third shot pinned Benniman down behind Crist's unmoving body, giving Josh barely enough time to pick up Benniman's pistol, scoop Mrs. Puissegur into one arm and dash with her over Stan's body and out the kitchen door. Assisting the doubly-stunned woman across the open space past where the helicopter had been, he dived them both behind a work shed.

Hank Benniman slowly raised himself off the floor and prepared to rush after Platur and the woman, but hesitated when he heard sirens closing rapidly in from every direction. *Fuck*, he mouthed in exasperation, realizing that no explanation he could concoct would satisfy the law. Hightailing it out the front door, he headed towards his car only to be caught in the middle of the street between three police cars screeching to a halt around him.

Two hours later, multiple ambulance crews were busying themselves treating Josh's wounds, while the police hauled Hank Benniman off in handcuffs, and the coroner's crew removed the sheet-covered bodies of Stan Meyers, Crist Marcus and Yousef Spasskov.

Sheriff Grant, who arrived immediately after the police, still appeared stunned by the nightmarish violence of the crime scene.

"John took off in Stan Meyer's helicopter with Leon Puissegur to… hell, I've really no idea *where* they were going. All I know is that John had a plan…" As he talked, Josh inched his way over to the blood-spattered attaché case lying open on the table.

"Sorry, Josh," Grant said, awakening at last from his shock. "That's evidence," he said, pointing to the attaché case in Josh's outstretched hand.

"That case is, practically speaking, the cause of all this," Josh explained, sweeping his hand around the shattered, bloodied room.

"It's still evidence," Grant warned. "It'll be safe locked up in the police evidence room," he added, nodding at several detectives to take it away.

"I'm not so sure of that, sheriff," Josh countered, watching one of the police detectives whom he didn't recognize carry away the case under his arm. "I'm not at all sure about that."

Josh plopped his exhausted body into a dining room chair and sat, staring at the television someone had turned on during the course of the investigation. A local news anchorwoman was informing her viewers excitedly that a British Petroleum International oil executive's email containing information vital to the nation's security had been leaked by an employee. The employee had been found mysteriously dead. The new CEO of British Petroleum International, a Mr. Shaun McClaussen, denied that the email was of any significance; however, he stated that BPI considered any breach of security serious. Appearing suddenly on the screen, he denied when questioned that the recent rash of oil industry deaths were in any way connected. Immediately following the report, the scene shifted to that of a very much alive and pissed off Crist Marcus being escorted away. A moment later the screen flashed to the front yard of Puissegur's house, where the combination of flashing sheriff, police and ambulance lights lent a surrealistic stroboscopic effect to the line of gurneys carrying one after another body from inside the house. *Good*, thought Josh. *With the media picking up on it, hopefully all of us will be the safer, as John suggested. McClaussen, on the other hand...*

An ashen-faced Shaun McClaussen was watching a rebroadcast of the same report on board an intercontinental charter jet halfway up the East Coast. His nemesis, Ms. Carol Bishop, now firmly entrenched as CEO of Dan Sogo Shosha Corporation, had called an emergency meeting of the key *daimyo* members. Undoubtedly she'd seen or was at least aware of the news reports that were coming out, one after another, and he wasn't sure how Carol would actually react. The meeting was set for less than four hours from now in the New York office where Greyson had first laid the plans for what had become known as the Email-Crystal Fiasco. It was the same office where Greyson had met his death. McClaussen shifted uncomfortably in his wide-body seat. One thing he was certain of: Carol Bishop, spurned ex-lover, would not make this meeting pleasant for him at all.

Howard Stein released his grip on the arm-rests with difficulty. His knuckles had turned numb and white. On either side, dense clouds whisked silently by the portholes of his private charter jet, the pilot having just announced their descent into New York City's Teterboro Airport, a mere twelve miles from Manhattan and DSSC's New York Office. McClaussen's witch-bitch, Carol Bishop, had successfully seized the reins of power at DSSC, and called an emergency meeting, *demanding* his presence. As Chief of Security, he would undoubtedly be held responsible for the mess that was unfolding minute by minute on the news media. He would also be held responsible for making sure the meeting went better than the last couple, the first involving the killing of several dissenting board members, the second, Greyson. What Stein feared most, however, was not what had happened, but what was *not* clear at all to him regarding the future, this meeting included. Bishop had chosen not to share the nature or details of the meeting with him. Stein shifted uncomfortably in his soft leather chair. One thing was certain: The meeting had to have been called in response to that fool McClaussen's inept bungling of the whole Email-Crystal Fiasco that was being aired nationally, an affair he, unfortunately, had played no small part in. One other thing Stein knew for certain: Ms. Carol Bishop was not the kind of woman who forgave easily.

John Marx sat next to Leon Puissegur on the private charter plane taking them from Louisiana directly to New York City to meet with the new CEO of DSSC. Carol Bishop had contacted him "out of the blue" on his cell phone, just after they'd lifted off in Stan's helicopter. She patiently explained how DSSC had, after hearing oil consultant Mr. Leon Puissegur's explanation of the likely presence of regenerating abiotic oil beneath the North American Strategic Oil Reserve, called in all the resources of DSSC to place at Puissegur's disposal in order to prove the theory. After calling an emergency meeting to discuss this, she became aware that DSSC had temporarily lost contact with the man. She was doing everything in her power now that Greyson and his henchmen were gone to locate and invite Puissegur to attend the meeting. In the meantime, it had come to her attention that John Marx had been the recipient of an important email that contained information that might be useful to the effort, and she wanted to personally invite him to attend the meeting, hopefully with the email and its contents in hand. A private corporate jet would be waiting for him at the Louis Armstrong International Airport. Unknown to her, Puissegur was sitting in the passenger seat of the helicopter confirming and denying the various parts of what she'd concocted with brief nods of his head. What was clear to both men was that Carol Bishop was telling them only what *she* wanted them to hear. In return, John chose not to disclose Puissegur's presence. Though it would be dangerous bringing the man back into the lair he had recently escaped, both agreed his appearance, given Bishop's stated interest in locating Puissegur, would provide John a substantial bargaining chip. There was, after all, only one way to sort out all that had been happening the past couple of days, and that was to get it directly from the apparent instigator's mouth.

It proved a short and wonderfully relaxing helicopter flight to the airport, and again from the airport, where John left Stan's helicopter in competent hands, on the private charter jet to New York City's Teterboro Airport. During the flight John located two duffel bags into which he placed their weapons, padding them in a couple of raincoats he found hanging in a flight closet for guests. At the airport, the two, each carrying a duffel bag, approached the waiting limousine.

CHAPTER 24

"How the hell did we get back here?" Hank Benniman asked his new partner, Howard Stein's new "number one hitman," Ralph Nooker, as the two sat together in the nondescript black Lincoln Town Car once again parked several blocks down the street from, but in clear visual sight of John Marx's house.

"Stein has contacts everywhere, including within the police and judiciary," Ralph stopped buffing his nails to snicker, tossing off the question as if too far beneath his station to answer.

"And within the best of the lawyer community," Hank added. "I was detained barely two hours for numerous charges of breaking and entering, assault with a deadly weapon...did I leave anything out? Oh, yes, can't forget the murders. What could the authorities do? It was the company's word against that crackpot Platur's. And he was caught with all three handguns. *And* his prints were everywhere. *And* who would believe a hysterical old woman, especially the admitted wife of one of the two other escaped 'criminals'?"

Ralph resumed buffing his nails. "Like I said, Stein's connected, and so is his pal, McClaussen. We may work for different bosses, but I think it's time we put our heads together."

"Agreed," declared Hank, offering his hand. "We're going to need to combine wits, given that we've now got a police tail following us wherever we..."

"Quick! Give me the binoculars!" Ralph Nooker interrupted. "Someone's walking towards the Marx house." Ralph grabbed the binoculars out of Hank's large hands and adjusted them as he spoke. "That's one of Marx's friends—Kelty Moss, the controller from Rustic Oil Rig Twelve. He's walking up to the door of the Marx house. It's just opened. He's talking with someone inside the house looking up and down the road. Damnation! It's Marx's other pal, Josh Platur! Now how the heck do you suppose *he* talked his way out?"

"Marx also has friends—like that pesky sheriff, and those policemen watching us from behind. We need to be careful..."

"Moss just walked into the house," Ralph continued, ignoring Hank. "You notify McClausssen, I'll notify Stein. They said they wanted to know about anything unusual going on at the Marx house, and I consider a reunion like this unusual."

Hank called McClaussen's cell phone, but didn't receive an answer. Ralph had the same experience with Stein.

Ralph shrugged. "Well, we've done our part. Marx and friends aren't as dumb as they put on. I know. Stein had me do background checks on all the oil derrick workers. Kelty Moss may look and act like a harmless geek, John Marx a wacked-out conspiracy freak, and his friend, Josh Platur, a 'wanna-be' James Bond, but Moss is an avid, dead-shot sportsman, and that Marx guy, a former Army special ops sniper. Both could put a man down quick and clean, if he wanted. Platur acts like the adolescent 'Robin' to Marx's 'Batman', but on more than one occasion he's cleaned out a whole barroom of drunken oilmen. He's also street-smart, that one. I was hoping we wouldn't have to deal further with any of them. Hey! I can't believe what I am seeing!" Ralph handed Hank the binoculars.

"That Platur guy's flipping us off!" Hank exclaimed.

"Like I said, those three are tougher *and* smarter than they put on. So, Platur's wise to us. What do you think we should do?"

Hank turned on the ignition and eased the car to within two houses of where Josh stood glaring at them from the front porch. "We sit where he can see us, and where we can see him, until we receive further orders," Hank replied.

Hank's cell phone chimed. To his surprise, it was his partner's boss, Howard Stein. The usually confident man sounded hesitant. Shaky. Maybe even scared. "I…I'm calling to let you know that Shaun McClaussen is…dead. From now on, you'll take orders from me. Put Ralph on the line."

Hank handed the phone blankly to his new partner. Ralph accepted the phone as if it were a talisman of death. "Yeah, boss?"

"McClaussen's dead. John Marx and Leon Puissegur are standing across the room from me; each has his cell phone out and a representative of the national media live on the other end. The two are threatening to tell all. Carol Bishop is next to me. In McClaussen's absence, she's assumed the CEOship of both DSSC and BPI. She just instructed me to call and tell you to take Marx's wife and children hostage."

"Bloody hell!" Ralph exclaimed. "Are you ordering me to…"

"*I'm* not ordering anything, you imbecile! Carol Bishop, the CEO of DSSC *and* BPI is ordering *me* to tell *you* to take Marx's wife and children hostage. Now. Call me back on this line as soon as it's done. Don't harm them for now, but don't let anyone else stand in your way. Anyone. You got that? Now do it and call me back…"

"Bloody hell," Ralph repeated, staring at the phone in his hand.

"You can't do it, Ralph," Hank, overhearing the conversation, said hoarsely. "Jesus, they're *innocents*. Removing corporate malefactors and reprobates, that's one thing. Kidnapping and holding innocents hostage, especially women and children, that's not part of my…"

"Bloody hell," Ralph said with disgust, throwing the cell phone onto the floor of the car as if it were anathema. "Let's go," he added with finality.

"Ralph, you can't!" Hank Benniman cursed quietly under his breath.

CHAPTER 25

Hank Benniman had not finished his sentence when Ralph Nooker ripped the field glasses vehemently from his partner's hands. Staring through them at the Marx house, he could see Josh Platur and Kelty Moss stealthily opening the garage door to reveal a sleek Four Winns 260 Fishing/Pleasure Boat on a trailer. The next moment, Kelty was directing while Josh backed up the Marx truck. Together they attached the trailer to the truck, then the two sprinted back inside the house. Unknown to Ralph, Josh and Kelty planned to help Ann Marx finish packing and herd together Jan, Jenny, Joan and the twin grandchildren, Karl and Kirk to the boat in preparation for their boating get-away.

"What the hell?" Hank asked his partner. "Looks like the two are taking the Marx family out for a boat ride. Should we take them or follow them? I vote for following…"

"Fucking right, we should follow them! You heard Stein just now. We follow them wherever they go, but we follow them from a distance. When the time is right, we take them hostage. They already know we're here, and will figure we're going to follow. They won't be able to do anything fancy hauling a boat like that and a truck full of children. I don't want to alert them as to our intentions, and we need to see what Platur and Kelty are up to. They're up to something, I'm sure."

"Okay, how about this for what they're up to: We're in Louisiana. Louisiana has more water than land. On land, we've got them wherever they go. On water, with a fast boat like that, they could disappear in the bayous and swamps, and we'll never find them! And, I should point out that, one, we don't have a boat, two, we've no way of following them unseen from a distance, and three, we're fucked," remarked Hank, perturbed by Ralph's lack of comprehension of the situation.

"To answer your second point first, we're going to use *this*," Ralph replied, fishing a small, button-like device out of his pocket and waving it in the air.

"That's a…"

"…single-frequency GPS transmitter. I never leave home without one," Ralph chided, pointing to the back seat where the briefcase-receiver rested. "All we have to do is drop this little device in the boat…."

This time Hank interrupted. "Yes, I can see it clearly now: We walk up to them and ask them, please, if they wouldn't mind us hiding a tracking device in their boat before they leave."

"Come on, Hank, use your head! Packing up a family for an excursion is a multi-trip task. I'll sneak down there and toss it in the boat between loads. You stay here and talk to my hat, which I'll put over the headrest, and my coat, which I'll drape over the seat. Just make sure Platur and Moss see you talking to 'me.' That way they'll think you and I are sitting here impotently on our thumbs wondering what they are up to, and what to do about it."

With that, Ralph worked his way into the back seat, created his front seat stick-man, then slipped unnoticed from the car and behind the nearest hedgerow of the nearest house. Ten minutes later, he reappeared, a look of success animating his dirtied face. "In answer to your first question, we don't want to alert them, right? So, when they leave, we follow briefly, then disappear like we got lost or something, tracking them from a distance while we get our hands on a faster boat. Then, when they least expect it, we appear out of nowhere and immobilize their boat. Bingo! Instant hostages like Stein—I mean, Bishop—ordered. They've brought plenty of supplies, so no problem with food or blankets or toilet paper. Platur and Moss won't chance a shootout with a mother and kids on board, so, no problem there, either. We won't have to do anything except hold them, until we're told to let them go."

Hank thought about what he was hearing. It was a plan he could live with.

The Oil Man

CHAPTER 26

"The kids are ready, Josh. What about all the supplies?" Ann Marx asked.

"All the supplies are stowed on board," Josh Platur echoed in answer. "And a surprise for those two thugs who've been watching us, should they try to follow."

"Let's go then," Kelty Moss said.

Ann nodded her reluctant assent, suddenly disliking the idea of abandoning her home and taking the children on what could turn from a much needed vacation getaway into a difficult, if not deadly, cat-and-mouse game. Worse, her husband, John hadn't returned from his "errand" with Leon Puissegur. On the other hand, lingering could end up being a death sentence.

She was worried. Worried about John, about their children, about their grandchildren, about their friends, about what the men in the car several houses down, as well as unseen others might be planning. John had said it wasn't over yet, and clearly he was right.

Josh and Kelty stood shotgun while Ann led the children into the truck, and fastened them in. Ann scrunched beside Kelty, in the outside passenger seat. Josh took the driver's seat. The truck was crammed, and the three adults felt vulnerable pulling the long, heavy trailer behind. All would feel much better when they could spread out on the boat and begin winding their way through rivers and bayous.

"Those guys are still watching," Josh said, noting sunlight flash off a binocular lens as Josh pulled away and made towards Colonial Boulevard.

"Without a boat, either they're going to have to call for help, walk on water, or follow us to the dock and wait for us to come back. They don't know where we're going to put in, so how could they pre-arrange a boat?"

After ten minutes, the car behind them disappeared from view. Josh drove another half hour, snaking his way from one backroad to another. Finally, he pulled off the road and waited to see if their tail would pass them. "Seems like we've lost them, though I can't imagine them not being able to follow us as slow as we are," Josh stated, fully expecting the two men to pull up beside them at any moment.

"Maybe they were supposed to keep watch on the home. They might be waiting for John," Ann offered.

"Good guess. Still..." Josh checked the rear and side view mirrors anxiously several more times. Any pleasure he felt at losing them was quickly replaced by anxiety at not knowing where they might be or what they might have in mind. Wherever the two men went, a police car would follow, lending a sense of balance to the situation. With the tail and police car no longer in sight, the situation felt unbalanced.

With Kelty's assistance, Josh aligned the boat and maneuvered the trailer into the water. Together they released it from the trailer. The children aboard and the truck and trailer parked behind some trees, Josh started the boat's 320 horsepower Volvo Penta engine and they proceeded without interference. After backing the boat away from the bank, Josh headed forward along a gradually expanding waterway towards Bayou La Loutre.

"I can't believe there's still clean-up people here from the BPI oil spill," Josh said as they passed boat after boat laden with oil recovery and spill mitigation gear. In the distance, two jack-up barges prickling with oil booms looked like they were preparing to head out to yet another place where some oil suddenly surfaced.

Josh and Kelty admired some low-draft airboats that sped by, envying their ability to go deep into the marsh without worry of being caught in unexpected shallows.

As soon as they cleared the no-wake zone, Josh pushed the throttle full forward. The boat roared, rising on step. Kelty and Ann hung on to the central console offering look-out advice while Josh directed the boat fast forward.

"So where we going?" Kelty yelled over the loud but reassuring growl of the powerful inboard motor.

"I figured we'd go to where Bayou La Loutre crosses Bakers Canal, then head out through Half Moon Pass, through Blind Pass and on to Bayou Eloi where it merges into Lake Eloi. We can stop there and see if anyone's following. It's distant, but open and public enough to be safe. If we're okay, we start a run for deep cover. We'll head over to an old camp I know of located just off Stump Lagoon and have an evening feast of fried fish. We can also gather and fry any oysters we find near the banks there."

"Sounds like a plan," Kelty acknowledged. Ann fell silent, staring back over her brood, thinking of John.

Josh led the boat across the old Ship Channel, which was now closed. Building the channel had caused the houses in St. Bernard Parish to sink underwater. Only five of the few remaining houses survived the subsequent floodwaters of Hurricane Katrina. The levees the Corp of Engineers had built were made of sand and when Katrina's five to seven foot waves hit the levees, they washed away. When the sixteen-foot surges followed, they plowed through what was left of the levees like the levees were made of wet toilet paper. Even now, years later, skeletal remains of houses, boats and ships were still poking through the mud along what little was left of the levees. It would cost more then it was worth to salvage anything.

Josh eased back on the throttle to make the right turn from Bayou La Loutre into Bakers Canal, which, as its name implied, had been cut through a marsh to reach a couple of oil wells erected back in 1950. Once in the center of the canal, Josh gunned the engine, taking a left bend at full-throttle, leaving the children laughing with glee. It only took a couple more minutes to navigate through Half Moon Pass, then into Long Lagoon and finally into Half Moon Lake. There, John carefully guided the boat through Blind Pass. Once through Blind Pass, he powered back up and made a slow, wide left turn to approach the mouth of Bayou La Loutre where it emptied into Bay Eloi.

"Shall we drop anchor or tie off?" Kelty asked, as they maneuvered into Bayou Eloi at near idle.

"Let's tie off on that pipe over there" Josh said, directing the boat towards the top of a grey plastic pipe sticking up from the water. Surveyors used the plastic pipes to first mark the channels, leaving the plastic pipes in place for recreational boaters to tie onto. Josh eased the motor into reverse as he came up on one.

Kelty tossed a rope around it, and Josh killed the motor.

"See anyone?" Josh asked, scanning the water and horizon for any signs of pursuit.

"Nope," answered Kelty.

"Then while we wait and watch, I suggest we look like a family on a fishing outing."

After Josh's suggestion, Ann had trouble restraining the twin boys, Karl and Kirk, who vied loudly for the right to be the first to begin fishing. The three girls, Jan, Jennie and Joanie rolled their eyes at the boy's hasty behavior, but were quick to find a place next to each to compete. All eyes eventually turned to watching the cork bobbers dance on the water.

"Let's see what Mother Nature will provide us for dinner," Josh said to Ann as he reached into a tackle box for a lure. By Ann's reckoning, Josh chose the single most disgustingly limpid piece of plastic possible. Furthermore, it reeked of rotten fish. *Men!* she thought, thinking of the many good times she and John had had going fishing with their daughters in this boat in the past. *No self-respecting fish would ever go for so foul looking and smelling a bait as that!*

Josh threaded a rusty hook through the bait-lure and cast it out into the middle of the bayou. The front of his line flashed silver as it touched the water. John always used a long steel leader just in case he hooked into a big red fish. If he did, he would need it.

No sooner did Josh's line hit the water than the float jerked under.

"Holy crap!" Josh yelled, yanking the pole back, instantly regretting his choice of fishing phrases when all the children turned their attention towards him. The fish on the other end jumped out of the water trying to shake off the hook. "That's a nice size fish, Josh," Kelty praised.

"Yes, it is," Ann agreed, adding to Josh's pleasure at having caught the first fish.

Pulling the fish in, Josh yelled excitedly back to Kelty, Ann and the children who were crowding near the side of the boat to watch the primordial fight between man and beast. "Try fishing near the middle of the bayou," Josh recommended to the avid audience, like the instant expert success had made him. "There are some big trout out there."

Josh pulled the fish out of the water and into the boat. "Looks like a keeper, doesn't it?" he asked hopefully.

Kelty unhooked the fish and placed it next to a ruler fixed to the side of the boat.

"It'll do. Fourteen inches by my reckoning," Kelty confirmed.

Kelty helped Karl and Kirk cast their lines out into the same general area. A few seconds later, both floats disappeared under water at the same time. Kelty and Ann helped the squealing twins set the hooks, then stood back to watch the twins as they yelped and tugged against their fish.

Josh placed his pole in a holder and got out the net. The twins appeared to be enjoying the moment almost as much as the three girls standing beside them, explaining to the twins moment-to-moment exactly what to do.

Everyone, even Ann, seemed to relax. The fishing was working its magic, preparing them, Josh hoped, for the next, more challenging part of their excursion. They were relaxed, but they weren't safe, and it would soon be time to run and hide.

CHAPTER 27

After following the truck and trailer for a distance, Hank Benniman made an abrupt u-turn and headed toward a charter boat shop he and Ralph Nooker had passed earlier on their way to Marx's house. It was at least thirty minutes since Josh Platur and Kelty Moss had left in John Marx's old truck, together with Ann Marx and five Marx offspring, hauling John's prized boat behind them. Hank gripped the steering wheel while Ralph clutched a small attaché case tightly to his chest. Hank was thinking about the two previous surveillance men who had abruptly met their deaths while pursuing John Marx and Josh Platur. Hank and Ralph were pursuing Marx's family and best friends. If John Marx had been dangerous before, he would be exponentially more so if and when Bishop disclosed that his family and friends were being held hostage. That worried him. A sane John Marx was dangerous, a frantic John Marx could prove unpredictably lethal.

Ralph held tightly onto the GPS recorder briefcase he was counting on to locate the transmitter he'd tossed into Platur and Marx's boat. It's function was key to his plan to kidnap the Marx family as ordered with minimum risk to himself and hopefully no collateral damage.

Both men were silent as they approached Captain Bob's Boat Charters. A pudgy, middle-aged man walked out of a dilapidated, white trailer office, almost but not quite hidden from view by numerous gaudy, hand-painted, weather-beaten signs, each exclaiming in a slightly different way that Captain Bob's had the best charter prices in Louisiana. Behind the rickety trailer, a barbwire-topped, chain-link fence surrounded a number of boats in various stages of disrepair. Wringing his grizzled hands, the balding man greeted them cordially. "Kin I hep yeh, gentlemen?"

"Yes, sir. We need to rent a boat. A fast one," Hank replied, rolling down the window of their costly-looking Lincoln. "Something dependable that can take us wherever we need to go in the bayous and swamps hereabouts," he added, scanning the contents of the fenced in yard with incredulity.

The man's hands, if possible, seemed to wring harder, as if he were engaged in counting bills. His face, however, betrayed no such greed; instead, only friendly cajun curiosity. "What chu need it fer, if yeh don' mind me askin'?" the man said spitting, a wad of well-masticated tobacco to the side. "If money is an object, then it'd be better teh charter," the owner suggested, feeling out the two "city-boys," his hands beginning to sweat with anticipation.

"We'd rather rent. My man here knows the area, and we have a GPS transponder. We don't need anyone with us." Hank explained hastily. Ralph stretched across Hank to the open driver's window and concurred with a smile.

"You boys ain't up to anything illegal, are yah, 'cause if yah are, I'd have teh call th' law, yeh see?" The man looked from Ralph to Hank and back and winked, returning his attention to their expensive car.

"Nope, nothing illegal. We just need to keep things to ourselves.

Oil business, you know? Price is no object to our employer."

"So, if'n ah said yeh kin rent yer pick of anythin' I have, say, with a $10,000 deposit, would that be a problem?"

"Not at all." Ralph pulled out his wallet and took out a BPI American Express credit card.

Captain Bob's eyebrows rose. "Okay, then ah have no problems with yeh renting. But it'll cost yeh, say, $2,500 a day, plus th' $10,000 deposit, which ah'll of course return when yeh boys bring th' boat back undamaged."

"Where do we sign?" Ralph asked, the eagerness in his voice suggesting irritatingly that the Captain hadn't asked as much as he could have, which Captain Bob immediately tucked away for future reference. After all, there's no profit in being too greedy. Most of his units had "minor" flaws that, unseen on the way out, could be made glaringly apparent on return.

"Come inside an' sign th' papers. Yeh have anythin' particular in mind, or do yeh want me teh choose one fer yeh?"

Hank scanned the derelicts in the fenced yard and shook his head in the negative.

"How about that one," Ralph said, pointing at a new-looking Midnight Express 37 Open Sport Fisherman with four slaved Mercury 300 outboards clamped on the back.

At last seeing his chance, Captain Bob whistled. "Yer partner's got good taste," he said to Hank. "That thar one's my own *personal* boat. Brand new, almost. Ah'd have teh charge yeh a mess more. Like, ah, $100,000 deposit, and $10,000 a day." The man paused to study Hank, then Ralph, knowing instantly by the unfazed looks on their faces he'd just made up his earlier mistake. "On th' other hand, that one's all gassed up an' ready teh go. Even comes with ship-to-shore radio. That beaut' kin go 75 miles an hour, and's so easy teh drive, a chil' kin do it." Captain Bob's hands writhed like two wet snakes in the throes of love-making, and he had to fight off drooling at the thought of the money he was about to make. Staring expectantly into Ralph's eyes, he waited impatiently for his answer.

Ralph looked at Hank with reservation, but Hank nodded affirmatively.

"Okay. Done. Let's finish with the papers and details. We want to get underway as soon as possible."

The triumphant salesman snatched Ralph's credit card, ran it through, and, as instructed, helped Ralph through the twenty-page contract quickly, avoiding having him read it. The Captain finally extended a hand and chortled, "Yeh fella's look anxious teh go, so's ah'll take care of all th' rest. Grab a picnic basket from the 'frige. It's on me. Ah know yeh two probably have cell phones, so's here's mah cell number, too, jes in case yeh should require emergency assistance. But listen. Ah have teh tell yeh that cell phones don' work past Bakers Canal. Jes fer yer information."

By the time Ralph had carried the picnic basket, replete with demi-sandwiches and a half-bottle of chilled champagne, along with the GPS receiver briefcase to the boat side, Hank already had it floating into the water.

"I take it you know a thing or two about this particular kind of boat in these waters," Ralph commented, stowing the gear and running a hand over the slick, shiny fiberglass frame.

"I was raised on one like this. It's big, powerful, fast, and, if necessary, can hold us and our guests. Let's get going."

Ralph castoff while Hank cranked up the quad-Mercurys. They growled, puffed out a grayish cloud, then began purring like kittens. The owner wasn't lying. This must be his personal boat, and it was perfectly tuned.

Hank put it in reverse and backed out from the dock into Bayou La Loutre. Turning the three-foot diameter wheel like a pirate captain, he headed the boat toward the Ship Channel where their GPS locator had last placed Marx' boat.

Hank kicked the motors into high and they tore off.

"How long before we catch up to them?" Ralph asked above the roar.

Hank smiled happily. In less than a mile, they would have to slow down to pass the Brenton Sound Marina and all the equipment lining the shoreline. "Once we get on the other side of the no-wake zone, it should take about twenty minutes to get close enough to put the binoculars on them. Then we sit back and act like we're fishing." Hank pointed to the fishing poles lying on the floor near the back of the boat.

Ralph's cell phone rang. "Hello?" Ralph shouted above the roar of the wind and engines.

"Mr. Nooker?" a dulcet female voice on the other end asked.

"Nooker here."

"This is Carol Bishop, acting CEO of Dan Sogo Shosha Corporation and British Petroleum International. I'm sorry to have to tell you this, but your supervisor, Mr. Howard Stein, is no longer with us. You and Mr. Benniman will, from here on, be taking orders directly from me. What's all that noise in the background? Where are you?"

Ralph looked wide-eyed at the cell phone, then Hank, then shrugged his shoulders, mouthing *Carol Bishop* to his surprised partner. "We're on Bayou La Loutre, following Platur, Moss and the Marx family. They took off in a boat and appear to be heading for less inhabited country, probably to hole up to wait things out. I was able to plant a GPS transmitter on their boat, and we're tracking them from beyond their visual range. My guess is that they believe they lost us,

237

and their current location is unknown to us, madam." Ralph almost said "sir," but caught himself, then afterwards wondered if he shouldn't have acknowledged the aggressive woman as "sir" anyway. He had to be careful with this one. Really careful. With McClaussen and Stein out of the loop, Hank and he were playing for high stakes. Who knew? Maybe if he played his cards right, he'd end up the next Chief of Security. "We should be in binocular range in about twenty minutes or so."

"Good work, Nooker. Let me know as soon as you make visual confirmation. Don't let them know who you are. That's an order."

"Yes, sir, madam," Ralph acknowledged, hoping the play on words wasn't lost to Bishop. The phone went dead. Ralph closed it up and tucked it in his pocket.

"What's up?" Hank asked, correcting course to keep the boat roaring down the center deepwater of the bayou.

"Stein is…gone," replied Ralph.

"You mean gone like in dead?" asked Hank.

"Don't know. All *Miz* Bishop said was that Stein was no longer with DSSC, and that from now on, you and I would be taking orders directly from her. I don't like it, Hank. That woman is really bad news. Stein wouldn't take a dismissal lying down. He'd have fought it tooth and nail. Besides, like McClaussen, he knew too much. My guess is that 'Miz Witch-Bitch' orchestrated a permanent removal."

"A loss for Stein, an opportunity for us, don't you think?" asked Hank coldly. Hank hadn't served under Stein, and, appropriate or not, felt nothing for the man's removal, permanent or otherwise.

"An opportunity or our death warrants, it's hard to know. So far everyone working for Bishop seems to eventually turn up dead or gone. Either way, we're to confirm when we sight Marx's boat, and lay low. We're 'not to let them know who we are.' Her orders. What do you

238

think?"

Hank didn't answer, so Ralph opened the GPS receiver case, and began studying the display. "We'd better hurry, they're a ways away and on the move." Ralph tilted the tracker screen towards Hank. It showed the Marx boat moving into Lake Eloi and heading north towards the mouth of Bayou La Loutre .

"No problem. We're much faster. We should catch sight of them anytime now. Look," Hank replied, pointing. "They're turning towards Mosquito Bight." The flashing cursor on the computer screen turned abruptly towards the electronic outline of shore then kept going until, at a point even with a pipeline canal, it stopped.

"They must've stopped to fish. My guess is they're stocking up on fresh food. We're almost in sight of them now. Get the bino's out and see if you can see them." Hank directed the boat to his left towards a distant shoreline. Ralph put the receiver down and brought the binoculars to his eyes.

"I see them! They're about a hundred yards into the pipeline canal. It looks like they're anchored."

Hank shaded his eyes with a palm and squinted. He could just make out a white hull against the darker background of the marsh. Pulling back the throttle, he slowed the boat and began circling as if looking for a place to fish. The boat burbled throatily, then stopped and began bobbing gently in the open water.

"Set the anchor, Ralph. Get out the poles and give me one."

Ralph handed one to Hank and reluctantly cast his preset lure. "Suppose we catch something?" To Ralph, it was bad enough bobbing like a cork out in open, unprotected water. Aside from the distant shoreline, there was nothing about them but clear, bluish-green-tinted water.

"Then we won't have to pretend anymore," Hank replied, casting his line on the other side of the boat. "What's the matter, Ralph?" he asked, noting Ralph's discomfort.

"I don't like open water," Ralph responded. "Makes me feel… naked."

"It's not all open water. If you look hard out there, you can just make out Deadman Island."

"Great. That makes me feel a whole lot better: Floating here out in the open next to an island of the dead. Does that say something about our situation, or not? I think we should do something about being so…vulnerable."

"You may have just gotten your wish," Hank said. The Marx boat was barely visible as a pin-point against the shoreline horizon. "I think they're moving again."

Ralph rechecked the GPS receiver and concurred. The two reeled in their lines and Hank cranked up the engines, heading the boat towards the pipeline. Halfway there, the Marx boat suddenly reappeared. Hank immediately shut the motor down, but not before they had been spotted.

"Shit!" yelled Ralph. "What're they doing? I think they're waving at us!"

"No, I recognize Platur's distinctive gesture from once before. He and Kelty are flipping us the bird. I think we can safely say they know we're here."

In the distance, Ann Marx was hurriedly instructing the children to pull in their lines while Josh and Kelty secured the boat for action.

"What do we do now, Ralph?" Hank asked.

"We might as well follow them as close as we can," Ralph replied morosely. It wasn't Miz Witch-Bitch's orders so much as the tone in which she issued her order that was trying to tug him into black depression.

Hank cranked the motors back up and began following when Ralph's cell phone squawked, albeit weakly. Ralph flipped open the protective lid of the phone. After a moment, he said morosely into the phone, "Somehow, they figured out that we were following them." Ralph had to move the phone away from his ear. Even from where Hank stood, he could hear the shrill female voice filled with anger castigating Ralph Nooker. When the vindictives diminished, Ralph closed the phone mechanically. "Change of plans," he said, looking at Hank as if he wished he could die now and save Miz Witch-Bitch the trouble of killing them both slowly and painfully later.

The Oil Man

CHAPTER 28

"See those two guys, Kelty?" Josh Platur asked, as he flipped the bird at the men in the distant boat. "I recognize the one at the helm. He's one of the two that were following us. I can't make out the other."

Overhearing, Ann Marx joined Josh and Josh's co-worker and friend, Kelty Moss, shading her eyes against the brilliant Louisiana sun to get a better look. "He's also one of the two 'computer repairmen' who tried to bully their way into my house. He's the one who later pulled a fast one, erasing everything on our home computer. He's one of McClaussen's men. Hank something. I don't recognize the other."

"Yeah. And I don't like the way the second one is looking at us. I've a feeling it's time to switch to Plan B," Josh added.

"Agreed," replied Kelty.

"I guess running and hiding in the bayous isn't going to be as easy as I thought. I wonder how they found us?" As the boat approached, Josh added, "That's a fast boat they've got. It's got quad-300 horse outboards! I think maybe we should take them on a tour of the less-traveled and more challenging areas of Louisiana, what do you think?"

Kelty responded immediately. "Just say the word."

Ann turned her attention to strapping down the children. "Where do you two plan to take them?"

"Those Merc's may be powerful, but they've got big props that sit rather deep in the water. Let's take them into Treasure Bay, then through Treasure Pass into Bayou Petre. If we can coax them into a high-speed chase from there into Flat Bay, I think we can maroon them high and dry in the middle of that bay. But first, we need to clearly establish who's in command." John woke the Four Winns to life, whipped the boat in a tight semicircle and aimed it directly at the open cruiser, pushing the throttle of the 320 horse power Volvo Penta engine full forward.

"What the...?" Ralph screamed as their target flew by them at full speed, the splash and wash nearly tossing ex-McClaussen muscleman Hank Benniman and ex-Stein muscleman Ralph Nookers into the water.

"Close, Josh, but not close enough," Kelty ventured, looking back at the wobbling boat.

"I could probably have done them in, but we've a woman and five children on board that we're sworn to protect," Josh retorted. "They've a lot more power than us, and will catch up shortly. I only hope the guy behind the wheel isn't intimately familiar with where we're taking them." Josh looked over his shoulder to see the fast boat come about and give chase.

"We also don't know their intentions," Kelty added. "If it's to follow or detain us, we're okay. If it's to...eliminate us...then we've an immediate problem as well."

Hank pushed the ganged throttles to half, seeking a safe position in the strong wake being generated by the boat before them. Looking briefly back over his shoulder, he saw Ralph, wobbling from side to side, attempting to hold on while unfolding and assembling a semi-automatic assault rifle. *Shit!* thought Hank. The weapon was an FNH SCAR 17S, a commercial version of the renowned military weapon, infamous for its precision killing capacity. *Is that what Ralph meant by a "change of plans? Were they to become women and children killers after all?*

Josh checked quickly behind, and, satisfied with the distance between the two boats, turned abruptly and buzzed around the point where Bayou La Loutre emptied into Eloi Bay. Directly in front of him was a thirty-foot pleasure craft he'd spotted out of the corner of his eye. The three men aboard were drift fishing. Josh slowed, maneuvering tightly around the boat and then pushed the throttle fully forward again. Behind, he saw the other boat nearly ram the fishermen, then awkwardly attempt to get around them, the three drift fishermen raining a hail of expletives and empty beer cans down on the two impolite interlopers. By the time Hank had successfully navigated around the fishing boat, Josh and his party were well distanced ahead.

"Power isn't everything on the bayous. That's twice I've caught them off-guard. Let's hope they get irritated, and don't learn their lesson." Josh grinned toothily at Kelty.

"I don't want to rain on your parade, Josh, but the man in the back is aiming a wicked-looking weapon at us."

"Hmmm," Josh worried, thinking to himself, *We'll soon find out their intentions.* Josh shouted at Ann: "Get the kids down flat on the deck! You, too, Ann! Kelty, John keeps a hunting gun locked in the cabinet below. Get it out and ready, just in case!" Josh tossed Kelty a second set of keys which Kelty caught in the air.

Kelty slid down to the cabinet, unlocked it and withdrew a sleek, black, long-barrel Harrington and Richardson Pardner 10-gage shotgun with sling. "Damnation!" Kelty shouted, chambering a monster slug and placing a handful of mixed slugs and double-ought buckshot shells in his pockets. "Their boat is big and fast, which means it'll be hard for them to slow down. Can you cut suddenly into a bywater and force them to pass us? I might be able to get a shot or two off while they're passing."

Josh purposefully directed the two boats into a quickly narrowing channel, knowing of just such a cut that only a seasoned traveler in these parts would know. The one in mind was particularly well camouflaged and about to come up. At exactly the right moment Josh made an abrupt right turn, forcing the other boat to go on ahead of them. The Four Winns shook to the sound and recoil of the huge shotgun, and then shuddered as a volley of bullets from the other craft struck home.

John continued maneuvering down the wash, threading his way toward Treasure Pass. The chase boat, constrained by the narrowing waterway, couldn't turn about and had to reverse engines, as Josh had anticipated. Just outside their pursuer's view, he slowed. He needed them to be close on his tail when he made his run through Flat Bay.

"What are you doing, Josh? We had them beat! I think I scored a hit to their boat, and maybe another to their engines. But irrespective of any damage, that ought to have scared the hell out of them. This gun fires like a blunderbuss. I'd hate to be on the receiving end," Kelty yelled, chambering another slug with a grin.

"I want them to catch up a bit. You remember what happened to you, me and John in the middle of Flat Bay last year when the tide was low like this?"

"Sure do: We got stuck in those damned shallows right in the middle of the bay! It took us *hours* to figure a way out of the mud. You're not planning to…?" Josh and Kelty laughed so boldly thinking of what was about to happen that a terrified Ann and her frightened children couldn't help but join in.

The moment he saw them coming, Josh thrust the throttle fully forward, bolting through Treasure Pass and Bayou Petre into Flat Bay. In the race across the bay, their pursuers noticed the boat in front of them cough and slow momentarily around the center before resuming it's full-out run. As Josh hoped, the men behind them took the bait, trying to shave the rest of the distance off by plowing full-throttle through the center.

To Hank and Ralph's amazement, Josh shut down his motor barely fifty feet away. The water over there was five feet deep. Their Midnight Express, however, jerked to a sudden stop in less than six inches of water. Their kinetic energy was enough to push the boat forward and raise it entirely out of the water, leaving it stuck solidly on the hidden mud flat. The loud screech of oyster shells ripping long gashes along the bottom of the boat was only the prelude. Everything on board not bolted down flew high into the air including the deadly assault rifle and two stunned men.

"Worked like a charm!" Kelty said, belly-laughing as the two men dropped out of the sky halfway between the two boats.

"Just like I hoped. They're alive, so they'll head back to their boat. The shore is too far away to swim. They're going to have to either hand-push the boat off the flat, or wait for the tide or owner to come and get them off. No matter which, by the time they break free, they won't have a clue where we are." Josh feathered the engine, ordering a quick inspection to see where their opponent's bullets hit. Ann reported everyone okay. Kelty noted three large bullet holes in the aft hull where it joined the deck. Inspecting the holes closer, he stumbled over a metal object the size of a quarter that rolled to a stop beneath his foot.

"What's that, Kelty?" Josh asked.

Kelty picked up and examined the small metallic cap.

"What *is* that?" Josh reiterated.

"At first, I thought it might be a flattened bullet, but it's not. It's a tracking device is my guess. That would explain how these guys found us."

Kelty was about to toss it overboard when Josh stopped him. "Don't throw it away. They don't know we know about it. That gives us another advantage."

Josh cranked the motor and waved at the two men struggling to gain a foothold in the mud around their boat. All six passengers went aft to watch the hilarious drama of the two mud-caked men attempting to slither their way back on board their grounded boat. Josh pointed at Hank trying to fire up the four outboard motors. The props together threw chunks of mud and oyster shells high into the air, splattering a second coat of mud and debris all over the boat and men. Ralph yelled at his tormentors and shook his fists at the receding boat. Josh, Kelty, Ann and the children waved congenially back as they disappeared across the bay. It would be a long time before their chasers got off the mud flat. Radio and cell phones didn't work in this particular location.

At the far end of the bay, Josh snaked the boat through several byways and on towards Lake Eugene, through Crooked Bayou and Stump Lagoon, and finally into Bayou La Loutre. There he spotted an oyster boat headed out to the gulf. Josh pulled up alongside.

"Listen. We've a game going on. If two guys in an expensive mud-splattered boat with quad-outboards stops you and asks about seeing us, they will be looking for this." Kelty held up the GPS transmitter. "If that happens, would you please return it to them?" Kelty tossed the device to a crewman on the oyster boat who touched two fingers to the brim of his sweat-stained hat and, grinning knowingly, slipped the tracker into a pocket.

CHAPTER 29

Eight o'clock in the evening along a dark shore of Bayou La Loutre, the fire-flies began lighting their luminescent flames within the recesses of some ancient-looking cypress trees draped in Spanish moss. The twinkling lights seemed to extend the reach of the heavens above into the Louisiana swamp. Josh Platur had tied the boat to a grey, weather-beaten, planked pier next to what had once been a sizeable camp. Aft, Kelty Moss talked quietly with John Marx's wife, Ann, while the two younger girls, Jennie and Joanie, played house with their begrudging male cousins, the twins, Karl and Kirk. The air hung sultry but was cooling, breathing lazily to the loud hum and buzz of swamp insects. The old camp had a ramshackle cabin, the doors and windows of which had long ago been torn off, but it offered an old but serviceable cast-iron cookstove to cook on, a rickety wooden table to eat at complete with an assortment of chairs and kegs to sit on, and a stone fireplace to ward off a late evening or early morning chill.

It was nine o'clock in the evening at the New York headquarters of Saber, the *nom de plume* of the newly reorganized multi-national energy-information *daimyo*. With McClaussen and Stein recently eliminated, unadulterated fear gripped the hearts of each of the members of the two corporate boards, as well as the representatives of the other organizations present. Carol Bishop, now thoroughly entrenched as CEO, had only to unleash the legal hell-storm she had so carefully planned to finish consolidating the various players into one board, with her firmly at the helm.

John Marx and Leon Puissegur had, in accepting her invitation, unwittingly played, as she had hoped, directly into her hands. She needed Marx to convince the new board members that the email affair, and thereby the resulting rash of killings, was over. She needed Puissegur to prove to everyone that she possessed the resources necessary to place the new corporation solidly in the center of its new role. She had only to control Marx long enough to finish the consolidation of power. She would have him quietly eliminated when the dust had cleared and the media, bored by the very monotony of the killings, turned to other, more morbid, larger-scale events going on in the world.

Marx, she planned to control by controlling the lives of not only his best friend and colleague, Josh Platur, the one who had somehow secreted out the email despite her best efforts to force it into the open, but also Marx's wife and children.

Puissegur was a different case. The same strategy wouldn't work on him. McClaussen and Stein's men had botched her attempt at kidnapping Puissegur's wife, and the woman now firmly ensconced within an impenetrable ring of police and publicity. Carol would have to resort to controlling Puissegur by maintaining in her possession the only known copy of his four-dimensional abiotic oil map which she had secretly had made before shattering the original.

Yet, despite the cards all being in her favor, she was having a devil of a time trimming the two remaining loose ends. John Marx had countered by securing himself, Puissegur and, through some quick-talking, Dresser Legend and his assistant, Joan Mistral, in the boardroom antechamber. Worse, in eliminating Stein, the former Chief of Security, Carol was temporarily without an experienced security man. The result was that Marx and Puissegur's dufflebags had not been searched, and now the two were armed. Afraid of the publicity that would inevitably result from calling in the authorities—the fledgling corporation by her reckoning couldn't survive any publicity at this time—Marx had effectively created a stalemate. The clever weasel had further solidified his position by revealing to everyone present that he had in his possession both a copy of the email and a fragment of the original crystal memory core on which the entire database was imprinted. The stalemate was causing some of the board members to rethink their positions, but the real sword in her side was the sudden loss of her newest lover, Stan Meyer. She was finding it hard to concentrate her mental powers on eliminating these last, final obstructions at the same time that a part of her, whether she liked it or not, was grieving Meyer's loss. *Was it her punishment to be forever denied a real man at her side?*

Less than twenty feet away, on the other side of the boardroom door, John, Leon, Dresser and Joan were huddled in thought. Their unstated leader, John Marx, looked tired and haggard. Leon and Dresser assumed it was par for the unstable situation in which they had staked their lives. Joan, however, knew without doubt that it was his not knowing about the safety of his family and friends that was taking the toll on him. Joan, Dresser and Leon needed John at his best. What she saw was half a man, dangerously close to breaking.

At Joan's suggestion, John had called and was continuing to call Josh Platur, Kelty Moss and his wife, Ann, on their cell phones without success. Either they were for some reason out of range, or…he forced the alternative from his mind yet again. The specter of their deaths, however, wouldn't budge. He was already beginning to grieve their individual deaths, whether he wanted to or not, and it was severely compromising him.

Less than two hours ago, he'd seen and heard Carol Bishop order Ralph Nooker, Stein's sociopathic right-hand hit-man, to close in on Josh, Kelty, Ann and the kids, and to choose one at random, shooting him or her to prove her determination. The suggestion had shaken everyone in the room to the core. The result was that John had bolted his group into an antechamber, leaving the board members huddling in terrified awe about their new CEO. The lines were now drawn, but the outcome uncertain to either group. The stalemate was, only for the moment, complete.

"John," Carol Bishop called from behind the boardroom door. "Our negotiations have entered a new phase. The stakes are unnecessarily high on both sides. Surely we can come to a... compromise."

Dresser shook his head in the negative. Joan, however, suggested negotiating with Bishop if just to buy them more time.

Choosing the latter, John replied loudly, "What is it you propose, Ms. Bishop?"

"I propose we lay down the weapons and talk, like adults, face-to-face. There's always room in a new organization like Saber for strong, capable individuals, like you and your friends."

Dresser shook his head more vehemently this time, running an index finger across his throat.

John acknowledged, but continued "negotiating" at Joan and now Leon's continued urging. "Exactly what roles might you have in mind?"

Carol signaled to the four of the eighth-floor security men in the boardroom to take positions on either side of the closed antechamber door. She had had to order the rest of the security men into another room, first, to decrease the number of collateral witnesses she might someday have to eliminate, and second, to keep the board members' fear for their own lives in check. She'd have to do a lot of work with this board to garner not just their fear but eventually their support. "I was thinking of you, Mr. Marx, as my working field representative, and you, Mr. Puissegur, as principal consultant to Saber—with stock ownership perhaps, in our new corporation. You, Mr. Dresser, I can envision as my right-hand man. Vice president, even. And Joan, with all the recent male attrition, I could use someone trustworthy like you beside me."

"She's trying to divide us," Dresser whispered.

All four could hear indistinct shuffling coming behind the closed door.

John ordered everyone back to the far side of the antechamber, John positioning himself to one side of the large executive desk where he sat on the floor and began chambering a buckshot load into his 12-gauge Mossberg shotgun. Leon positioned himself at the other end of the desk, and, kneeling, loaded six .35 caliber rifle bullets into the lever-action Marlin, and trained the sight on the wall just left of the door. If Bishop was preparing a rush, anyone clamoring through the narrow doorway would fall to Marx's shotgun, while, with his lever-action rifle, Puissegur would hopefully pick off up to six who might be waiting in the wings on either side of the door. Dresser and Mistral pressed against each other in the middle, waiting.

CHAPTER 30

"I know what you mean, Kelty," Josh continued, turning another of the sizzling fish filets over on the cast iron stovetop. "Since Vietnam, I've wondered why the American people think more about themselves then about their country. Mark my words, there will come a time when this nation will fall flat on its face, and the same greedy people that brought us there will be asking how it could possibly have happened and where all their freedoms went." Josh's face appeared flushed and red in the firelight. Kelty, Ann and the children watched Josh finish cooking the fish and oysters. After a silent dinner, Josh got up and drifted over to the boat, where he ran a hand along its side below the gunnel.

"What are you doing?" asked Kelty, who'd followed close behind.

"This line of bullet holes says it all. I don't know what to do right now except hide. We can't call John from here, or him us. He was supposed to have joined us, but he never showed up. I've no idea what he's doing, or if he knows we're safe. I'm not like those two guys chasing us wanting to do harm, but I'd prefer to be doing something other than…"

"I know the feeling," Kelty cut in. "Those bullet holes, however, are nothing compared to the damage we wreaked on their boat, and to whatever plans those two had. I'd like to see the look on the boat owner's face and on the faces of those two men's bosses when they're rescued. Given what we've seen so far, I can't help but think those two won't be around long enough to get at us again. At least, that's my hope."

CHAPTER 31

"Damn, Ralph. Why the hell'd you shoot at them?" Hank Benniman asked, hoping to pry from his mud-caked partner, Ralph Nookers, what he had meant earlier by a "change of plans." Their boat was stuck firmly in the same muck they were stuck up to their knees in.

"Hey, I thought you knew these waters, and all!" Ralph replied, trying to rock their damaged boat forward without success.

"I know the more widely traveled area on the other side of Bayou La Loutre well, but I never came through here."

"I'd just like to know where they are right now. That phone call I got was from our mutual boss, Carol Bishop. The 'change in plans' was that we were to close in on Josh Platur, Kelty Moss, Ann Marx and the children, and I was to randomly select and kill one. Right now, I'd settle for beating the hell out of Platur, and killing him first just for fun."

Further inspection of the hull inside or out was equally hopeless with everything covered by a dual layer of mud. Working their way back on board, Hank raised the motors to where they were just above the muck. Using a couple of emergency paddles as poles, the two began to make slow but visible headway. The tide had reached its minimum and would soon assist them in their efforts as it started coming in.

Ralph was the first to note a low roar coming from behind. A long, thin, flat boat with a huge, rumbling onboard car engine connected to a long shaft descending at a 45-degree angle into the water pulled up alongside.

"You guys look stuck good," the captain and sole passenger of the odd-looking craft laughed.

Ralph smiled angrily, swallowing his pride. "Yeah, some friends stopped near the opening over there and signaled for us to cross the bayou to join them. To them, it was a big joke."

The tall thin man dressed in jeans and checkered linen shirt, his hand on the tiller, laughed louder. "You ain't the first ones got hung up here. That's why they call this place Flat Bay. Anyone who tries to cross the bay full bore through its center during low tide gets right stuck where you are in the goop. The first time I came through here, I got stuck. I was investigating what I thought was a bunch of seagulls feeding on bait fish. Turned out the gulls were cooling the bottoms of their feet in the mud. There wasn't even enough water for bait fish to swim in. Took me four hours to get off the mud. You're lucky. The tide's coming in. Even if I hadn't come by, you'd have been able to float off in a couple hours or so."

The thin man tossed Ralph a line then turned his boat about and adjusted the long shaft of the motor so the propeller just disappeared beneath the surface. Restarting his engine and giving it full throttle, both boats slowly moved together away from the center and towards the far side of the bay. Even so, it took thirty minutes to work the v-hull of the Midnight Express 37 into deeper water. Finished, their helper turned his needle-like boat around and pulled back his rope.

"You boys take it easy, now. If you want to get back the way you came in, you'll have to do it at idle when the tide's a little higher by creeping carefully around the center. By the way, it looks from here like you've got some gashes running the length of your hull below waterline. I'd be sure to check the boat for leakage before running her out in deeper water."

"Thanks," Ralph replied, disinterested in any advice. "By the way, what kind of hook-up is that you're piloting?"

"This here's a 'mud boat' set up. She can go slow across very shallow areas like Flat Bay and is plenty fast in open, calm water. Not as flexible or maneuverable as an airboat, but I like to use it out here for going into some of the small bays to fish for big redfish and gather soft shell crabs. Works fine, though it's not really made for towing boats." The man laughed his infectious laugh. "You know, you were lucky that the boat stopped when it did. Had you ended up in dead center in the muck, I would have only been able to wave at you. Your friends knew what they were doing when they goaded you. You'll probably be wanting to get them back sometime for that trick."

"You better bet we will," Ralph answered as Hank dropped the four large motors back into the water and started them up. They growled hungrily, though slightly out of tune, one snorting a large cloud of black smoke. Hank headed the boat out Bayou Petre, weaving back through Treasure Pass into Treasure Bay. Continuing on through Bayou La Loutre and out, they passed Dead Man Point and sped across open water towards Gardner Island and Grace Point. It took them almost an hour at full throttle to get back to the old Ship Channel, cross it, and head towards St. Helena Bay. While Hank drove, Ralph cleaned the GPS receiver and, just in case, re-calibrated it. Satisfied it was still working, he took a redundant reading as they approached the entrance to the bay. It showed the Marx boat nearby. Looking around, all they saw was an oyster boat in the far distance dredging for oysters.

"You sure that thing's working?" Hank asked, continuing to search the horizon for any sign of the Marx boat.

"It shows them right where that oyster boat is. You think they spotted us and are hiding just on the other side of it?" Ralph replied, watching the oyster boat pulling its rake behind, digging up the oysters from the muddy bottom.

"It's possible. Let's have a look."

Moments later, Ralph was waving at the captain of the oyster boat, who, recognizing the expensive, mud-covered boat he'd been alerted to earlier, waved back. The captain ordered the rake pulled up and slowed down long enough for Hank to maneuver around the other side and, his disappointment showing, next to them.

"You fellows happen to see a white fishing sport-about with two men, a woman and some children on board?" Ralph asked.

"Sure did," the first mate standing nearest them replied, "They gave us this thing and said that a couple of fellows in a boat like yours would be asking for it." The mate held up the device, then tossed it to Ralph.

"Thanks," Ralph replied, red with rage. "You didn't happen to notice where they were headed, did you?" he asked, reddening further when Hank let out a loud guffaw.

"Sure did," The mate said, between ordering some of the deck hands to pick out the big oysters and to pile the others up to be dumped back overboard. He was developing a bad feeling about the arrogant fellow questioning him.

Ralph wished he still had the semi-automatic assault rifle and could teach the mate some manners. "Mind if I ask which way they went?" he said, gritting his teeth.

The mate decided he *definitely* didn't like this fellow. "They said they were heading back home—wherever they came from, I suppose. Didn't say exactly where that was though. They did mention two men getting stuck in Flat Bay. Say, that wasn't you they were referring to was it?" the mate continued, baiting the pompous ass standing in the boat next to him.

"Yeah, they were playing a practical joke. They lured us there. We just broke free and are looking to rejoin them…"

Before Ralph could finish, the captain, who had been listening intently in the boat house to the conversation between Ralph and his first mate, cut in. "You got stuck in Flat Bay? Hey, Tom, they got themselves stuck in Flat Bay!" The captain let out a loud belly-laugh, as did Tom, his first mate.

Before Ralph could respond, Hank cut in. "Yeah. A great joke. Thanks for your help."

Ralph, wordless, his mouth fixed open, stared daggers at the captain and his mate, finally saying, "Yeah! And thanks for returning this device." Waving it threateningly, he tossed it angrily into the bay.

Hank cranked up the motors and pointed the boat towards the old Ship Channel on his way back to Bayou La Loutre and the Charter boat dock. Ralph sat, arms folded, fuming with rage. As they crossed Half Moon Pass, Ralph jumped when the wet cell phone in his pocket vibrated weakly. Ralph brushed the mud off, flipped the phone open and stared at the display.

"Who's calling?" Hank asked, knowing full well it would be their newest boss.

The number on the display, like before, indicated it was from Stein. "Hello," Ralph answered hesitantly.

"Mr. Nookers?" Bishop asked.

"Yes, sir, madam, it's still me," Ralph replied awkwardly.

Hank slowed the boat as he navigated from Half Moon Pass into Bakers Canal.

"I've been trying to get you for several hours. Did you accomplish your task? Who did you...choose?" Carol Bishop asked crisply.

Ralph hesitated, gathering his wits, imploring Hank with his eyes to help. Hank ignored the frightened sadist, wanting the blame for their failure to fall squarely on his sadistic "partner's" shoulders. "I...we lost them. We've been out of cell phone range. I..."

"You *lost* them? How the hell could you lose a boatload of children?" the voice on the other end screamed. "You have five minutes to locate them and follow my orders. On second thought, don't kill the mother. Shoot someone, anyone but her, as soon as you get one of them in your sights. I want her on the phone begging her husband to surrender before you kill the next hostage. FIVE MINUTES, you hear?" Bishop screamed, cutting off the call without waiting for an answer.

Ralph hung up looking utterly forlorn. "Fuckin'..."

"Are we to understand that your plan includes murdering children?" one of the female board members asked the newly-appointed CEO. Corporate liability laws didn't exonerate board members from murder, and murdering children would get each of them a guaranteed non-appealable death sentence.

"Yes," Carol Bishop admitted bluntly, staring down the cowering board member.

"And your men have *lost* the hostages?" a man asked carefully from the center of the crowd.

"This Platur guy is no dummy, and neither is his friend, Moss. Somehow they located the tracking device my two men placed on their boat. I've ordered them to shoot someone on the boat as soon as they relocate it…"

"You don't even know where they are?" interrupted a third man, emboldened by Bishop's momentary show of weakness.

Carol Bishop swung her body towards the source of the voice and thrust the heel of her hand forward directly into the man's chest. The man looked down with surprise at the hand on his collapsed ribcage, then his eyes widened and he opened his mouth as if to speak. A wet burble and a gush of bright red blood was all that issued.

"Any other questions?" Bishop asked, abruptly withdrawing her hand, allowing the figure to collapse in a heap to the floor. "Listen to me! All of you! What those four yahoos behind this door have and don't fully know it yet is all that we need to get our hands on the North American Strategic Oil Reserve. If we hesitate and this information leaks out prematurely, we're *all* going to die. We're standing on a cusp. We have to seize them, finish establishing our cartel, and gain control of the oil fields—not another oil cartel, a global energy-information cartel. Once we do that, and drive oil up to the 150 dollar a barrel mark, the people on that boat and behind this door will become totally irrelevant. Immaterial. *Unnecessary.* If they speak out now, we lose *everything*, including our lives. Oh, yes! You're all implicated at this point just as deeply as I am. Can't you see that these few lives don't matter any more than whether there's really any abiotic oil or not? It's all about belief and control. We need only control the *information.* Once we convince or eliminate Marx, then Puissegur and Dresser will come back to our side. Why? Because they have no choice. All we need do for the moment is prevent Marx from talking and neutralize him one way or another and all our troubles are over. I thought to bargain for his cooperation using his friends and family, but there's more than one way to resolve this crisis. We only need eliminate Marx, and everything we've planned for will be ours!"

Eyes blazing, Carol Bishop turned to the four armed men crouched on either side of the antechamber door. "Take Marx out any way you can, just make sure nothing happens to Puissegur. Save Dresser, too, if you can. I don't care about the girl. It's time to end this!"

"And if we don't take Puissegur alive?" another board member hidden in the mass asked with trepidation.

"I still have a copy of his entire database on another crystal, and we have the necessary technology to read and project the four-dimensional abiotic oil map on it. We've got all the resources in place. We know the email didn't go any further than Marx. If we get rid of him, we get rid of the *real* threat. We don't *need* Puissegur or Dresser, really." Returning her attention to the security men, she continued. "Save Puissegur and Dresser if you can, but don't hesitate to lose them if it means taking out Marx. I want that man dead! On my signal!"

The two men closest to the antechamber door repositioned to smash it down. Their plan was, once through, to fall to the floor, guns blazing. The remaining two, one on either side of the doorway, would position themselves above the two on the floor, adding firepower. "You!" Carol Bishop commanded the closest board member. "I want another four armed security men in here now! They'll be backup, just in case. Go into the next room and bring them. Just four!"

The businessman she pointed at, an Asian executive representing one of the largest energy conglomerates in the world, hesitated, then bowed slightly and departed. Moments later, the four additional men took positions in a semicircle yards ahead of the CEO and board members who were pressing themselves against the far boardroom wall as far from the antechamber door as possible.

Carol Bishop separated from the huddle in the back and strode defiantly forward, then stopped in the middle of the long, rectangular room to the right of the conference table and prepared to give the signal.

CHAPTER 32

Inside the boardroom antechamber, John Marx settled into firing position, directing the full force of his shotgun at the center of the door. "They're preparing to attack," he stated.

Leon Puissegur, crouching at the other side of the heavy wood desk, nodded in acknowledgement, zeroing his scope at a spot chest-level on the wall to the left of the door. The .35 caliber bullets from his lever-action deer rifle would easily penetrate the wall without losing any of its striking power.

"I agree," Dresser Legend said.

Joan Mistral reached for a wooden lamp stand, ripping off the shade and upending it, brandishing it like an axe in her hand. If she was going to die, she would take everyone bold enough to approach her with her.

John Marx's cell phone chimed. "Yes?" he asked quietly.

"Mr. Marx? This is Captain Allen Stolby, Chief of Special Operations, NYPD. We got word there's something radical going on up there on the Dan Sogo Shosha Corporation floor where you're at. A Mrs. Puissegur had called and alerted us earlier that you and her husband may be there and in trouble. It took us a bit of time and effort to piece everything together.

"Apparently your wife, Ann, alerted Ms. Puissegur just before your wife, a Mr. Platur, a Mr. Moss, and your five children left together to seek refuge in the lower Louisiana swamps. She gave Mrs. Puissegur the name of the sheriff of Violet, Louisiana, who confirmed seeing the group leave in your old truck pulling a boat. A black car with two men in it that the Violet police had been watching followed the truck for awhile. Mrs. Puissegur also related another most unusual story, so unusual that we had trouble believing her at first. She suggested that the rash of murders in the news were all connected to some sort of secret plot within a company her husband had consulted with: A plot to seize control of the North American Strategic Oil Reserve.

"At first, it all sounded pretty far-fetched, but police from different states were called in and confirmed the basic facts about the murders. They all pointed a finger at British Petroleum International and what the state and federal attorney general quickly discovered was an international shell corporation called the Dan Sogo Shosha Corporation in control. Recalling the results of the 9/11 conspiracy, that was enough for the feds and us. At my request, the Mayor of New York called the Governor, who alerted the FBI, who, with NYPD assistance, have cordoned off the area around the Empire State building. We're finishing up the orderly evacuation of the building as you and I speak.

"The Governor of New York also called the Governor of Louisiana, who has agreed to provide Louisiana Air National Guard reconnaissance and support to locate your friends and family. The officer in charge of the Guard unit has just reassured me that they are safe and secure. It was your friends, Josh Platur and Kelty Moss, who put it all together and convinced us this was for real. It was your wife and children, however, who convinced us of the eminent danger you and Mr. Puissegur are in. What is the situation up there...?"

John had barely time to sigh with relief, before the door on the other side of the room crashed open. Leon reflexively pumped two shots to the left of the doorway and two more to right of it. As the door fell to the floor, two men fell with it to the floor, two more kneeling to either side of the doorway, all of them leveling their .357 magnum Ruger Security-Six revolvers at John. The two kneeling on the sides fell wide-eyed and lifeless to the floor. John squeezed the trigger of his shotgun, which issued a sound like a cannon in the small room. Both men on the floor in the doorway slumped, their weapons falling, unfired, from their hands.

From far inside the boardroom, a female voice yelled, "Stop!" and John and Leon paused, weapons at ready, ready to unleash another rain of bullets and buckshot at anyone on the other side of the open doorway. "Stop!" two male voices boomed together, one distinctly Asian, the other with an unmistakable Louisiana accent. Both spoke with authority and command. "The fight's over! Ms. Bishop is dead!"

A trick? John asked Dresser with a flick of his eyes.

"I don't think so," Dresser replied aloud, shaking free of Joan's grip. "I recognize those voices. They're all three board members."

The Louisiana voice from inside the boardroom continued. "Bishop was struck in the chest by one of your rifle bullets and died instantly. There's four more armed guards out here, but they're no longer after you, they're protecting us. I'm ordering them to stand down." The resonant male Louisiana voice continued, "Please, don't engage further. Several rifle bullets passed through the back wall where we're gathered."

His open cell phone that John had dropped when the shooting

began came back to life. "What the hell's going on up there?" It was Captain Stolby of the NYPD.

His initial surge of adrenaline diminishing, John rested the barrel of his shotgun on the edge of the wooden desk, but kept it leveled at the doorway. Despite Dresser's admonition, it *could* be a trap, and he wouldn't put such a thing past the infinitely clever and ruthless Carol Bishop. She would be desperate now that his family and friends were safe and the situation was rapidly shifting in his favor. John picked the cell phone up in his free hand and brought it to his ear. "We were rushed while talking. There's at least five dead here, four guards and, I'm told, the CEO of DSSC/BPI. I'm told there's four more armed men in the next room guarding a group of executives."

"Shit," the voice on the other end of the phone exclaimed. "Are you okay? We've got our men on the floor. Can we send them safely into the boardroom?"

"I don't know. I'm told the mastermind, Carol Bishop, is dead, but I've no way of confirming if this is true without exposing ourselves. It might be a trap to flush us out..."

A wave of blue-and-black-clad figures with "FBI" and "NYPD" in bold white letters stenciled across their chests poured into the room. Momentary sounds of scuffling were followed by a loud, "Clear!" in a distinctly Bronx accent. "Hold your fire!" the same voice boomed as its owner approached the open antechamber doorway, hands above his head, one still carrying an automatic pistol.

John tensed.

"Hold your fire! It's all over!" the man said, the white FBI letters across his chest finally sinking into John's brain. "It's all over, Marx. Bishop's dead like they said. The boardroom is secure. You're in no further danger, but I have to ask you two to lower your weapons. Now."

John and Leon slowly complied.

Dresser and Joan stood up, despite John's hesitation. "It's alright, John. Like the man said, it's over now."

One part of John wanted desperately to comply, but the other kept entreating him in mind, *Yeah, it's over, and the moment you lower your gun, you're a dead man.* The voice in his head sounded amazingly like that of Carol Bishop.

"I need you to let go of your gun," the officer repeated, more firmly this time, and John, against his own better judgment complied. Leon followed, and the two slowly stood, hands raised, palms open and facing the officer. "Thank you, Mr. Marx, Mr. Puissegur. I assure you it's all over."

The man in black slowly leveled his weapon at John, but instead of firing, said, "I need to know that there's no other weapon threat. Please, assure me you've no other weapons, and if you do, place them on the desk next to the shotgun and rifle. You're safe. This is a necessary precaution, Mr. Marx. There's too much adrenaline in the room, and that can result in actions everyone will later regret."

John took a long, deep breath and let it out slowly. "We've no other weapons in here or on us."

"Good," the officer said, his eyes entreating John to reassure him a second time.

"There are no other guns," John replied flatly, while Dresser pealed the lamp stand from Joan's pale, shaking hand and placed it onto the desk.

"Clear!" the officer called into his shoulder mike and into the boardroom, visibly relaxing at last.

The Oil Man

CHAPTER 33

News of the hostile takeover of Dan Sogo Shosha and British Petroleum International, the formation of Saber, and deaths of Ms. Carol Bishop and her two colleagues, Mr. Howard Stein and Mr. Shaun McClaussen, hit the eagerly waiting news media like a bottle of nitroglycerine tossed at a million-gallon gasoline storage tank. The lurid details of the shootout at the top of the Empire State Building in New York City and later, the attempts at taking the Marx family hostage and murdering them, including the children, one by one, only fanned the flames higher.

Over the next week, the press progressively turned its attention to linking the boardroom fiasco to the deaths of DSSC's retired computer genius, Dr. Alexei Solokov, BPI's corporate helicopter pilot, Mr. Stan Meyers, Dresser Legend's surveyman, Claude Askins and Askins' survey crew, New South Wales Petroleum oil man, Mr. Chris Longley, and finally, Rustic Oil Central operator, Mr. George Franks. Nothing in corporate news history had ever peaked public interest like this; the media made millions on the stories, and millions more on the collateral stories of mastermind Carol Bishop's former involvement in the CIA, her violent love affair with the power-hungry McClaussen, her thwarted love affair with Meyers, and the grisly murders ordered by corporate sociopath Stein and his "hitmen." Only after exhausting the full potential of this secondary news did the media turn to the issues at heart: the attempt by a *daiymo*, a super-national consortium of international and domestic oil corporations, to perpetrate a hoax on the President, the American government and the world of unparalleled proportion. It was only then that the sensational, four-dimensional holographic map of the world's abiotic oil generation hotspots and the question of abiotic regeneration of existing oil fields began to be addressed publicly.

Amidst the weeks and weeks of investigative hoopla, Dresser Legend was quietly voted CEO of Saber, and he quietly appointed Leon Puissegur as chief consultant.

John Marx, Josh Platur and Kelty Moss were quietly elevated to heads of divisions of international oil exploration, information and security respectively.

Several months later, Dresser Legend called a private meeting in Saber's new Asia Office, in the recently-acquired seventy-seventh through eighty-eighth floors of Hong Kong's Two International Finance Centre building located on the Hong Kong Central District waterfront. The "Big Five" as CEO Legend had taken to calling Puissegur, Marx, Platur, Moss and himself met in the auspicious seventy-seventh conference room overlooking picturesque Victoria Harbor. For John Marx's wife, Ann, it was a Louisiana shopper's dream come true. For Dr. Leon Puissegur's wife, Betty, it was an attestation to the years of her husband's work developing and supporting the abiotic oil theory of oil field regeneration for which he had recently received numerous honorary doctoral degrees and been nominated for a Nobel Prize. For CEO Executive Secretary Joan Mistral, it was the culmination of her employer and lover's dreams.

"You're undoubtedly wondering why I've called this meeting, now that Saber has weathered the storm of public scrutiny and worked its way out of the darkness. I'll come right to the point: It's time to put Dr. Puissegur's theory to the test."

All nodded approval.

"I thought it didn't matter, as long as there was the *possibility* it could prove correct," Puissegur ventured.

"True," replied Legend, turning to look out the floor-to-ceiling windows at the vast expanse before them, hands clasped behind his back. "True, indeed. But now that the public eye has finally turned elsewhere, we've been able to begin negotiations with this administration to do exactly what Greyson, and later Bishop planned, only we're going to do it right and on an even grander scale. In the open. No threats, no conspiracies, no collusion. Whether our talks will lead to the eventual opening of the North American Strategic Oil Reserve or not, I can, at this time, only guess. What's more important and symbolized by this new office in Hong Kong, and our other new offices in Moscow and Dubai, is that *all of the world's governments* are interested, maybe more so than what meets the eye given the competitiveness of the energy-information industry we're building."

Legend gave everyone in the teak-lined office a moment to reflect on the last few months, Leon on the unexpected international fame his abiotic oil theory had brought, Kelty on his sudden appearance in the new world of global security, Josh on his welcome insertion into the world of informatics, and John to his personally unwelcomed rise to fame in the petroleum world, and himself over his sudden rise to CEOship of what had now quickly become one of the leading super-national corporations in the world. Of all the people reflecting, only John still wished for the "good old days" before he had become "The Oil Man" extraordinaire.

"Like I said," Legend continued. "It's time to test the abiotic oil theory, and, if we are as lucky at unlocking it's secrets as we've been in resolving the DSSC/BPI mess, begin sharing it with the world—at a profit, of course." Dresser nodded to everyone in the room. "But first, I'd like to share with you what your combined efforts during the past couple months have already yielded, and upon which I base this decision." Dresser walked to the middle of the room, picked up a remote control and pushed a button. The room hummed and a four-dimensional hologram of the world with it's predicted abiotic oil areas hovered in the center of the room. The image rotated on its axis and the oil areas began moving like fingers and snakes as the years indicated above the ghostly display advanced. With another button push, the world stopped rotating and the Western United States as a block rose and expanded; alongside the caricature-image, a stream of numbers began scrolling.

"Based on a limited analysis, if Leon's theory is correct, our best current estimates are that under Colorado, Utah, Wyoming, North Dakota and Montana, the so-called Green River and Bakken Formations, lies some two *trillion* barrels of oil that could be recovered for around fifteen dollars a barrel over the next 50 years. This is, of course, only an estimate, and a low estimate at that. The *minimum* the United States could expect to extract *without any depletion of the North American Strategic Oil Field* would be nine hundred and fifty billion barrels of oil. Based on what the United States uses today, without any further foreign oil, that represents a two hundred and forty-five year supply just waiting to be taken from the ground. All we have to do is build the oil refineries necessary to bring this oil to fuel for our nation, and make certain we have the necessary technology to burn these fuels without damaging our environment.

Hopefully our current President and the ones to follow will allow us to do this."

Dresser paused to let the enormity of what he was saying settle in, then he continued.

"Compare that with current Chinese, Middle Eastern and Russian reserve estimates of 500 billion, 12 billion and 10 billion barrels respectively. If Leon's theory is correct, these previously-considered 'static' reserves might be able to be increased by ten to a hundred times. If his theory is correct, the balance of power in the world could change in one day—and that would be the day we prove the theory correct. We, here, would know the numbers before anyone else. I don't think I need to say any more, do I? The rewards, and the dangers, are immeasurable. *That's* why I invited you here today: To find out if you're ready to take on the grandest challenge of all time. So then, are you with me?"

ABOUT THE AUTHOR

A writer since his junior high school days, Leon Puissegur is a happily-married Vietnam Veteran with a wonderful wife, three children and nine grandchildren. He has three books in print, not including this one.

If you enjoyed *The Oil Man* consider these other fine books from Savant Books and Publications:

A Whale's Tale by Daniel S. Janik

Tropic of California by R. Page Kaufman

The Village Curtain by Tony Tame

Dare to Love in Oz by William Maltese

The Interzone by Tatsuyuki Kobayashi

Today I Am a Man by Larry Rodness

The Bahrain Conspiracy by Bentley Gates

Called Home by Gloria Schumann

Kanaka Blues by Mike Farris

First Breath edited by Zachary M. Oliver

Poor Rich by Jean Blasiar

The Jumper Chronicles by W. C. Peever

William Maltese's Flicker by William Maltese

My Unborn Child by Orest Stocco

Last Song of the Whales by Four Arrows

Perilous Panacea by Ronald Klueh

Falling but Fulfilled by Zachary M. Oliver

Manifest Intent by Mike Farris

The Mythical Voyage by Robin Ymer

Hello, Norma Jean by Sue Dolleris

Richer by Jean Blasiar

Charlie No Face by David Seaburn

Number One Bestseller by Brian Morley

My Two Wives and Three Husbands by S. Stanley Gordon

*In Dire Strait*s by Jim Currie

Wretched Land by Mila Komarnisky

Chan Kim by Ilan Herman

Leon Puissegur

Who's Killing All the Lawyers? by A. G. Hayes

Ammon's Horn by Guerrino Amati

Wavelengths edited by Zachary M. Oliver

Almost Paradise by Laurie Hanan

Communion by Jean Blasiar and Jonathan Marcantoni

Scheduled for Release in 2011:

Blood Money by Scott Mastro

In the Himalayan Nights by Anoop Chandola

Random Views of Asia from the Mid-Pacific by William E. Sharp

Isla Vista Crucible by Reilly Ridgell

Perverse by Larry Rodness

On My Behalf by Helen Doan

Rules of Privilege by Mike Farris